THE CONQUERING HEROES
PETER GENT

Million-selling Author Of *North Dallas Forty*

"Gent's storytelling abilities…serve him well in a novel that moves with speed and precision."
— *Publishers Weekly*

"*The Conquering Heroes* is the *North Dallas Forty* of college basketball. But it's much more. It's about a whole generation of kids who came of age in an America that I grew up in. It's also a spectacular read."
— Bill Walton, former UCLA All-American and NBA All-Star

Pat Lee—the star player on his high school team, now the recruiting coach of an NCAA powerhouse—is badly shaken when the school's star player rapes one of the students, and the university's athletic department's response is to cover up the crime. This sets in motion an explosive series of events in which Lee winds up confronting the corrupt system he has, against his will, been a part of for twenty years, ending in open warfare against the powers-that-be, who go far higher than one might imagine.

Not since *North Dallas Forty* has Peter Gent written a novel of such power, such intensity. *The Conquering Heroes* is a genuinely compelling human drama—and a novel readers will never forget.

"A scathing look at college sports just beyond the bright lights of the hardwood arena."
— *South Bend Tribune*

"Peter Gent has written a powerful novel about the dark side of college athletes."
— *Wichita Falls Times Record News*

PETER GENT

THE CONQUERING HEROES

LEISURE BOOKS **NEW YORK CITY**

For Carter, who just keeps on

A LEISURE BOOK®

March 1995

This edition is reprinted by special arrangement with
Donald I. Fine, Inc.

Published by

Dorchester Publishing Co., Inc.
276 Fifth Avenue
New York, NY 10001

For further information, contact: Donald I. Fine, Inc., 19 West
21st Street, New York, NY 10010.

The name "Leisure Books" and the stylized "L" with design are
trademarks of Dorchester Publishing Co., Inc.

Printed in the United States of America.

And a man's foes shall be those of his own household.
—Matthew 10:36

He jests at scars, that never felt a wound.
—William Shakespeare
Romeo and Juliet, II, ii, 1

*If you think your BACK is against the wall,
you're facing the wrong way.*
—T.P. Winner
Sports as Irony and Exception
H.S. Publishing, 1992

The Rain

It began to pound steadily on the sidewalk as Cathy Sullivan left Baker Hall on the way to her humanities class across campus.

In her second year at Southwestern State University in Dallas, Cathy planned to major in psychology and work with learning-disabled children.

Small and slender with her blonde hair tucked up under her rain hat, she opened her umbrella on the steps of Baker Hall and set out to cross the campus. Falling in sheets, the water could not drain rapidly enough from the pavement so that soon Cathy Sullivan's Top-Siders were soaked through. Even though there was a test scheduled, Cathy decided to seek shelter in the nearby

Student Union and forget about her humanities class. She had just turned to cut across the street, when the blue Z-28 pulled up next to her and the passenger window buzzed down electrically.

"Hey, little girl." The driver leaned over and spoke above the pounding of the rain. "Hop in and I'll hook you up where you want to go."

Cathy studied the face of the driver and recognized him immediately. Chuck Small was the most famous basketball star at SWS and considered one of the best players in the nation. Two years earlier he had led the SWS team to the Dixie Conference title and a trip to the Final Four.

"Come on." He flashed a brilliant smile and opened the door. "I'm just offering to get you out of the rain. I don't want to marry your sister."

Cathy hesitated a moment longer, then laughed and slid onto the cool leather of the seat, pulling the door shut behind her.

Sitting behind the wheel, Chuck Small was massive at seven feet one inch and 270 pounds. It was easy to see why he could be a dominant man on a basketball court. His blue Z-28 now fishtailed slightly on the wet pavement, then headed off down Circle Drive.

"Hey," Small yelled over the sound of the rain pounding on the car and the rap music blaring from his compact disc player, "what's your name?"

The Conquering Heroes

"Cathy," she spoke up against the jarring noises. "Cathy Sullivan."

"Let's find us some shelter from this storm and have us a party, little girl. Where should we crib? I got me a kicking disc player. Bust us a few? Whattaya say?"

"No . . . thanks, I've got a class . . ." Fear crossed her face. Nervously she smoothed her damp shirt, tried to force a smile.

"Come on, woman, loosen up." Small talked rapidly, his big hands pounding out rhythms on the steering wheel.

"Take me to Abbott Hall, please." Her voice was a tight monotone. "I've got a psychology course—"

"You don't really want to go to class on a day like today. Besides, a pretty girl like you don't have to worry about grades."

"Oh, yes, I do." She stared straight ahead and tried to control her body language. "I've got a test today."

"Come *on*, babe." Chuck grabbed her leg. His hand wrapped completely around her thigh. "I'll talk to your professor and give him a couple of season tickets."

Cathy Sullivan looked desperately for an exit, but Small raced the car across the campus.

"Please, you just passed the turn to Abbott Hall."

"I just have to run by my apartment and pick

something up." Small accelerated through the intersection of Circle Drive and the Drag. "It'll only take a minute."

"Look . . . please just drop me off here and I'll walk—"

"Don't be crazy, momma."

"I'm not your momma, damn it, and I'm not crazy." At least she was determined not to act the victim. "Either you let me out now or I'll have you arrested for kidnapping."

Small turned and faced her. "Oh, you gonna have me arrested?" His voice turned cold, flat. "That's real funny. I give you a ride and now you gonna call the law on me. I don't think so."

"Please . . . don't do this—"

He hit her against the temple with his fist. Her head banged off the window and she slumped down in the seat.

It was dark when Small finally fell asleep. He had raped Cathy Sullivan four times and beaten her severely.

Battered, she waited until his slow even breathing assured her he was sleeping. Her lips were cut and swollen, her right eye was blackened, her body was bruised. Blood was seeping down the inside of her thighs. Quietly she pulled on her torn blouse and skirt. She could not find her underwear, socks or shoes. She moved painfully to the door and slipped out into the night.

The Conquering Heroes

*   *   *

Campus police Sgt. James Cash was half awake as his patrol car cruised slowly down Circle Drive. Suddenly the battered and bloody figure of Cathy Sullivan stumbled into the car's headlights. To miss her Cash had to swerve and slide his car into the shrubbery lining the campus road.

It took Cash some five minutes to get Cathy Sullivan to the SWS campus police station, where she told desk sergeant Jack Moore she had been raped and who had raped her.

That was her second mistake that day.

"And you're willing to swear that it was Chuck Small who raped you. It couldn't have been somebody who just *said* he was Chuck Small?"

"I *know* what Chuck Small looks like. Everybody knows what he looks like."

Moore avoided her eyes and pretended to be writing something down. What he was doing was making bigger and bigger concentric circles on his notepad. He had yet to write down a word.

"Now calm down, lady. These are pretty serious charges. We've got to be real certain you know what you're talking about."

Cathy gave him a look. "Who is *we?* You have a mouse in your pocket?"

"She's hysterical," Jack Moore said as he turned to Sgt. Jim Cash. "Check her into the medical center under a Jane Doe. Don't let anybody see or talk to her. I'll call Barry Sand—"

"Wait a *minute*." Cathy tried to pull back as Cash took her arm. "I want to see a rape counselor . . . it's my right . . ."

Cash turned her loose and looked at the desk sergeant for direction. Jack Moore kept his eyes down on his ever-growing doodle and waved them both away.

For a moment Moore wished he could just dive headfirst and disappear into the whirlpool of ink lines he had drawn. This was a delicate matter; he didn't want to be left holding the hand grenade when it went off. Chuck Small had already pulled the pin. The trick now was to toss it to somebody else before the explosion.

As Sergeant Cash left the station with the grenade in tow, desk sergeant Jack Moore picked up the telephone and dialed The Man.

The pink Princess phone on the nightstand in the bedroom of Barry Sand's house buzzed like a deranged house fly. Mrs. Geena Keats Sand reached up, grabbed the phone and poked Barry in the ribs with it without opening her eyes or mouth.

Head basketball coach Barry Sand sat up, wiping the sleep from his eyes.

"Yeah." He picked up the phone.

"What!" Suddenly he was wide awake. "You *sure* it was Small? . . . Well, she could be wrong . . . I don't care. She could still be wrong. All right, I'll take care of it. Don't write anything down."

Coach Sand slammed the receiver against the mattress.

"Trouble with a player?" His wife mumbled without opening her eyes.

Her husband punched in a phone number, waited for an answer. "Doc? This is Barry . . . I don't care what time it is. Get your ass up. We got a problem."

Cathy Sullivan sat on the hospital bed, face bruised and scratched. Her upper thighs were caked with streaks of blood. Still barefoot and wearing her dirty clothes, she was staring at the wall and appeared to be in shock. It had been more than an hour since she had staggered into Sgt. Jim Cash's headlights, but nothing had been done to ease her suffering or deal with her trauma.

Sgt. Cash stood by the door now and studied his shoes.

Suddenly there was a loud knock. "Who is it?" Cash did not open the door, he yelled through it.

"Dr. Mel Knight. Let me in."

Cash opened the door just wide enough to let the basketball-team doctor Melvin Knight into the hospital room, then stuck his head out the door and checked out the hall.

"All right," the doctor said to no one in particular. "What happened?"

Cathy continued to stare at the wall.

"She claims she was raped . . . by Chuck Small."

"Well," Knight said with irritation, "let's first determine if she was actually raped before we start jumping to conclusions about who did it."

Cathy took in the figure of Dr. Knight.

"I *was* raped, and it *was* Chuck Small."

"I'll be the judge of that—"

"Why, doctor? Did Chuck Small ever rape you?"

"That attitude of yours is not going to get us anywhere. Let's get you out of those dirty clothes and clean you up. Okay?"

"I want a nurse in the room."

"There aren't any available." Knight pulled on a pair of latex gloves. "Let me just—"

"I want to call a rape counselor—"

"There'll be time enough to do that later. Now, just cooperate and let me do my job here."

"But . . ."

"Look. I *am* the doctor here." Dr. Knight looked at Jim Cash and nodded toward the door.

"Sergeant, please wait outside."

Cash left the room and closed the door behind him, then waited in the hallway outside like a palace guard, arms crossed, stone-faced, trying not to think about what was happening, and what he should be doing, what he should have done.

This is basketball business, he repeated to himself like a mantra. It's basketball business . . . the captain will tell me what the hell to do later . . .

The Conquering Heroes

It seemed hours before the door opened, though Cash knew it was some forty-five minutes. His stomach churned. He was out of his depth. Way out. This was athletic-department trouble and it was always handled differently. He had to be careful. He had heard the stories about campus cops who hassled the wrong athlete and were instant history. This could be a class-A felony. He fought the urge to take off, then heard the doorknob turn behind him as Dr. Knight stepped out and patted Cash on the shoulder.

"I cleaned her up and gave her a shot to make her sleep. We'll be okay. Did you check her in?"

"Yes, under a Jane Doe."

"Did anybody see her?"

"Just the admitting nurse."

"I'll talk to her."

"Was she raped, doc?"

"That's none of your concern."

He didn't like the doctor's tone. "What are you talking about? I found her. If she was raped I'm the investigating officer, it's my job to find out who did it to her. We've got to do an AIDS test . . ."

"Sergeant, your job is to stay outside this room and make sure nobody is admitted. You think you can handle that?"

"But she said she was raped. We have a procedure—"

"We have another procedure, sergeant." Knight smiled. "I'll get back here in a couple of hours.

The investigation is being handled at a higher level. You can relax."

"You already called the captain in on this?" Cash felt his skin tighten.

"Somebody more important than your captain is now personally involved."

"Who?"

"Coach Sand. Your captain is taking care of the paperwork. Any information you've got is to be communicated only to him."

"What about the girl?"

"I gave her Demerol and Valium. She'll sleep until I get back. You just do as you're told and be careful about making accusations."

"Is she gonna be okay?"

Dr. Mel Knight turned and walked off down the corridor.

Geometry

1960

Steve Lee put backspin on the ball. The leather kissed off the hardwood and bounced back and up, snuggling into his brother Pat Lee's hands.

Pushing hard off his toes, Pat was in the air.

The two defenders had no chance. Pat had beaten them to the baseline. It was perfect geometry and timing. The ball was in the right place and time. So was Pat. Steve knew he would be there. It was what made the brothers so good.

Steve put the ball on the baseline because it was where it had to be. Steve knew the moment Pat knew. They knew when, where, and how.

Now Pat rose toward the backboard, rolled the

ball off his long fingers, let it bang off the glass, through the hoop and slash into the net.

Before Pat had returned to earth the buzzer sounded.

They had won.

Like they had won all year long.

Yet each time seemed like the first time.

Even the last time would seem like the first time.

Time. They were experts at using it. But even for them, it was running out.

Soon they would be playing their last game. All they could do was try not to think about it. But it was coming, just like death.

Losing was a small death, a homicide in a tiny part of a player's soul. But to stop playing, to have no more games, was death. It was an ending, a crossing over from a world that was bright with joy, skills, knowledge into a world that was dark and unknown.

The world of the game. The life of the game. The art of the game. The game was life telescoped and they had been *living* it.

On the court they were one mind with ten arms and ten legs—a ten-legged, ten-armed monster that was terrorizing the hardwood in western Michigan in the year 1960.

They had played together since the fifties in junior high school when they were all elbows and knees and the bigger, richer schools beat them like stepchildren. Now, they were nearly grown and pounding down every team in their path. But it was almost over, it had all gone by so fast. Their first game had seemed like yesterday.

It was said they were unbeatable. Maybe. The next few weeks would tell. Win or lose, it would all be over in a few short weeks.

When Pat thought about it he was frightened. He panicked, like he knew old people must panic when death became real and palpable. Close. Bearing down on them like a train with nothing between them and the collision but prayer.

"Prayer never stopped no train."

"What?" Steve asked his brother as he pulled on his shirt, his hair still wet from the shower.

"Nothing." Pat stripped off his uniform and walked to the showers. He was always the first one there and the last to leave. He loved this place, its sounds and smells, the feel of the locker room. Soon they were going to force him to leave for the final time and would never, ever, let him come back and do what he loved doing most in the world.

He was helpless to stop it. He would have prayed if he believed it would have helped.

But prayer never stopped no train.

He let the water beat on him and felt his energy drain. A strangely euphoric exhaustion always descended on him in the shower after a win. If the feeling would continue as long as the water pounded his body he would stay under the spray forever. It was an incredible high, but like a narcotic, it had the same side effect. It wore off. And he came crashing down. Still, the going up was worth the coming down. But what about that final fall? Where would he land? How hard? And how long would he stay down?

For the next few weeks there could still be another game to take him into the stratosphere. But what would happen after that last game? The Final Permanent Splashdown.

Pat turned off the shower and wandered back into the locker room. Now, after a game, win or lose, the bottom fell out of his heart. Until the next game.

The games were his life. He just marked time between them. And time was getting short.

"Is that all it does, Steve?" Pat said to his younger brother. "Just gets shorter and shorter?"

Steve stopped combing his hair. Familiar with his brother's unanswerable questions, he responded with a grin. "You're getting worse, Pat. You never got over 1949."

"Time's running out."

"That's the deal, brother. Come on, let's go to the dance. You can listen to music and won't have to think."

"I'll be out in a while," Pat said, and watched his brother leave.

Alone in the locker room, he could dress slowly,

deliberately, trying to stretch out the feeling as long as possible. It would take him another twenty minutes to dress, then, reluctantly, he would leave and it would be over.

God, how he hated the endings.

Pat Lee's first encounter with time had been New Year's Eve, 1949. He was seven years old. He knew he was seven because he had birthdays, but birthdays were about parties and presents and getting bigger. Birthdays were not about time.

He had vague recollections of other New Year's Eves, when his parents let him and his brother stay up until midnight. When they all went out on the front porch and yelled "Happy New Year," banged on pots and pans and listened to other people around the little farm town of Wood, Michigan, all doing the same thing. Until his father shot off both barrels of his twelve-gauge Stevens Blue Goose and they went back in and went to bed.

But December 31, 1949, had been different. His parents were going out somewhere. Uncle Jake was going to stay with Pat and Steve. Pat wanted to know why.

"Because, we are going to a party," their mother explained. "It's the end of a decade."

Pat had no idea what "decade" meant but he wasn't going to let that keep him from boring in on his mother.

"So what?"

"Well, we're going to celebrate with some of our friends. You can stay up until midnight if you like. It's going to be 1950, honey!"

"No, it's not," Pat argued. "It's 1949."

"Of course, it's 1949 today, but tomorrow it will be 1950."

"*No*. It's always 1949!" Suddenly Pat was angry and scared. He didn't know why. "It's *always* 1949!" He felt threatened and fought back. Even at seven he was like that.

When he woke up the next morning it was January 1, 1950, and life wasn't the same. He had found out about time . . .

Now it was March, 1960, and Pat knew what decade meant. An end and a beginning.

Pat had liked the *fifties*. What kind of decade would the *sixties* be? 1960 threatened him like 1950 had. Because he had learned one hard lesson about time—just when something had gotten great and wonderful, it ended.

The *fifties* had just ended.

Pat Lee hated endings.

With good reason.

Time

Coach Pat Lee clawed out of his sleep like a drowning man.

He had been dreaming about high school again. Over thirty years ago and the dreams made it seem like yesterday.

The head recruiter for Southwestern State University, whose boss was his ex-boyhoodfriend, and now the famed SWS head coach, Barry Sand, was soaked with perspiration. He looked around the hotel room, his mind scrambling across three decades for a foothold in the present. Fuck me.

The room looked familiar, but all hotel rooms looked familiar. He could be anywhere in the United States or Canada. But, was he where he was supposed to be?

Pat tried to sit up and his head felt as if it had split open. His mouth tasted like someone had promoted a circus in it. He eased his head back on the damp pillow and searched his cratered mind for some dim memory of the night before. Lately, he could remember things that had happened in the fifties and sixties like it was yesterday. It was yesterday he couldn't remember like it was yesterday.

The drinking didn't help him remember yesterday, but at least it made today easier to take. The last thing he recalled was flying into Detroit from Dallas and driving to Medgar Evers High to meet head basketball coach O.K. Free and his star point guard Jamail Jenks, who some said could be a future Chuck Small, SWS's current superstar. Jenks was Michigan's Mister Basketball and Southwestern State University of Greater Dallas was one of the fifty schools that Jenks was "seriously considering."

Lee had taken the six-foot-seven-inch Jenks and Coach Free to dinner to discuss Jenks's prospects and Free's demands. O.K. Free was the kind of coach who "shopped" his best players, always demanding something for himself for steering the player to the most agreeable college, and Lee had already paid Coach Free $15,000 in cash money just for setting up the dinner meeting. Some goddamn hors d'oeuvre.

After dinner Pat gave Jamail Jenks the keys to

his rental car to go visit his girlfriend while Pat and O.K. Free retired to the bar to work out the nuts and bolts of the deal. If Free agreed to the deal he would make certain that Jamail Jenks signed the letter of intent to attend Southwestern State.

Pat remembered ordering a double Stoli and asking O.K. Free what it would take to get Jenks. After that, his mind went blank.

Pat tended to recruit especially heavily in Detroit because it was familiar territory, where he and SWS head coach Barry Sand had once been teammates on a Michigan high school state championship basketball team back in 1960. God, how he'd loved those days, how he'd hated to see them end. He'd gone to Southwestern State in the Dixie Conference on a basketball scholarship from 1960 to 1964, and Barry Sand had come along on scholarship as a student assistant—a twofer deal, with Barry strictly segundo. But Barry Sand, over the years, had changed all that, and now the roles were reversed.

Twofer deals might include teammates like Pat and Barry, or they could be father-son deals with the father getting a job in the area, on campus, or hired on as an assistant coach. Some twofer deals included the player and his girlfriend. Now in the nineties Pat wondered when he would be asked to make a twofer for a player and his boy-friend.

In the sixties the first thing Pat and Barry discovered was that no blacks were allowed to play in the Dixie Conference. Or, for that matter, in most of the big conferences in the South. The Lily White Leagues, Pat had called them. As a revenue-producing sport in the sixties and seventies, Dixie Conference basketball was a stepchild to football, because without access to the talent pool of inner-city black players Dixie Conference basketball was actually below the level of top high school play in states like New York, Indiana, Illinois and Michigan. Even Barry Sand could have played at Southwestern if he hadn't hurt his shoulder in the regional finals game in Kalamazoo. To make basketball a major sport in the Old Confederacy, college coaches would have to find a way to tap into that huge untouchable pool of black players. Not surprisingly, when Barry Sand took over as head coach, recruiting blacks, thanks to Pat Lee, was top of the agenda of the Southwestern State basketball program.

It had made SWS a national power. It was why Pat Lee had gone to the well again in Detroit.

What worried Pat this morning was that he couldn't remember what had happened at the well. These blackout binges were becoming frighteningly common in his life as head recruiter for SWS. Trying to stop time, as usual. Trying to deny what seemed to have happened to him since those golden oldie days before . . .

The Conquering Heroes

*   *   *

He slid out of the hotel bed and staggered, head bent below shoulders, to the small refrigerator next to the television, grabbed a beer and drank it down without taking the can from his lips. Back in bed, he was beginning to feel a little better. The pain in his head had subsided and he no longer felt like his nervous system was on the outside of his body.

He turned on the television, where a newscaster was describing the traffic conditions on the freeway coming in from Galveston Island to Houston.

"Oh, shit," Lee intoned. "Something tells me we ain't in Dee-troit no more."

Panic began to set in, and he made and drank a Bloody Mary.

After fixing a second he dialed his office at Southwestern in Dallas. The phone rang five times before his secretary Jan answered.

"Basketball offices," Jan Dayton sang out. "Coach Lee's office."

"It's me. I'm in Houston."

"How did it go in Detroit?"

"Great." A lie. "I just about got Jamail sewed up."

"Well, you better. You know, Barry says he'll fire you if you don't bring in Jamail *and* Eddie Sanford from Houston Country Day."

"Hey. Don't worry," Pat said, relieved by her

29

reminder that he was supposed to go to Houston on this recruiting swing. "I got Jamail and I'll nail Eddie Sanford today. Barry will be kissing my ass in front of the Student Union at noon."

"Good." Jan sounded genuinely pleased for him. "Well, Barry told the press yesterday that it was your inadequate recruiting that cost Southwestern a berth in the NCAA tournaments last year for the first time in six years."

"Barry wouldn't even have a program if it wasn't for me spending my life beating the bushes and the ghettos for talent."

"I'm afraid that's not the way he tells it," Jan said. "He's spent the last two days covering his ass at your expense. *Sign* these guys, will you? I like working for you."

"No sweat. So what else is new?"

"Avis called from Detroit. They want to know why you haven't returned your rental car."

Pat slapped his forehead and restarted the ache behind his eyes. "I totally forgot, I lent it to Jamail Jenks."

"That was real brilliant, Einstein." Jan was good at cleaning up after him on recruiting trips. "You better get it returned. If the NCAA finds out he's driving it . . . well, you know the drill."

"I doubt they'll ever find the car." Pat pressed his forehead with the heel of his left hand to ease the pain behind his eyes. "It's probably nothing but two axles and a frame sitting on cement blocks somewhere in the Woodward Avenue corridor." He drained the last of the second Bloody Mary. "Anything else?"

"Nothing I can put my finger on"—Jan's voice took on a hushed air of mystery and concern—"but Barry's been on a rampage all morning. Dr. Knight and some campus cop met with him this morning. He's got his boy DeFor Clark trying to find Chuck Small."

"Barry's still trying to figure a way to keep Chuck from declaring early for the NBA," Pat said. "Either that or he got caught pawning the TV from the athletic dorm again."

"Well, stay in touch, boss."

"Sure, and call me if anything big breaks." Pat gave her his room and phone number. "I'll be out after Sanford later this afternoon."

Drinking Bloody Marys, he went out and sat on the small balcony of the high-rise hotel staring southwest at the Houston skyline.

It was 10:30 A.M. He had calmed down some since waking in this strange room, but he still had no recollection of the late night drinking and bargaining session with Detroit Medgar Evers High School coach O.K. Free.

Nor did he know how he had gotten from Detroit to Houston. But at least he could take some solace from the fact that he was to fly to Houston to recruit Eddie Sanford, a white seven-foot center from Houston Country Day after closing the deal with Coach Free for Jamail Jenks. Trouble was, he just didn't know if he had closed the deal for Jenks, or if he had, just what the deal included.

He thought of Barry Sand laying the blame for last season's poor showing on him. It was another of the many deceits courtesy of Barry Sands that had started long ago with Geena Keats in high school. "*Trying* don't get the hay in the barn," Barry would say. No shit.

He picked up the phone and dialed Rachael's number in Houston. He would slip down there and see her today. Maybe go to Galveston, have some drinks at the Galvez, talk about old times and good memories and walk along the breakwater.

Take some time off. Relax. Quit worrying.

Rachael's lawyer-husband, Benjamin Pankin, was always out of town on some real-estate or oil deal, a nuevo-Texas George Bush/Ronald Reagan/Richard Nixon Republican. He'd left the Democrats and joined the Republican Party during Watergate, one of the few known instances of a rat swimming *to* a sinking ship. Pat could smile at that. What kind of man votes for guys like that, Pat liked to ask himself, unconsciously helping to justify his adultery.

He let the phone ring fifteen times before slamming down the receiver. Next the asshole would be supporting Ross Perot, the billionaire populist . . . He checked his watch. Rachael was probably at the Houston Galleria shopping and having lunch with the River Oaks crowd.

He drained his Bloody Mary and decided to take a quick nap and regroup before heading out to see Eddie Sanford.

As soon as he closed his eyes, the memories came flooding back. Back to when it had all seemed so simple and there was nowhere to go but up. Back to the golden days when they were young and indestructible and were going to play forever. Every day in every way, things were getting better and better.

The Sock Hop

March, 1960

The gym was transformed. The bright lights were off, everything was in shadows. The screaming crowd was gone. The bleachers had been folded up into the walls. The backboards and rims had been cranked up into joists in the ceiling. Sawdust had been sprinkled lightly across the floor and couples clung to each other, dancing in their socks.

Fats Domino's "Blueberry Hill" was playing. It had been Pat's favorite song when he was a freshman. He had seen lots of blueberries. His grandfather had grown them in the peculiar sour soil of the fruit farming country of west Michigan . . .

The Conquering Heroes

Now his eyes began to adjust to the dim light and he scanned the darkened gym for his teammates. His brother Steve would be off with Barb, as usual. Steve was a lover. But the rest of them, Ron Waters, Barry Sand, Chuck Stanislawski and Larry "The Frog" Grant, would be huddled somewhere rehashing the game.

They were six-men deep, a little thin but as long as no one got hurt or in foul trouble it would be enough to take on the big-city schools if they got that far. Kalamazoo, Grand Rapids, Lansing, Jackson, Flint, Detroit had deep teams. They could go to their ninth and tenth men without a drop in talent. But they could only play five at a time, and Pat would match up his five against any combination the big schools wanted to put on the floor.

Well, they would all know soon enough. The state tournaments started next week.

Somehow Pat Boone's "Love Letters in the Sand" had bumped Fats Domino as he felt the touch of soft fingers against his back.

"Hi," Geena Keats said from behind him. "I wondered how long you were going to stay in there. Everybody else has been out for twenty minutes."

"I'm a slow dresser." He turned to face Geena.

"You couldn't prove it by me." Geena smiled. "Not that I'm trying to get you to show me."

But in fact she was, and had been for the several months they'd been dating. And he had been tempted many times. Geena was tall, slender, her face was surrounded by thick blonde hair, clear soft skin stretched tight across sharp cheekbones and jawline. Her green eyes seemed to glitter.

Pat liked Geena Keats, probably more than he had ever liked any girl, but that wasn't reason enough to have sex with her. Color him old-fashioned? In a way it was more that it involved the kind of beginning and ending that Pat had *some* control over. And that was getting to be more and more important to him.

Pat's role-reversal, being the one to say no, not surprisingly intrigued and excited Geena. Most other guys were out to score, or at least claimed they were.

Pat also figured his life was complicated enough without taking on the responsibility of sex with Geena, no matter how attractive that prospect was. He was, after all, a normal male. But the fact that Geena Keats was Catholic made it even more complicated.

"You wouldn't respect me in the morning," Pat said, smiling, trying to defuse things by making the joke.

"I haven't got that much respect for you now," Geena came back at him.

Pat acknowledged the dig with a shrug but didn't remind her that by the end of March the 1960 Michigan state tournaments and high school basketball would be over. By June he would graduate from high school and in September he hoped to go to college, which one he didn't know. Well, he wasn't going to start sleeping with Geena just to end sleeping with Geena in a few months.

Pat Lee didn't need any more endings in his life.

Carl Perkins was asking how come you say you do when you don't? for Geena and she began to smile. Pat loved her smile. She just lit up. Her eyes turned an even brighter green and she always seemed genuinely happy when she smiled. He wanted her to be genuinely happy. He didn't want to cause her pain. He told himself that, and meant it. Was he being too damn noble? Was he a phony? Was he just plain scared? Truth was, he didn't really know . . .

"Where's your brother?" Geena was asking.

"Where do you think?"

She nodded. "He and Barb make a nice couple." She slid her hand into Pat's, tickling the palm with her nails.

"Have you seen Ron or Barry?" Pat said, trying to cut her off at the pass.

"They're over by the door there with Chuck and the Frog." Geena was pointing toward a lobby doorway, where Pat could make them out huddled together against the wall.

Larry "The Frog" Grant, long and lean.

Ron Waters, the shortest at five feet, eight inches, the best pure athlete ever since junior high.

Chuck Stanislawski, average height and weight, his special talent knowing when, where, and how many great plays were needed from him during a game. They had won two games that season on last-second shots by Chuck. In each game it was the *only* shot he took.

And then there was Barry Sand, the bull, six feet tall, thick through the chest and shoulders, a farm kid with an alcoholic father. Barry Sand was street smart, a survivor, a force. He wanted to go to college, and he wanted to be a coach. Nothing was going to stop him, he said. Nobody was going to stand in his way. They'd better not. Barry wasn't the greatest athletic talent, and he knew it. But he was near-maniacal about making it. Barry Sand would not be denied. Just ask him. Nothing and no one would be allowed to stop him. Hell, he couldn't even stop himself, if it came to that.

"Let's dance," Geena said, nudging Pat.

"I just ran my legs off on this floor, I'm not gonna dance on it too."

Pat took her by the hand and walked her over to join his teammates. Nobody said hello. They just exchanged glances, nodding to Geena, and absorbed them into the group.

The Conquering Heroes

It was a warm, comfortable feeling, one Pat treasured.

"I thought they had us there at the end," the Frog, the team pessimist, was saying.

"They had to be more than four points ahead with a minute to go," Ron Waters, lead guard in the offense and natural leader, said. During a game, he seldom spoke; he led by his acts.

"Hey, Barry, you beat the shit out of their big forward," Chuck said. "He was bitching to the ref all night."

"I got four fouls," Sand weighed in, his dark brows pulled together.

"That's one for every three times you knocked him down," Chuck Stanislawski said, careful to smile when he said it.

"It's a contact sport," Barry said. "What the hell they expect?"

"I thought football was the contact sport," Geena cut in.

"No." Barry's voice was hard. "Football is a *collision* sport."

Pat Lee's brother Steve and his girl, Barb Coles, came into the gym now from the lobby, Steve buttoning his shirt and tucking it into his pants.

"Christ, Steve, how many times you going to get dressed tonight?" Ron Waters said.

Steve grinned, glanced at his brother and said nothing. Her face turning red, Barb walked over and began whispering to Geena.

Peter Gent

"We were just watching the satellite go over," Steve said finally.

"You can do that with your clothes on, buddy."

Somebody had put Sanford Clark's "The Fool" on the record player. It was time to leave.

"We're going to my place," Pat announced, touching Geena's arm. "We'll meet you guys there."

Everybody nodded and Pat led Geena from the gym, the song echoing in his ears, about a fool telling his baby goodbye.

The Derrick Lounge

The song was echoing again in Pat Lee's ears as he woke up from his nap in the Houston hotel room three decades later.

It was 2:00 P.M. by the time he showered and left his room, taking the up-elevator to check out the Derrick Lounge on the top floor with its panoramic view of Houston and the surrounding urban sprawl that covered the rice fields of the coastal plain, buried under the overbuilt housing developments, empty shopping centers and unleased office-industrial parks, hallmarks of the Reagan Revolution and George Bush's Voodoo Economics, the same he had once criticized Reagan for. The supply-sider's taxpayer-financed nightmare lay out in all directions as far as the eye could see.

In the eighties people like Rachael's lawyer-husband had built up and written down properties everywhere. On top of the rice fields exclusive housing developments grew up overnight while the FDIC and Federal Flood Insurance protected the hustlers with tax dollars. And flood they did, of course. Rice fields were designed to flood. Three-hundred-thousand-dollar houses would fill to the second floor with muddy water and the taxpayer would pay the bill. Down on Galveston Island they built $200,000 condominiums without a thought to the hurricane of 1900 that pushed a tidal surge completely over the island to a depth of some twenty feet and killed 6,000 people. A once-in-a-lifetime fluke, they said, it would only happen this once. But for those people once in a life was all they got.

Finally the savings and loan industry, which had based its real-estate paper on supply-side economics and The Greater Fool theory, began to teeter. The oil loans went bad and the house of cards collapsed, just this once. A five-hundred-billion-dollar fluke. Next would come the commercial banks and the insurance companies. But, the politicians were hiding the coming disaster as long as possible.

Pat Lee may have been only an assistant coach in charge of recruiting but he wasn't ignorant.

The Conquering Heroes

His job may have made him crazy; it didn't make him stupid. He had been dealing with star mentality since he was seventeen. What did everyone expect? he had said when the economy collapsed. "Reagan let an ex-pro football player and David Stockman from Benton Harbor develop economic policy." Pat himself had grown up thirty miles from Benton Harbor, a once thriving little industrial city on Lake Michigan. Now Benton Harbor was looking like Germany and Japan in 1945 without any hope of a Marshall Plan or a MacArthur regency. This time the winners picked up the marbles and went home. They left the tab for the losers. The Greater Fool theory was a reality.

"Remember the difference between brilliance and stupidity," Jim Lee liked to tell his sons Pat and Steve once he quit buying Fords and switched to Volkswagens. "Brilliance has its limits, stupidity knows no bounds." You wanted proof? Reagan was an unemployed actor, the Great Communicator without a thing to say.

The world was upside down.

Pat couldn't get a head coaching job, although he had played twelve years of basketball. At the same time his youngest son's high-school coach had watched the movie *Hoosiers* before every game, hoping to pick up coaching tips and inspiration from Gene Hackman and Dennis Hopper. Kids all over the country thought

Kevin Costner was a pro baseball player, Wesley Snipes and Woody Harrelson were world-class basketball hustlers, and there was a chance the Cleveland Indians could get to the World Series if Charlie Sheen got glasses and Tom Berenger could just bunt.

Tom Selleck played Japanese baseball in a Japanese movie. The Japanese were buying American culture and selling it back, taking the cash and leaving the trash.

And the fans were coming out of the stands after the players. The rules had changed, the boundaries were disappearing.

Playing The Game was becoming more and more dangerous, Pat thought as he walked to a table near the floor-to-ceiling glass wall on the south side of the Derrick Lounge, sat down and gazed through the hot smog toward downtown Houston.

The lounge was empty.

"We just opened." The woman's soft voice startled him.

She had a sort of exhausted beauty about her; small lines wrinkled the corners of her green eyes, her dullish blonde hair was tied back. Green eyes and blonde hair . . . reminded him some of Geena Keats. Pat felt himself immediately attracted to her.

"The waitresses won't be in for another hour. I'm the bar manager. What can I get you?" A white tag over her left breast read ANNE. She was well-shaped, about five feet six.

Pat studied her body and face, a habit from over twenty-five years hunting down physical talent to feed the ever hungry basketball program at SWS. Behind the rather gloomy aura that surrounded her was an attractive woman in her mid-thirties in good physical shape.

Except he felt a deep pain clouded her eyes.

"Well"— Pat paused, glancing again at her name tag—"Anne? I'm Pat. It's nice to meet you."

"Likewise." She nodded, looking down to study her long delicate fingers and the well-kept nails covered with clear polish.

"Could you make me a tall Bloody Mary with three shots of Stolichnaya?" Pat stared into her face.

The request seemed to surprise her. She looked up, for a moment their eyes met; then they looked away.

"Sure. Anything else? Corn chips? Potato chips? Silicon chips?"

"What?" He looked at her. Now he was surprised.

"A little postindustrial service-economy humor." She half-smiled. "Sort of a high-tech riff on 'do you want fries with that?'"

"That's good. I like it."

"You're the first." Anne drew her lips together tightly. "But then, you're the first customer I've had since Bush threatened to beat the piss out of Saddam Hussein. Sorry, it's my America as third world humor."

"Let's see what the first drink does and maybe you'll have time to do your complete stand-up act." He smiled when he said it.

"You want to run a tab?"

"Please. Room 1201." He watched her move back behind the bar. She carried herself well, denying the fatigue in her eyes.

While she was working on his drink Pat tried to organize himself for his recruiting run at Eddie Sanford. He had already scouted the kid's game, talked to him several times on the phone and in person and sent him hundreds of pieces of mail.

Eddie Sanford. He came from what the sociologists would call a lower-class white family shattered by divorce. He lived with his mother, but his life was still dominated by his father Jo Don, a crude, intimidating tool pusher who worked on offshore rigs. Pat had met Jo Don once, at one of Eddie's games. The man was so abusive and foul that Pat had changed his basic recruiting strategy and decided to avoid involving himself in the domestic side of the kid's life.

Usually recruiting a kid from a broken home was easiest when Pat inserted himself into the single-parent (read: mother) household and bcgan playing the father figure. Flattering the mother, offering emotional support as a surrogate dad to the recruit was an effective route to a kid's trust, and eventually convincing him to come to SWS. Okay, he was no saint, but in spite of himself he was no cynic either. Hell, he even liked some of the kids. Some a lot, too much.

Pat learned to read his prospects. They all wanted to be told they were great, would play a lot and go on to lucrative careers in the NBA. He didn't *promise* that last, but he did let it lie there. He knew the odds against a college kid making it in the pros were about five hundred to one. The odds against a high-school kid were astronomical. The kid had a better chance of becoming a nuclear physicist than an NBA player. But they wanted to believe it, and, deep down, so did Pat Lee, even though he knew better.

The parents always wanted to know that their kid was special and would be handled with kid gloves. "I'll treat him like he was my own kid," Pat would say, and even if he couldn't always keep that promise, he believed it when he said it. Hell, these recruits had a better chance to claim his attention than his own kids, who were subjects of benign neglect. Like his wife Sara. Ex-wife. His recruiting job kept him away from his family, and one day he came home from a two-week recruiting swing to an empty house and a note from Sara. It wasn't an angry note. She had loved him, probably still did, but he was married to the road, and her jump shot wasn't what it used to be.

47

Sorry Pat, she and the kids needed a man around the office . . .

After meeting the six foot five inch, 225 pound Jo Don Sanford, dealing with his mercurial and dangerous personality, listening to the constant threats he made about his ex-wife or people messing with Eddie, Pat took himself out of the family loop and recruited Eddie outside his home. Jo Don Sanford plain scared the shit out of Pat.

During the twelve months he had been bird-dogging Eddie Sanford, Pat had never met the kid's mother. He knew that could be a fatal mistake and this trip planned to rectify the omission, no matter the risk from Jo Don. His devout hope was that Jo Don was offshore somewhere pushing tools or drowning.

Eddie was a decent, hard-working kid, with a great attitude—he didn't have the star mentality and kept his dreams and goals within reason. He wanted to graduate from college and his B+ high-school record indicated he had every chance of doing it. He had scored in the high 1200s on his SATs, so he would be eligible to play his freshman year. Since Proposition 48, the SAT scores were important. Prop 48, for example, was a major stumbling block in Jamail Jenk's path to playing as a freshman, and it was Pat's job, like it or not, to remove the obstacles. Head coach Barry Sand didn't care how.

The Conquering Heroes

Because of Prop 48, Barry Sand was always telling Pat to be on the lookout for JUCO (junior college) kids who could play immediately. Also "somebody else has already bought 'em a car." Pat didn't much like recruiting junior college players because he would have to find someone to replace them in two years.

For Barry what most counted was kids who could immediately contribute to his quest for the glory *and* the money a trip to the Final Four would bring. The NCAA bid alone was worth $250,000 and reaching the Final Four would bring in well over a million to the basketball program. And that didn't include ticket sales or television and radio contracts negotiated for the regular season with the networks and cable sports. The network had paid a billion dollars for the rights to televise the NCAA tournaments. Major money. The previous year Southwestern State basketball had netted $2.5 million *without* a bid to the NCAA tourney.

But never mind what you did for me, what have you got coming up? That was Barry Sand's heavy hand on his recruits. Well, Eddie Sanford was a recruiter's dream and SWS and Pat Lee needed him next year real bad. Chuck Small, Southwestern's all-American center, was planning to declare early for the NBA draft, which would leave a huge hole in the middle of the Southwestern offense. Coach Barry Sand hadn't given up on Small and was using all the

49

pressure he could muster, from promises of love and money to threats of retribution, to keep the kid on campus, but so far Small was unmoved and Sand was pushing Pat even harder to land Eddie Sanford.

"I want this kid," Barry had told Pat. "You want to keep your job here, old buddy, you'll bring me this Sanford kid *and* Jamail Jenks."

Pat tried not to take Barry's threats seriously. Barry Sands was no Bobby Knight. Pat had played against Bobby in college. As a player, Knight was a good seventh man on a great Ohio State team. As a coach, Knight had taken everything Fred Taylor had taught him to another level. Pat knew Barry needed him, not just to bring in talent but also to teach the system. Barry hadn't played past their high school days, and was a poor fundamental, tactical and strategic coach. Barry coached by threats, which didn't exactly endear him to his players. But Barry Sand did have one great talent—politicking, jawboning athletic directors, rich alumni and trustees. When he wanted to he could even turn on the charm, and he was a past master of the blame game. And now, Jan told Pat, Sand was publicly blaming Pat's recruiting for the previous year's failure to get an NCAA bid.

Barry Sand, unlovable as he was, was no fool. He had never failed to recognize where his bread was buttered, and that dated back to junior high school in Michigan. He understood that Pat had the ability to recognize, recruit and develop talent, and that that ability was mostly responsible for making Barry Sand the "Dean of Dixie Conference Coaches." On the other hand, if it was his ass or Pat's, if the heat got hot enough, Barry would decide that somewhere there must be another Pat Lee and fire him.

Pat knew this, though he hated to admit it to himself, just as he'd hated over the years to acknowledge that he probably long ago should have cut loose from Barry and SWS. Why the hell hadn't he? His wife had asked him that. His friends, too. Even his secretary Jan once put it to him when she'd had a couple of drinks at an end-of-the-season party. He rationalized, like most human beings. And he had his points . . . he really loved the job, he got his greatest satisfaction finding and developing kids with talent, even though increasingly they were getting greedy and arrogant, and some were straight-out scumbags. But then there were the Eddie Sanfords that reminded him why he was still doing what he did. And nobody had the perfect job, and so forth.

But right now, with Barry Sand putting the heat on him like never before, he could literally feel the sweat running from under his arms.

Anne, the Derrick Lounge manager, appeared with his drink and set it in front of him, a huge celery stalk sunk in the glass of red liquid.

"You look like you need some nourishment,"

she said, shaking her head. "I've seen people trying to drink themselves sober before. During the boom years I watched oil tycoons, junk-bond brokers, swampland developers and freelance swindlers swill alcohol like it was a miracle drug."

"Where are they now?" Pat made an exaggerated motion of looking around the empty bar.

"Downtown." Anne pointed south. "Drinking Mad Dog 20/20 and sleeping in old refrigerator boxes." She studied Pat's face. "You have a bad night?"

"I'm not sure. What day is it?"

"Thursday."

"Shit! I had a couple of bad nights *and* days. The last thing I remember was Tuesday night."

"That's not too good." She wiped the table.

Pat shook his head. "I was in Detroit. I don't know how I got to Houston."

"Better rethink your lifestyle, cowboy. Pass out in Detroit and come to in Houston two days later . . . It's the nineties. Drunks are out of style."

Pat took a long pull of Russian vodka and Mexican tomato juice.

"I hate the nineties," he said. "Everybody wants to live forever and look beautiful."

"Seems like a decent idea." Anne's hair fell over her left eye and she brushed it back with her slender fingers.

"Well, I'm a sixties survivor looking to share my golden years with a codependent in a warm alley in a decent welfare state." He said it with a straight face.

"Well, survivor, you better get the hell out of Texas." She placed her fists on her hips, her arms akimbo. "The old safety net went south."

"I'm not worried, I used to drink with the governor. And, Attorney General Laude VanMeer was my college roommate."

"That ought to tell you something right there." Pat nodded.

"Well, go straight to Waco, do not pass GO and do not collect $200 unless you use it to bribe an ATF Agent. That's my Apocalypse Now humor, sorry."

"Very good." Pat nodded. "Actually the Branch Davidians are an offshoot sect of the old House of David in Benton Harbor, Michigan. I grew up near there. Me and David Stockman." He saw her questioning look and quickly explained that Stockman had been a financial whiz kid in Reagan's administration, had admitted he screwed up with supply-side b.s. and now, naturally, was making a million per on Wall Street.

"Anyway," Pat said, "as far as my recent behavior is concerned, I'm supposed to be here. I think I've learned to time travel and space shift."

"But I bet if you ever backtrack you'll find some big muddy prints of your screwups in airplanes, taxicabs and hotels from here to Detroit."

"Probably." Pat took a long drink of the Bloody

Mary. "Here's to short-term memory loss."

Anne rolled her green eyes and walked back to the bar.

Pat finished his drink and decided to try Rachael's number again.

The day was still young, even if he wasn't.

He used the phone at the end of the bar and charged the call to his room.

After ten rings he gave up and ordered another drink.

Anne looked at him. "Even if you don't know how you got here, I'm still responsible for how much damage you do to yourself, and others, if you drink too much."

"You a lady cop? Social worker? Hey, I made it to here, and once upon a time I was damn good."

He walked back to his table. Anne brought his drink and sat down with him. Pat reached for the glass and touched her fingers.

"What is it you were so damn good at?" She drew her hand away.

"Basketball. I was a hell of a player. High school, college and professional."

"And now?"

"I'm supposed to be a college basketball coach, but I don't get to do much coaching."

"I can see why." Her eyes followed the glass up to his lips and back to the table.

"I'm a *good* coach, lady." He held up the glass.

54

"This is just a . . . symptom."

"What's the disease?"

Pat stared at his glass. He almost said Barry Sand. "Instead of teaching kids to love the art and the passion of the game I spend my time convincing them that to play basketball at Southwestern State is akin to a state of grace."

"Is it?"

He finished off his drink. "I got to go to work."

"Look, miss," Sgt. Jim Cash was saying to Cathy Sullivan in her hospital bed. "You really don't want to press charges . . ."

"But he *raped* me. He beat me up and raped me."

"That's your story," Cash said, trying not to be sympathetic. He had his orders. "His story is very different. He said you were a groupie that always hung around the basketball team—"

"He's *lying*." Tears appeared in spite of herself. Her face tightened. "He beat me and raped me. He kidnapped me and kept me a prisoner. What more do you need to hear?"

"Like I said before, that's your story." He paused, then said, "Small said you've slept with half the team—"

"A *lie*. I only accepted the ride to get out of the rain. He—"

"Look, this isn't the place to give testimony." Jim Cash didn't want to hear, he didn't want to know. It was a shit job but it was his. "As far as I know, if you had sex with him it could have been voluntary, you could just be trying to extort money from him." He cut off her protest. "Look, I'm not the judge or the jury. I just report what I know, and all I know right now is that it looks like you're just another white girl who likes to hang around nigger ball players."

Jim Cash looked away as he said it. A shit job, no question. "The newspapers will love it—"

"Why are you doing this?" Cathy Sullivan demanded, still fighting the tears.

His answer was to press harder. It was an opening. "A pretty girl like you must have a boyfriend, think what he's gonna do when he hears about this? What about your family?"

She looked away, covered her face with her hands.

"Now, I'm not saying anybody else has to know. We can end this thing right here and now." And as he said it and saw her face, saw what he was doing to her, the anger built against Barry Sand and the orders to protect Chuck Small. A real hero, that one.

"I haven't filed a report." His face was getting red. "Nobody has to know anything." He was sickened at the sound of his own voice.

"If you make trouble, well, you can't imagine what trouble you'll be in." He tried to sound caring. He hit somewhere around ironic. He was telling the truth this time. They'd really dump on her . . .

"But . . . I . . ." She struggled to form whole thoughts. She couldn't believe the horror of her situation.

"They'll bring out other players to say you hung around the basketball team. Everybody in Texas will hear about this. Chuck Small is a big hero. He's a star. Important people will protect him. They'll say you were a whore and slept around—"

"Why can't I at least see a rape counselor?"

"Believe me, the more you stir this, the worse it will get." Which was true . . . "Look, miss, I'm not gonna file a report. Dr. Knight admitted you without any records. You can stay a couple of days and the school will pick up the bill—"

"Who *are* you people? You're supposed to help me?" Her voice was getting weak in spite of herself.

Cash looked out the hospital window at the campus that looked calm and serene. "I'm trying to help, Miss Sullivan. You don't want your name and picture splashed all over television."

"But . . . why? . . ." She kept up the struggle, still not able to accept what was happening to her.

His job was to convince her. Cathy Sullivan had to be stopped from making any trouble for Barry Sand, Chuck Small, the basketball program. Sam Watts had told the captain and the captain had told him.

"You seem like a nice girl . . ." Cash winced inwardly as he considered what he was going to say next. "It would be a shame if people thought you were just a whore fucking niggers all the time."

Which finally did the job.

Sgt. Jim Cash could hear Cathy Sullivan sobbing out of control as he walked down the hall.

He hated the captain, Sam Watts, Barry Sand. Most of all he hated Chuck Small. He was ashamed of himself and prayed that his wife and children never learned about his part in this sordid mess.

And as her sobs still sounded in his ears, Sgt. Jim Cash had to wonder who was really the whore.

Eddie Sanford was leaving Houston Country Day School when Pat Lee caught up with him in the parking lot.

"Got a ride, Eddie?" Pat was sitting in a new Cadillac convertible that had been left at the motel for him by an SWS Booster Club member from Houston. "I left the top up, we can ride air-conditioned."

"Well . . . dad was supposed to . . ." Eddie scanned the lot for Jo Don Sanford's Ford Ranger pickup and didn't see it. "I guess he got called out to the rig. He thought he might."

"Good," Pat blurted, then quickly moved to recover. "I don't mean it's good he isn't here, I mean, it's good that I *am* here to give you a ride home. I've been wanting to meet your mother. I hear she's a wonderful woman."

"She's working." Eddie paused. "She won't be home until two in the morning. You look like you've got a hangover, Mr. Lee."

"Oh? Well, I've been on the road for weeks. I'm beat. I flew the red-eye from Detroit to see you, not that I wasn't glad to do it."

"What's in Detroit?" Eddie still hadn't moved to the passenger side of the car.

"My brother Steve," Pat lied. "He's a high-school coach and . . . he had to have surgery. I went up to see him. He was on the team with me and Coach Sand that won the Michigan high-school state championship." Well, some of it was true.

"You told me. Are you sure you don't have a hangover?"

"Come on, Eddic. You think I'd risk driving the top blue chip in the nation if I'd been drinking?"

"It's okay," Eddie said, smiling. "You're a coach, not a preacher."

Pat reorganized. He opened the driver's side door.

"You drive, kid," and Pat slid over to the passenger side.

Eddie considered the offer for another moment, then folded himself behind the wheel.

"Well, it's too far to walk and the buses aren't air-conditioned." He adjusted the seat as far back and as low as it would go, but his knees were still jammed under the steering wheel and his head touched the top.

"So, did you get the stuff I mailed you?" Pat asked.

Eddie nodded. They were driving through the crazy quilt of subdivisions and industrial developments of Houston, the only unzoned city of its size in the United States.

"Did you read any of it?"

"I glanced through it. I already told you I was interested in Southwestern. You've got Jax Morrow and I'd like to play on the same team with him. We had a great rivalry in high school. Why don't you believe me?"

"I *believe* you, Eddie. It's just that I know about all the pressures that can be brought to bear on a great talent like you. I also know about the corruption out there." Pat was warming up. "Some schools will offer anything to get a talent like you into their program."

Silence.

Pat's heart sank. "Has somebody made you an offer?" Panic started to take over. "You can't accept . . ."

Eddie fixed Pat with a flat stare.

"Well, I mean," Pat started over, "you, of course, can accept anything you want. It's just that I'd hate to see you do something that wasn't in your best interest."

Eddie steered down Westheimer.

"We're on national television fourteen times next year. With you in the middle we're a definite Final Four team. That's a fact."

"What about Chuck Small?" Eddie asked. "He's a two-time all-American and he's only a junior."

"I'll tell you the truth. Chuck's gonna declare early for the NBA. So center is all yours."

Pat looked to see what effect he was having. Not much, if any. Pat pushed it toward the edge, even considered crossing the line. Until now he had never offered any "inducements" to Eddie and the boy hadn't asked.

"Eddie, did somebody offer you money? If you need . . . maybe we could set up a job or something. You say your mother works hard. I know people here in Houston that would help her find a better paying job with better hours . . ."

"What are you talking about?"

Pat realized he had indeed overreacted. He had his toes on the line.

"Nothing really." Pat's head started to ache. "I was just surmising. We wouldn't ever offer you anything improper. We've got too much respect for you." At least he, Pat Lee, did.

Pat paused, squinting against the headache. "It's just that we've never fully explored all the options available to a kid with your brains and talent."

"What options? A scholarship is all anybody's allowed, isn't it?"

"Well, it is and it isn't." Pat felt mountain goats butting heads inside his skull. "If you would commit to us I could explain in more detail what's available."

"What's that supposed to mean?" Eddie steered the Cadillac convertible into the parking lot of the Palms Apartments, a ramshackle building where he and his mother shared a two-bedroom unit.

"It's just that we've never sat down and really talked. I would love to meet your mother. The three of us need to sit down and discuss your future." Pat pressed his thumbs against his temples, trying to stop the throbbing behind his eyes. "This is the biggest decision you'll make in your life and your mother should know all the details. When you make your campus visit to meet Coach Sand you should bring your mother with you."

"I don't know if she could get off work." Eddie was searching the lot for a parking space. "Oh, oh, there's my dad. He looks drunk."

Pat Lee's body went to full general alarm and his mind scrambled for battle stations. Jo Don Sanford was no one to take lightly, especially stoked on alcohol.

"I thought your mother had a restraining order on him." Pat's voice had risen an octave.

"She does, but he gets drunk and breaks it." Eddie slowed the car. "She won't call the police because the judge threatened to give him six months the last time. She would never put my father in jail."

"Why the hell not?"

"Because"—Eddie frowned at Pat—"he's my father."

Pat scanned the lot for the hulking figure of Jo Don Sanford.

"He hasn't seen us, yet." Eddie pulled the Cadillac into an empty space a hundred yards from the entrance to his apartment.

Pat could see Jo Don's pickup near the entrance. He still hadn't spotted the man himself.

"What should we do?" Pat spoke in a low voice.

"Why are you whispering?" Eddie shut off the engine. "He's not going to hear you. I'll get out, you better leave."

"Sure." Pat silently damned Jo Don to the depth of his soul. "I certainly don't want to cause you any trouble."

"It's not me you ought to be worrying about." When Eddie opened the door and got out, his seven-foot frame stood out like the Harbor City lighthouse.

For a mad instant Pat wondered if the SWS boosters would supply a hit man. I've finally gone crazy, Pat thought, as he kept searching for sight of Jo Don Sanford.

"Damn, he's seen us," Eddie was saying.

And Pat now picked up Jo Don as he lurched

across the lot toward them. Pat got out of the car and waited for the end.

"What the hell's going on here!" Jo Don Sanford's nose almost touched Pat's nose. His thick index finger pounded on Pat's sternum.

"Dad . . ." Eddie came around the Cadillac. "What are you doing here, you were supposed to meet me at school—"

Jo Don stopped punching his finger into Pat's chest but stayed right in Pat's face. "I got held up." He never took his eyes off Pat. "I've got to go out to the rig tonight, I'll be gone for two weeks. Now what is this sonofabitch doing with this Cadillac?"

"He just gave me a ride home from school."

"You were driving. Why?"

"I asked if I could. I've never driven a Cadillac."

"So? That's my fault? Has Mr. College Man been talking to your mother?"

Jo Don's finger began punching into Pat's chest again. "You've got some fucking nerve, buddy. You come around my kid and make me look bad. Make promises to my wife, sniff around like a dog in heat—"

"Dad!" Eddie grabbed his father's shoulder. "He's never even met mom. Get off him."

Jo Don shrugged off his son's hands, but he did back away from Pat, who by now was soaked with sweat. He knew Jo Don Sanford was a major lunatic. Something had to be done.

The Conquering Heroes

"I better go, Eddie," Pat said. "I'll talk to you later."

"You won't be talking to the boy *or* his mother. You talk to *me*. I decide where this boy goes and what he gets for going. Eddie, go wait by my truck. I want to talk to Joe College alone."

"Dad, if you start a fight I'll have to call the police," Eddie said, shaking his head, then slowly walked off.

"Okay now, Mr. Bigshot." Jo Don studied Pat with bloodshot eyes. He had a three-day beard. "What are you gonna give my kid?"

"A scholarship, an education and the chance to play in a world-class basketball program with TV exposure. He makes out at SWS, an NBA contract—"

"Fuck that. What about right *now? How much?*"

"The scholarship is all we can give him." Pat wasn't about to deal with Jo Don. "The NCAA has rules—"

"Yeah, so does the EPA and we're still doing what the fuck we want in the Gulf. I ain't stupid. I *know* you pay for players."

"We can't pay him."

"Then pay me."

"What?"

"You brought that nigger kid's father to Southwestern as an assistant coach."

"That's because during the recruiting process

we got to know Mr. Hampton and realized he would be a good addition to our staff. It had nothing to do with LeJune Hampton playing at Southwestern—"

"Yeah, and a three-peckered goat ain't horny. Don't shit the shitter. You pay me $75,000 and I'll make sure Eddie signs with you."

Pat shook his head, quietly amazed at how cheaply this guy was selling out his own son. Sam Watts would pay $250,000 for Eddie Sanford if Pat trusted Jo Don. Jo Don Sanford was not a man to be trusted.

"I'm sorry," Pat said. "We can't do that."

"You'll be sorry, then. I'll find a school that will pay and *that's* where Eddie will go."

Pat knew Jo Don could easily find a school that would pay him. Could Jo Don make Eddie go? Pat didn't like the risk; the boy was clearly intimidated by his father.

"If you sell your kid"—Pat clenched his teeth—"I'll know and I'll turn the NCAA and IRS loose on you. Eddie'll never play *anywhere*."

"You just try it, Mr. College."

"Listen, asshole . . ." Pat was about to lose it. His own personal frustrations surfaced. "Don't *fuck* with me. You may beat up your wife and kid but you don't *ever* fuck with Pat Lee." Talking about himself in the third person, Pat knew he was getting out of control. This guy had really pissed him off, but he had gone too far. Now he waited for Jo Don to beat the shit out of him.

Instead, amazingly, Jo Don Sanford proved to be a trueblue bully—when someone stood up to him, he backed down.

"Listen," he said, "I been drinkin'. You know how it is. Me and the wife ain't been getting along. The job sucks. I just want what's best for Eddie. Hey, give us a break."

Pat nodded and frowned, recovering fast.

"Just remember"—and Pat's tone was almost paternal—"you send him to Southwestern and I'll look after him like he was my own kid . . ."

Back at the hotel, Pat decided his luck was changing.

And with that decision, he also decided to go up to the bar to celebrate.

"I'll take a triple Stoli on the rocks."

"You really pound 'em down." Anne was still on duty, and the Derrick Lounge was still nearly empty.

"I had a long day."

"A couple of those will cut it short."

She brought his drink and again sat down at the table.

"Did you have any luck today?"

"Luck? Recruiting's about lies and greed, television money and prime-time exposure. Oh, yeah, and some talent too . . ."

"And you just go along?"

"I'm no virgin." Pat sipped his drink. "Hey, I can remember when I felt like I belonged, when being an athlete was about *playing*. It wasn't part of some scenario to get to the NBA, fill your bankbook by endorsing junk food, soft drinks and shoes. Or to get a job as a TV analyst."

"What's wrong with that?"

"It makes the money, not the game, what counts." He drained his glass. "That sounded like some two-bit idealist who doesn't practice what he preaches."

Anne got up to fix him another drink. "Well, I can tell the difference between horsesense and horseshit."

"What?" Pat rocked back in his chair and stared at this strange woman.

Anne smiled. "Maybe playing for free wasn't a matter of choice?"

"It was. I played ball with guys who would have played for free. We loved to play. And that's no bullshit."

He waved his hand at Anne, as she began to pour his drink. "Bring me two triples and save your legs. The legs are always the first to go. At least mine were."

"You seem to be one unhappy fella," Anne said from the bar, where she poured his vodka. "What's different now than when you played?"

"The entertainment dollar. Coaches and players

step all over one another for it. The NCAA is a marketing operation." He was pushing it with this man-of-conscience spiel and he knew it. Was he mostly trying to impress this woman? He hadn't been able to get Rachael on the phone, and a long lonely night in Houston stretched out in front of him like a bad road. Well, maybe that was part of it, but he believed it too . . .

"Well," she called out from the bar. "Somebody was making the money when you played. Why didn't you get your share? This is America!"

"Because once you put a price on playing the game you're just whoring. Selling out." Pat was beginning to feel positively righteous. And horny.

Anne returned with three drinks and took one for herself. If you can't save 'em, join 'em, she thought ruefully. Besides, she liked this man.

"Now," Pat continued with booze-enhanced wisdom, "television has taught junior-high kids to get their hands out for money. High schools recruit kids with money and jobs for mom and dad."

"You're telling me that television is turning these kids into little hookers?"

"Television and people pimping twelve-year-olds for a chance to ride their backs to Division I coaching careers."

"Is that how you got into coaching?" A low blow, or was it?

"No, but I guess I'm not surprised you asked.

I did it the old-fashioned way. I played until I had no other choices. I'm not sorry. I loved the game. It's just that the money has gotten so big, it's making everybody crazy."

"Well, you can't expect people to work for free. And without money there wouldn't be sports—"

Pat's cheeks reddened. She had hit a nerve. "Colleges don't need 60,000-seat-domed basketball arenas and $500 designer warmups, $300 uniforms, $200 shoes. It all started with a couple peach baskets, you know." It was a sensitive area for Pat, who had to fill those huge domes and raise the money to buy the expensive equipment. It was why he spent most of his life on the road. He stopped to drink and dig into his shirt pocket for a Marlboro. Arguing with her had thrown him off, screwed up his timing. Also, he might not even get laid. He took a long drag on the cigarette, trying to calm himself. Anne watched his change of mood.

"It doesn't sound like a very good way to run a college basketball program," she said.

Pat nodded. "With the exception of the Chicago Cubs, people don't pay to see losers, especially on television."

"You make it sound pretty down and dirty."

"Well, today I had a father offer to sell me his son for $75,000."

"That's awful."

"What's worse is I probably would have made

the deal if the father wasn't such an asshole."

"You're pretty goddamn judgmental for a guy on a continual lost weekend."

"The wisdom of alcohol . . ."

Anne glared at him. "Like there's truth in wine? You're a fucking jerk. I guess you can justify your life that way if you're a used-car salesman. All your holier-than-thou I'm-drinking-to-kill-the-pain bullshit doesn't cut it for a coach entrusted with the well-being of kids."

"I was just trying to explain the contradictions . . . the complexities of my business . . ."

"You're given, you ask for this great responsibility and you get drunk and turn it into bar-babble. And you end up hoisted on your own petard."

"What?"

"You know what that means, but you're surprised I do. You think I'm just some dumb divorced broad in a bar?"

"No, I never thought that, I was enjoying our conversation—"

"Save it . . . my son plays basketball, he's pretty good and I don't know what to do about college. Now you—"

"Don't ask *me*." Pat held up his hands. "I don't know either. I am sorry I ever brought up the subject."

"You just figured a little sportstalk might get you laid?"

Of course she was at least partly right.

"You asked me," he said.

She cooled some. "I guess I did. I was interested. My son—"

"Please," Pat said. "Let's just change the subject."

He didn't want to talk about her kid. He'd already made a big mistake. He was sorry he'd told her what he did. This happened in bars when people found out he was a coach.

She ignored his request. "I told him it was his decision," Anne went on, "but I wonder if I'm avoiding my responsibility."

"What about his father?"

"I told you I'm divorced, and anyway, he doesn't think much of his father. I'd tell him to forget about basketball but I can't pay for his college education."

"Look, Anne, I just open my mouth to change feet," Pat said, and drained his glass.

"All right, I've calmed down. I'll even buy you another drink. I want to know what you think. Truly."

Pat took a long, deep breath.

"The odds against him at any big basketball power would be like playing Russian roulette with five loaded chambers."

"That bad?"

"That bad. Is he a big kid?"

"Seven foot."

72

The Conquering Heroes

"What!" Pat knew all the Houston prospects. There were no other big men available this year. Eddie Sanford was it. Anne's kid must just be tall and untalented to escape the notice of the college chicken hawks. Including Pat Lee.

"Does he have any scholarship offers?"

"I'm not really sure," she said. "I told you I've stayed out of it. He gets a lot of mail and phone calls."

"When does he graduate?"

"This year."

"From where?"

"Country Day."

Jesus. "You're Eddie Sanford's mother?" His heart sank; he slumped in his chair.

"Yes." Anne nodded. "Do you know Eddie?"

"Look . . ." Pat hurried to collect himself. "Could we start all over at the beginning?"

"I don't think so . . ."

"Come on, I've had a real bad day. Now I've shown my hand to you, what have you got to lose?"

"I'm not sure, but listening to you I'm sure it's something."

"I'll help you make sure it isn't your son that—"

She walked off to the bar, came back with a beer and sat across the table from him.

"Okay, coach. Let's have it."

"It's simple," Pat said. "You have to get involved in helping your son choose a school. Because if you don't, somebody like your ex-husband will. I guarantee you."

"Or somebody like you?"

"I'm already there. I've been in contact with Eddie for over a year."

"So what am I supposed to do?"

"You ought to be monitoring what's going on. What schools are interested, who he's talking to and what offers are being made."

"I work twelve hours a day, six days a week. Where am I going to find time to do all this checking up?"

"Get a good lawyer. Eddie is so talented that a good sports attorney would represent him for free, gambling on the back-end chance that Eddie would be a top NBA draft choice."

"I don't know any lawyers."

"There's a good one here in Houston," Pat said. "His name is Benjamin Pankin."

"He's probably a classmate of yours."

"Actually he went to Northwestern," Pat said, not mentioning that he knew Benjamin Pankin's wife Rachael very well. "Ask around about him. I think you'll find he's got a very good reputation."

"I don't trust lawyers."

"Well, you better trust somebody and quick. It was your ex-husband that asked me for the $75,000."

"Jo Don asked you for $75,000?" Anne's face went white. "For Eddie?"

Pat nodded.

"I don't know what to do." Anne was truly upset now.

"Go home and talk to Eddie. He's a bright kid."

"Okay, I'm on my way. Last call, I'm closing the bar."

"Well then, give me a beer to cry in."

Pat Lee returned to his room and slept. Again he dreamt of years and people long ago. Mostly, he dreamt of 1960 and those last days in high school.

Of the people and times that had just seemed to slip away.

The News That Fits

1960

... Secretary General Dag Hammarskjöld said the United Nations was against confiscations of Israeli cargo in the Suez Canal ..."

Jim Lee was watching the eleven o'clock news when his son Pat and Geena Keats walked into the house from the postgame sock hop at the Wood High School gym.

" ... Nasser, president of the two-year-old United Arab Republic, insisted the Arab boycott of Israel would continue, threatening war to 'liberate the stolen parts of the Arab nation.' Also in Egypt, work continued on the Aswan Dam to be financed in three stages by the Soviet Union . . ."

As Pat and Geena entered the bookcase-lined living room Jim Lee looked up from his easy chair.

"What's the latest news, dad?"

"The Middle East is going to hell in a handbasket." Jim Lee shook his head. "Not that that's news."

"You're still pissed at Eisenhower for sending the Marines into Lebanon," Pat said. "Ease up on Ike. He brought 'em back home from Korea, didn't he?"

"When I was in the Corps they sent us down to Nicaragua to put that creep Somoza in power," his father shot back. "Imagine, killing people over bananas. We can't keep doing that kind of crap! Hey! You and your brother played great tonight," Jim Lee said, quickly changing the subject. "Your mom and I could eat and drink free out at the Black Lake Inn for the next month just on that final play. I'm proud of the two of you."

"We had a lot of help."

"Are they coming over?"

"They're right behind us," Geena said.

"Hello, Geena." Jim Lee quickly stood. "Excuse

my bad manners. I get so damn mad at the news."

Geena smiled and squeezed Pat's hand. "Where's Mrs. Lee?"

"In the kitchen." He waved toward the back of the house and Geena walked off to find Pat's mother.

"I hate to think of you having to register for the draft this summer." Jim Lee frowned at his son. "At the rate they're going, those idiots in Washington will have us in a war before you get a chance to finish college."

"You think so?" Pat plopped down on the couch. His legs were beginning to hurt. "Where?"

"It's hard to tell." Jim Lee sank back into his chair. "Maybe Indo-China. We already paid for France's disasters in Vietnam and that goddamn John Foster Dulles did everything he could to piss off the Chinese."

"Well, as long as I stay in college I get a 2S deferment."

"Can you imagine any man in his right mind insisting that a country of over half a *billion* people doesn't exist? That's what Dulles said. Mainland China is Commie so it doesn't exist. We don't recognize it. Jesus . . ."

Pat couldn't imagine it but the truth was he'd never thought much about it.

"Where's your brother?" Jim Lee asked and drained his glass of bourbon, then lit an unfiltered Chesterfield.

The Conquering Heroes

"Barb and him were out watching the satellites go over, the last I heard."

"I hope that boy can keep his pants on long enough to finish college."

"He's okay, dad. Steve's not dumb, he just thinks he's in love."

"He's got to learn the difference between being in love and being in heat." Jim Lee took a long drag off the Chesterfield.

". . . President Eisenhower finished up his two-week goodwill tour of Latin America with huge, enthusiastic crowds welcoming him at every stop . . ."

Jim Lee pointed at the screen. "They sure liked Ike a lot better than they did that jerk Nixon. He sure won't make the president that Eisenhower did."

"*If* he gets elected," Pat put in. "Geena's sure that Kennedy is going to be the next president."

"She's Catholic, son. What else is she supposed to think?" Jim Lee stubbed out his cigarette. "What do you think of Senator Johnson from Texas?"

"Don't ask me." Pat shrugged. "I don't know why anybody votes, it just encourages the sonsabitches. You said that yourself."

Heavy footsteps sounded across the front porch, the hall door swung open and the living room was immediately filled with Pat's teammates.

"Where's the food?" Chuck Stanislawski was the first into the room.

"The kitchen's where it always was, you starving Polish prince," Jim Lee growled good-naturedly. "Someday I want to see that tapeworm you're keeping."

"Where's Steve and Barb?" Pat asked when Ron, Barry and the Frog had sprawled out in chairs and on the floor.

"They went over to Harbor City to watch the waves hit the pier," the Frog told him.

"They're having submarine races in Lake Michigan again," Barry Sand added. "You know your little brother, he sure loves the submarine races."

"I'm gonna get that kid a chastity belt," Jim Lee said, "and I'm going to have the only key."

"Dad," Pat said, "you'd be surprised what a girl can do with a hairpin and a nail file."

"Hey, I spent four years in the Marine Corps. Nothing surprises me." Jim Lee lit another cigarette. "You boys looked pretty good out there tonight. Who do you play first in the districts?"

"Don't know," Barry Sand said. "The drawing isn't until Monday morning."

"Doesn't matter," Jim Lee said, picking up his copy of John P. Marquand's *Women and Thomas Harrow* and putting it on top of *Anatomy of a*

Murder. "You guys can beat anybody in this district. The regionals will be tough, though."

"Colins'll be tough," Pat said. "Those black kids love to run and gun. If they got the hot hand we could have big trouble . . ."

" . . . despite continuing prosperity, Italy is still in a state of political chaos, the Christian Democrats failing to form an effective government. . . ."

" . . . riots continued in Argentina as followers of exiled dictator Juan Peron . . ."

" . . . and in South Vietnam opponents of the government accused Diem of running a family dictatorship . . ."

Pat came alert when he heard "Vietnam." His father said the United States might go to war there, but Pat had no idea of Vietnam. All he could picture was Yul Brynner playing the King of Siam.

" . . . accusing the United States of interfering in Cuba's internal affairs, Castro said he would accept missiles and weapons from the Soviet Union to defend against invasion . . ."

Cuba? Hell, if the U.S. didn't like Castro why didn't it just turn out everybody at Guantanamo on a five-day pass? No country that small could survive for long that many drunken sailors and marines. But his father was right, Pat decided seriously. America was building up an inventory of antagonists, beyond the Soviets and the Red Chinese.

World War III?

Pat still remembered Uncle Jake coming to live with them after World War II. Jake had been with the 101st Airborne at Bastogne and it had taken an awful toll on him. He lived with them for five years, stayed up nights, drank beer, painted the walls and varnished the woodwork. Over and over. In 1950 he took a construction job in the Al-can Highway, finally ending up working out in the Alaskan bush. Uncle Jake died of a heart attack in 1957, and it took three weeks for the word to reach them. He was thirty-seven years old. Pat still had a snapshot of Jake taken during the war, smiling and leaning against a Messerschmitt jet.

Pat just couldn't imagine it, life was too good. Who would be stupid enough to start a long destructive war when things were going so well?

Sure, but why did he have this sudden chill? Was this one of those endings he hated?

They were heading west toward Lake Michigan in Geena's white-on-blue '57 Chevy convertible. Geena was driving. Pat leaned against the passenger door, his body tired but his mind racing.

The Conquering Heroes

The Coasters were on the radio singing "Charlie Brown."

His father had sent them on a mission of celibacy—Pat was to find his brother and Barb Coles before things got out of hand and on to other parts of the anatomy.

The Chevy dropped off the bluff, down the narrow single lane road that led to the Point. Over the Coasters Pat could hear the sound of the waves. As they pulled out of the woods onto the openness of the Point, Pat began scanning the beach for the distinctive shape of his father's '59 Volkswagen.

"There they are." Geena swung the car hard to the right and headed toward the dark hump that broke the straight lines of the beach, water and distant horizon.

The vastness of Lake Michigan stretched out in front of them as Geena pulled up next to the Volkswagen, whose windows were all fogged up.

"It's probably just as well we can't see them," Geena said.

"They're both gonna be pissed at me."

"What about me?" Geena said, sliding across the leather seat. She put her hand on the back of Pat's neck. "Let's give them a few minutes to notice us."

Pat turned and Geena leaned up and pressed her lips against his, her soft breasts on his arm and chest. He kissed back, inhaling the sweetness of her and slipping his left arm around her waist. She felt so fragile, but there was an urgent strength to her kiss. Now she had both arms around his neck, hugging herself tightly to him.

In spite of his physical exhaustion, Pat felt himself responding. He could feel it beginning, and except for the painful constriction in his jeans, there was nothing in him that wanted it to end.

Geena guided his right hand under her cashmere sweater, then began fumbling with the buttons of his jeans—

Suddenly a fist was banging on the window.

"Aw," Geena said, "damn you, Steve!"

Pat felt her pull away from him. He turned and looked into the grinning face of his brother Steve as he stepped back and pointed his left index finger at them, rubbing his right index finger across the top.

"Shame . . . shame!" Steve yelled through the closed window over the sound of the surf.

The door on the driver's side opened and Barb Coles clambered into the back seat. She was wearing only a skirt and a short sleeved blouse, buttons askew. When Pat last saw her at the gym Barb was wearing a sweater and her cheerleader's jacket over the blouse. Now she was half undressed in the back seat, shivering.

"God!" Barb exploded, "tell your father to buy a car with a better heater. Get some Dee-troit iron."

"Most people wear more clothes in the winter," Pat said. "It works for them."

"Oh, sure." Steve pushed into the seat behind Pat. "Like you guys were helping each other bundle up just now." Steve was jacketless, his shirttail hanging out.

"We're here looking for you."

His brother laughed. "Riiight . . ."

"If you were looking for us you were sure looking in the wrong places," Barb said.

Suddenly Elvis blared "Hound Dog" out of the radio.

"Oh, God!" Barb squealed. "Turn him up. I just love this song!"

Geena leaned over and Elvis boomed out of her stereo speakers.

You ain't never caught a rabbit . . .

Elvis carried on as Pat stared out at the dark water and tried to shut down his mind. He felt some unknown fear. Something seemed to be stalking him. At times, out of the corner of his eye, he caught a shadowy movement. But, when he turned to fix his gaze on it, it was always gone.

"Is that WLS?" Barb interrupted his wonderings.

"I think so," Geena said. "Only Chicago stations are still on this late."

"Come on, Steve, let's go." Barb started crawling out of the car. "They're going to play the Everly Brothers next. I want to hear the whole song."

"Hear it on the way home, Steve." Pat gave the instructions from their father.

"You too, big brother." Steve pushed out of the Chevrolet convertible and hurried through the cold wind to the tiny car.

Hearing the booming surf of Lake Michigan, Pat felt somehow small, even fragile. Strangely, in a way, he liked the feeling. He would have to lose it before the Colins game, but for now he wallowed in the vastness of things beyond control. Scary but relaxing all at the same time. Strange . . .

Geena leaned over and kissed him hard one last time, then put the car in gear and they pulled away.

By the time they were back on the lane through the woods, the lights of the Volkswagen were behind them and Don and Phil were on the radio singing bye-bye to love and happiness, saying hello to loneliness and fully expecting to die.

The death of the fifties, the birth of the sixties.

It was an awesome time.

It would have terrible and wonderful consequences.

Time would tell what they were.

But Pat would always feel, like now, that he was moving against the wind.

Protecting
the Program

Disembarking from the Houston-Dallas shuttle, Pat Lee drove directly from the airport to the Southwestern campus, to the Greg Dunne Memorial Field House and basketball offices.

He was wearing the hat he had bought in Houston to cover the balding patch and the fact he hadn't washed his hair. The hat was red with BOOMTOWN silkscreened in white across the front of the crown. It was, he knew, a stupid-looking hat, but the only other one he could find in his size said OILMEN DRILL IT DEEPER.

His head ached but he felt relatively confident about his meeting with Eddie Sanford. It would take persistence to patch up any mistakes he had made with Anne Sanford and to keep Jo Don

Sanford at bay. His persistence and dedication that had once made him a superior basketball player had served him well as assistant coach in charge of recruiting. Well, he'd use these qualities to land a seven-foot kid in spite of his family, if you could call it that. Thinking about it raised his boiling point. If that was possible.

It seemed he was constantly angry, a dangerous, free-floating sort of anger that he had to fight to keep under control. He knew where it came from, all right. It came from where he'd once been, and where he was now. They gave him a pimp's job, enticing kids. He fought against the seamier side, tried to tell himself he was giving a kid a chance for dollars and glory he'd otherwise never have. And often that was no lie. But he also too often reminded himself of the kind of man his father told him not to hang around.

Angry? Sure, angry at himself. How did he fall for this? An old story . . . He was an out-of-date idealist, purist. And when life fell short of his expectations, his—and his father's—standards, he settled for at least trying to do something for the talent. But, face it, mostly he was in the service of Barry Sand . . .

He parked his car now in his space in the field house lot and walked into the locker room entrance, stopped and stared out at the portable basketball floor marooned in the middle of the dirt arena and indoor track like a spit-shined island. At

The Conquering Heroes

the north end of the field house baseball players were taking batting practice inside the cages. The pitching machines hummed and whipped the balls across the plates at one hundred miles an hour.

Pat liked the solid crack of the wooden Louisville Sluggers that the pro prospects were using, learning to adjust from the aluminum, graphite and ceramic bats allowed in high school and college. He himself had only known wooden bats when he played baseball for Wood High School, and the idea of paying $150 apiece for shoes and a glove was as incredible as paying $250 for the latest high-tech, space-age bat. Give me that good old ash, Pat thought as he turned and headed upstairs to the basketball offices.

Standing at head coach Barry Sand's open door, Pat waited while Sand, seated at his desk, his back to him, yelled into the phone:

"I don't care *what* she says. You tell her that we'll make her look like the biggest whore in Texas if she tries to go public or file charges."

Sand listened and shook his head violently.

"How can she prove who it was? Doc Knight cleaned her up. There's no clinical evidence."

Sand paused, then laughed.

"Tell her nobody will accept her identification. They all look alike and she can't prove how tall he was 'cause he was lying down." The coach laughed at his wit.

"Now, goddammit, Sgt. Cash, you handle this or I will. If I have to handle it you'll be looking for a patrolman's job in the Panhandle."

Sand slammed down the phone and spun around in his big leather judge's chair. His eyes widened at the sight of Pat Lee.

"What happened in Houston?"

"I got into a little hand-to-hand recruiting with Jo Don Sanford over his son Eddie."

"I don't send you out to come off second best." Sand looked down at his daily calendar.

"I did okay," Pat said. "I finally met Anne Sanford and I'm making real progress with the kid and his mother."

"Well, don't make so much progress with the mother that the father shoots you."

"They're divorced."

"What happened in Detroit?"

"It's gonna take a little more time."

"I'm getting tired of waiting on results. You better deliver pretty quick, Pat. *Everybody* is after Eddie Sanford and Jamail Jenks."

"I've got Jenks all but signed," Pat lied. "I'm working out the financial details with his coach right now."

"That slime bag O.K. Free is making a fortune off kids."

"So are you . . ." It just slipped out. Pat was too beat to censor himself all the time. He was immediately sorry he hadn't.

The Conquering Heroes

"What the fuck does that mean? If you don't like it I got a hundred guys waiting to take your job."

"I've heard all the threats, Barry. We're not strangers, you know. Anyway, about the details on Jenks ..." He spoke as if he knew the details.

"Hey!" Barry held up his hands. "Don't tell me anything. You know better than that. I don't want to know. If you need something go to Sam Watts."

"Right. Look, I'd like to get home. I've been gone a long time. I'd like to see my kids. James is in town and—"

"I know, I know." Barry shook his head. "But no can do. We got a major fire to put out. Goddamn Chuck Small raped some coed the other night. I want you to go to his apartment and scare the shit out of him."

"Small is seven foot tall and weighs 270," Pat pointed out. "He has the mindset of a Nazi, the brain of a hummingbird and a $200-a-day cocaine habit. How do you suggest I communicate, leave alone scare the dumb bastard?"

"Tell him he's looking at fifteen-to-life in the can."

"And then what?"

"Advise him that the only way out is to give up his idea of declaring early for the NBA. If he does that we'll hush this thing up. If he doesn't, it's hello Huntsville."

"What about the girl?" Pat asked. "Won't she press charges?"

"Not if she knows what's good for her. She's nobody. Her father's a San Antonio high-school teacher and her mother is dead. We'll pay her off. It shouldn't be a problem for anyone."

"Except her."

"What the *fuck* is the matter with you?"

Pat shrugged and shook his head.

"Your *job,* old buddy, is protecting the program, not worrying about some cooze who was stupid enough to get in a car with Chuck Small. Now get out of here and roust Small. He'll be at his apartment counting the links in his gold chains."

"And loading his nine millimeter," Pat mumbled, then turned and walked back out through the main office bullpen.

"Pat." Suzie, Barry's secretary in charge of passing out the cash-filled envelopes to the players, called out.

Pat turned to face her across the outer office. "Yeah?"

"I got a call from Avis in Detroit," Suzie said. "You never returned your rental car."

"Shit!" He had again forgotten that he'd given Jamail Jenks the keys to the rental. "Don't worry, tell them it'll be turned in tomorrow."

"But, Pat . . ."

"Goddammit, Sue." Pat was disgusted with himself and angry at Barry. "Please just do what I tell you, okay?"

This was a bad situation. He would have to call O.K. Free and ask him to get Jamail to turn in the car. More than likely, Jenks would keep the car and Pat would have to fly back to Detroit to get it. If, by some miracle, Jenks hadn't totaled the car and *did* turn it in, there was always the danger of him being recognized by some fan who worked for Avis who would notice that a Southwestern credit card had been used to rent the car.

He was committing an NCAA violation from 1,500 miles away and relying on Jamail Jenks's discretion to keep him from being caught. Which was like relying on Charles Manson to babysit with your kids.

Pat Lee walked out of the Greg Dunne Field House into the bright Texas sun. The light, and what he was facing, made him squint and his eyes hurt.

Pat hammered on the door of Chuck Small's $1,500 a month apartment, paid for by a no-show job at Sam Watts's Discount Mart Headquarters close by the campus. Most of the favored players had similar "summer jobs" at the ten Watts's Discount Marts in the Dallas area. Depending on the player's talent and value to the team, the "work" paid various sums from $6,000 to $12,000 for the summer. Better than counselor at the Boy Scouts. Any other money paid to the players came in the white envelopes Barry's secretary Sue dutifully filled and handed to the players when they dropped by the office for their weekly chat with Coach Sand.

A four-time high-school all-American from the Bronx and winner of the McDonald's Slam Dunk Contest three years running, Chuck Small had received $200,000 cash for signing his letter of intent to Southwestern and was promised an additional $200,000 if he stayed the full four years. The money was provided by Sam Watts in one hundred dollar bills.

But after two years as the top college center in the nation, Chuck Small was a huge attraction to the NBA with, unofficial, of course, promises of $12.5 million. After accepting $200,000 from the Southwestern basketball program with a promise of $200,000 more, Small was now crying hardship and asking to be allowed to declare for the NBA draft. Come on, his mother needled him . . . only a fool would stay in college and risk injury when the NBA was willing to pay millions of dollars, but fortunately for coach Barry Sand and SWS, Chuck Small was, at the very least, a fool. Right now, as a matter of fact, he was on the verge of being a felon.

It was now Pat's job to convince Small that

staying at Southwestern, although against his financial interests, was in his *legal* interests. Pat was obliged to make him an offer only an idiot would refuse.

But, of course, therein lay the problem . . .

As Pat continued to pound on Chuck Small's door he could hear rap music and smell marijuana. He listened to Small lumbering and dancing around the room, banging into furniture. Something crashed onto the floor. Glass shattered.

Pat kicked at the door with his foot.

"Who is it?" Small's voice boomed through the door.

"Coach Lee."

"You ain't no coach, you is a pimp. Get the fuck outta here."

Pat tightened his jaws. "Look, you sonafabitch, talk to me or talk to Coach Sand."

Pat considered threatening Small with the police but he knew the players were more frightened of Barry Sand than the police. The police were Sand's instruments. He was the power, so long as he kept winning.

"Go away." Small's tone was less confident.

"You've got a problem, Chuck," Pat said through the door. "I'm here with the only solution."

The door swung open and Pat looked up into the bloodshot eyes of all-American center Chuck

Small, surrounded by a blue-white cloud of marijuana smoke.

"That's real brilliant, Chuck," Pat said. "Smoking dope and playing music that can be heard all the way to the field house."

"What?" Small did not move from the doorway.

"You better let me in," Pat said. "This isn't something we want to be talking about in front of God and everybody."

Small moved away and Pat walked in, closing the door behind him. The apartment was a mess; beer bottles littered the floor, old pizza boxes and half-eaten Big Macs covered the tables. Traces of white powder were sprinkled on the kitchen counter.

"Chuck, you got big trouble." Pat touched his finger to the white powder and tasted it. "What did they cut this with, Ajax?"

"Don't be talking trash to me, pimp." Small was still high.

"You raped that girl and put her in the hospital."

"What you talking about?" Small was lighting up a roach. "I didn't do nothing."

"She identified you."

"The white bitch is lying."

"Who said she was white?"

"What?" Small stopped trying to light the roach. "If she was white she's lyin'. I know no black bitch would be saying I raped her. They all want some of what I got."

Small grabbed his crotch to make his meaning perfectly clear.

Pat shook his head. What a waste. A million-dollar talent with ten cents' worth of smarts. How much of the responsibility for that waste was his? How much was Barry Sand's? How much the system's that made billions out of adolescents whose skill in putting a leather ball through an iron hoop was hardly matched by any clear idea of what the hell real life was about?

Forget it, he ordered himself. A conscience and racial guilt were luxuries he could not afford.

Life is not a slam dunk. Who said that? Some wiseass sports writer, he thought.

"Chuck, I'm tired and I've no time to waste on you."

"Then," Small said, resuming his attempts to light the roach, "git."

"You damn fool. You got everything going for you and you go rape a white girl . . ." Pat was startled by his own anger. But anger was point-less, like being mad at a coyote for killing a rab-bit. Small just did what he did. He didn't think about consequences. It was what made him so easy to recruit. All it took was the most money.

"Hey! You can't talk to me like that." He was, after all, a hero, especially in his own mind.

"The hell I can't. You're up to your nose in a

lake of shit and I'm driving the speedboat." Pat liked the sound of that one. He almost smiled. Instead he pointed his finger at Small. "Now, shut the fuck up and listen. I'm not gonna repeat this. We'll get you out of this, as soon as you tell the NBA to take a walk and guarantee to finish out your career at Southwestern."

"Fuck you, man, I ain't—"

"I told you to shut up!" Pat was surprised at his own forcefulness.

Apparently Chuck Small was too, because he did shut up and stared at Pat.

"You do what I'm telling you," Pat said, "or Coach Sand is promising you fifteen-to-life in Huntsville for rape. And in Huntsville the Aryan Brotherhood will tear off your dick and feed it to you."

"He wouldn't—" Small's eyes had emptied of confidence.

"You're as good as convicted. A seven-foot black man raping a five-foot white girl in Dallas, Texas." Pat shook his head and stared at Small. "You'll be lucky you don't get the Big Needle. No more Lucky Chuckie. No more NBA career. This is Dallas, fella. They give thousand-year sentences here."

Chuck Small seemed to shrink.

"*Comprende?*"

Small nodded, slowly.

"Coach Sand will call you later," Pat said. "You

stay here and don't talk to anybody. I mean *anybody*."

Pat turned, opened the door and went out, slamming the door behind him.

He felt sick to his stomach.

"Goddamn, how did I end up doing *this*?"

And then he began to remember.

Saturday Morning

1960

After every Friday night Wood High School basketball game, Pat was wide if painfully awake at seven on Saturday morning. His broken nose and a night of mouth-breathing saw to that.

The most recent damage to his nose was a tear-dislocation suffered against Hickory Corners. It had healed with the cartilage at an angle that nearly closed both nasal passages. There wasn't much sense, he figured, in getting it fixed. He would just break or dislocate it again.

He lay stretching and groaning for half an hour before he finally crawled out of bed.

Steve was snoring blissfully in the next room.

The Conquering Heroes

Steve could sleep through anything. In 1956 he'd slept through the tornado that tore off the kitchen roof.

"Can I fix you something for breakfast?" Katherine Lee said from the kitchen.

"No, thanks, mom." Pat was pulling on his red and gray, leather-sleeved varsity jacket. "I'm going down to the drugstore. You just rattle them pots and pans."

His mother gave him a worried look as he went out of the house.

It was a cold, clear late-winter Michigan day. Pat walked the two blocks to the blinking light that marked the beginning of the two-block downtown district of Wood. Reaching the corner, he cut past the pumps at Angelo's Service Station. His first job had been working for Angelo on weekends, washing cars and pumping gas. He jumped up and down on the hose that snaked across the service drive, ringing the bell inside, until Angelo looked up from behind the cash register and waved.

Gas was thirty cents a gallon.

Next to Angelo's Pat walked in front of the Wood Dairy. From inside the dairy came the rattle of quart milk bottles as they were run down the line, sterilized and refilled to be ready for the next day's early-morning home deliveries.

Just past the Wood Dairy was the IGA grocery;

everybody called it the Leader. One of Pat's football teammates, Rick Cane, worked there as a carry-out boy.

Beyond the IGA was William's Hardware with its selection of snow shovels, sleds and space heaters packed in the front window. And then the Smoke Shop featuring shelves of cigarettes, cigars, chewing and pipe tobacco and, in the back, the nonstop card game, the players barely visible through the blue white haze of smoke.

Further on was Gold's Five and Ten, where Pat as a young boy would wander, awestruck, among the toys and gadgets that were "made in Japan" and cost less than a dollar.

Pat looked now at the window display in Wood Men's Shop, at a mannequin in a green corduroy jacket with elbow patches, brown corduroy pants and dirty bucks. He didn't know whether he liked the outfit or not. He did know he couldn't afford it. In the window he saw the reflection from across Main Street of Don's Barber Shop, the Liquor Store, Red's Hobby Shop (where he bought model airplane kits of balsa wood, then failed to build even one correctly), Dee's Beauty Shop and the Wood Elevator and Fruit Exchange.

The Elevator was next to the railroad tracks and extended back off Main for three blocks along the boxcar siding that ran past the Elevator to Wood Trucking and the pickle factory before returning to the main track at the Birch River Railroad

Bridge. All the local farmers hauled in their corn and grains, their apples, peaches, pears, plums, grapes, blueberries and sold them to the Wood Elevator and Fruit Exchange, then bought their seed, baby chicks, ducklings, seedlings, fertilizer, feed, pesticides and herbicides.

The Wood Elevator and Fruit Exchange shipped the produce out by train or truck. Top-grade fruit went by train to Chicago markets, the rest by truck to the Benton Harbor Juice and Canning Company owned by U.S. Representative Fred Thomas, a member of several of the House committees and subcommittees on agricultural policy, price controls and supports, and farm export-import controls. A man to be reckoned with, no question.

Across the tracks from the Elevator was Jon's Ford dealership that carried Ford cars, trucks and tractors. In 1956 Jon and the Ford Motor Company pissed off Jim Lee with shoddy workmanship, and then their refusal to stand behind their product sent Pat's father running into the open arms of Kalamazoo Volkswagen and ruined his sons' teenage driving years. A Volkswagen was hardly to be desired over a Ford—which, after all, was made in Michigan. From in front of Water's Grocery Store across Main Street Pat stared through the showroom window at the 1960 white Ford convertible with the blue interior. Jon was asking some twenty-one hundred dollars for the car. For Pat, it might as well have been twenty-one thousand.

Sharpe's Drugstore was just up the street between Dan's Pool Hall and Long's Furniture and Floor Covering. Every Saturday morning Pat met his teammates at Sharpe's, and Mr. Sharpe always fed them baked goods and milkshakes while they hashed over the Friday game one more time.

Now Ron Waters, Barry Sand and Chuck Stanislawski were already there and Pat walked in and sat down at the counter. The Frog, like Steve, was a late sleeper. Both wouldn't arrive for another hour. Barb Coles and two other cheerleaders were sitting in a booth at the back. Geena would be along later. The David Keats family had a sit-down breakfast every morning and attendance was mandatory for Geena, her two brothers and two sisters.

It had been almost 1:00 A.M. when Pat had walked home from Geena's after hunting down Steve and Barb at the Point on Lake Michigan south of Harbor City. Which meant Geena would now be getting lectured by her mother. Her parents liked Pat but they didn't encourage the relationship. Pat wasn't Catholic. Pat wasn't anything, which probably made it even worse to people as devoutly successful as Mr. and Mrs. David Keats.

David Keats owned Keats Metal and Coil on the Birch River north of town. He had moved the company to Wood from Chicago after World War

The Conquering Heroes

II. Subcontracting from the Big Three in Detroit and the booming television manufacturers in and around Chicago, Keats employed half the people in the area who weren't full-time farmers.

David Keats had the first television set Pat Lee had ever seen—a huge Admiral console with a tiny ten-inch black-and-white screen. Mostly, they watched test patterns and waited for programming to catch up with technology.

"You did fine last night, Pat," Mr. Sharpe said as he set a chocolate milkshake and a plate of fresh donuts on the counter.

"We'll see how good they do in the districts when the pressure's on." The familiar voice came from behind.

Pat turned to see Mr. Marks, the math teacher, standing and studying the laxatives.

"I see shithead is up early," Pat whispered to Chuck Stanislawski.

"The prick has been here half an hour putting us down," Chuck said. "I thought Barry was gonna punch him out."

"What are you guys whispering about?" the math teacher demanded.

"None of your business," Barry Sand shot back. "If we wanted you to know, we'd put it in the paper."

"Not you, Sand," the teacher said, "you'll be too busy cruising the bars for your old man."

Pat saw the mounting hurt appear in Barry's

eyes. The remark was close to home. Marks knew how to inflict pain. Barry sometimes asked for trouble, but not this. Adults, teachers and coaches that Pat had known in his short life hurt kids because they could. That's the way it seemed to him, anyway.

"Did you hear me, Sand!"

"We all heard you," Pat broke in. "Why don't you go talk to the trees and see if they hear you?"

"I don't need any of your smart mouth, Lee. You aren't a big shot just because you get a few scholarship offers."

"Asshole!" Pat spun on the stool and spat out the word.

Marks's face twisted in shock. "I'll fix your wagon, Lee. I'll—"

"In three months I'm out of here."

"You may be out sooner than that, buddy!"

"You should go easy on those laxatives, Mr. Marks. It's dangerous. You've already got shit for brains."

"All *right*, Pat." Mr. Sharpe leaned over the counter and put his hand on Pat's arm. "That's enough."

Pat was surprised at the depth of his anger. His hands were shaking.

The druggist then steered Marks away from the boys. "They're just kids . . ."

"Goddamn, kids!" Marks said, not wanting to be appeased, and left.

The Conquering Heroes

"I see your math teacher uses the Socratic method." Mr. Sharpe smiled as he returned to his place behind the counter. "I'll get some hemlock and mix it in with his next batch of stool softener."

They all laughed; the tension was broken.

"What are you and Geena going to do tonight?" Ron asked Pat.

"Going to the show in Harbor City, I guess."

Wood didn't have a theater. It had burned down, suspiciously, when Pat was in fifth grade. He remembered that *Abbott and Costello Meet The Harlem Globetrotters* was playing. Television had driven the owner of the Wood Theater to near-bankruptcy, and arson, most people said. He and the other kids could see the smoke from the fire through their classroom window.

"What are you going to see?" Barry Sand reached for a donut. If it weren't for Mr. Sharpe and his teammates' families Barry would literally have gone hungry through most of high school.

"*Paths of Glory*. Kirk Douglas is in it. Geena loves Kirk Douglas. I guess it's that weird chin. What else could it be?" He smiled and sipped at his milkshake. "What did you guys do last night after you left my house?"

"We went for burgers and played the pinball machine at Cap's," Ron Waters told him. "Barry stayed at my place."

Barry looked embarrassed, and suddenly angry.

"Yeah, my old man was at Cap's when we got there. He was drunk. Mr. Keats fired him for drinking on the job."

"Well, I heard him in the crowd," Pat said. "At least he made it to the game."

"By the time we got to Cap's he'd forgotten the game. Fuck him. Let's talk about something else," Barry said.

Geena Keats's Chevy convertible nosed up in front of the drugstore just as Pat's brother Steve and Larry the Frog Grant crossed the street from the post office. Geena got out of her car and began talking to Steve and the Frog. She looked great, Pat thought, in a suede coat and jeans. No wonder . . . Geena bought all her clothes on North Michigan Avenue in Chicago.

"I've got to get a ride out to my house and pick up some clothes," Barry Sand said. He lived on Duck Lane, one of over a hundred small inland lakes in the county. "When my old man starts drinking like this he stays drunk for days."

"You can stay at our place," Pat said, his eyes on Geena, Steve and the Frog all laughing and scratching there in the street. "You better get enough clothes for the week. If we don't draw a bye we'll play three games between Tuesday and Friday night."

"Assuming we win," Chuck put in.

"Lighten up," Ron said. "The Frog is our pessimist-in-chief."

The Conquering Heroes

Geena walked into the drugstore, Steve and the Frog tagging along behind.

The Frog was rubbing his thigh and wincing. The Frog had at least one imaginary injury a day. He earned his moniker as a sophomore when he complained about a sore arm in biology class, and Pat and Barry asked the biology teacher if they could dissect Larry Grant instead of the dead frog. Now nobody even bothered to ask the Frog why he was limping. It was what he did.

"Well," Geena said, waving at the girls in the booth and sitting down next to Pat, "my folks were really *nuts* this morning."

"We weren't that late."

"It's not that . . . my dad is still all bent out of shape about the steel strike so he took it out on me."

"The steel strike? That ended in January," Pat said.

"I know, but my dad thinks the Communists are taking over the unions and everybody in this country is going to go broke. He actually talked about moving the plant to Mexico!"

"Don't they have Commies in Mexico?" Barry Sand asked.

"Sure." Geena ran her fingers across the back of Pat's hand. "But they work cheap."

"They'll strip his Cadillac in a New York minute," Chuck added. "He'll have to get a new one every week instead of every year.

He's been watching too much Herb Philbrick on television."

The Frog grabbed a donut and started eating while he kept right on rubbing his leg.

Steve slapped his brother on the shoulder and continued on to the back to sit with Barb and the cheerleaders.

"Geena?" Mr. Sharpe was setting down the Frog's milkshake. "Can I get you anything?"

"Please, a cherry fountain coke."

Mr. Sharpe nodded and noted the Frog rubbing his leg. "Say, Larry, I've got some aspirin. I could tape one to that leg."

Everybody laughed except the Frog, who stood motionless for a long moment, the donut halfway to his mouth.

All heads at the counter swiveled toward the back of the store and the jukebox, where Steve and Barb were playing "Little Darlin."

"I hope they're spending her money," Pat said. "Sometimes I think one of us was adopted."

"Jesus, Steve!" Ron Waters called out to him. "It's still morning! Give it a rest."

Steve never turned his head, just put his hand behind Barb's back and gave them all The Finger.

"Well, what did you think of it?" Geena asked.

They had just come out of the Harbor City theater into the wind that roared off Lake Michigan and up the mouth of the Birch River, forcing Geena to snuggle her chin down into the fox collar of her coat. The wind had even blown several letters off the marquee so that it now read ATHS F GLO.

"Everybody got killed in the end." Pat shivered as the wind knifed through him.

"Kirk Douglas didn't!" Geena sounded as if Pat had just tried to kill the Kirk. "God! I just love Kirk Douglas. I can't wait for *Spartacus*."

"You won't like it."

"Why not!"

"Because they'll kill him in the end."

"How do you know?"

"My dad has the book and I read it."

"Well, thanks a heap for ruining it for me."

"*I* didn't kill him."

"You might as well have." Geena increased her pace toward her car.

"You know, Geena, in Mexico it's considered proper behavior to beat women. Maybe your dad has good reason to move."

"Oh, be quiet and hurry up, I'm freezing."

Walking alongside her, Pat knew that Pope John XXIII could hold all the Ecumenical Councils he wanted, but things between him and Geena weren't going to get any easier.

"How was your date?" His father was reading in the living room when Pat walked into the house.

"Weird." Pat shivered, still cold from the walk home from Geena's house. "Steve and Barry already asleep?"

"Your brother went up at nine all worn out from an afternoon with his girl." The disapproval showed clearly in Jim Lee's face. "Barry just went up about an hour ago. We had a long talk about the Marine Corps."

"Why?"

"He's thinking about joining if he doesn't get a scholarship. I offered to shoot him in the foot."

"Good."

"How was the movie?"

"Everybody got killed in the end."

"I know how you hate unhappy endings." Jim Lee put down the magazine. "I hate to be the one to tell you, son, but life is full of them."

"I'm learning, dad." Pat shucked his varsity jacket and shivered again.

"You know, *Paths of Glory* is based on a true story," Jim Lee said.

"Jesus, dad, don't tell me that!" Pat threw his jacket over the back of a chair. "I'm going to bed . . . in the *dark*."

Jim Lee took a drink from the tumbler of straight bourbon. "Take it easy, Pat. You look like I just slapped you away from the table for farting."

"What are you reading?"

"You don't want to know."

112

The Conquering Heroes

"Tell me. Things couldn't get any stranger tonight."

"Well," his father eyed him, "it says here that the United States and the Russians are both developing a nuclear weapon that just kills without damaging buildings and factories. You know, property, the important stuff."

"You're kidding." Pat grabbed his head with both hands. "All that time in grade school crawling under our desks and remembering not to look at the flash was wasted?"

"So it seems. The desks will come out without a scratch, the kids won't." Jim Lee rubbed a thick hand across his face.

"They call it the neutron bomb. Now they can start a war without worrying about property damage. With the insurance companies and the rich off their backs, that gives these lunatics a free hand."

"A bomb that just kills people without doing any damage?" Pat sat down on the couch still holding his head.

"Christ"—the cigarette smoke streamed from his father's nose—"now, even the goddamn French have an atom bomb. They'll probably drop one in Algeria before that mess is over."

"Those were the French in that movie," Pat said, as though that backed up the stuff his father was giving him. Another reason to shiver.

"Jim? Who are you yelling at?" Pat's mother

said as she came into the room dressed for bed. "Oh, hi, Pat. Is your father telling you about the end of the world again?" She put her hand on Pat's arm and squeezed. "Are you hungry? I've got some chicken left over from dinner."

"Thanks, mom." Pat pulled his lips into a thin line and stared at the floor. "No, I'm not hungry. Not much sense in eating if the powers-that-be are going to turn me into a pork rind by morning."

Katherine Lee glared at her husband, then said to Pat: "You haven't opened your mail. You've got letters from the University of Michigan, Michigan State, Notre Dame, Southwestern State University and Drake."

"They're all form letters, I'm sure, mom." Pat already knew enough about college recruiting to know that this sudden interest in him from the major colleges was coming too late to be taken too seriously. He would probably end up in Kalamazoo at the small college there that had been after him for two years. They had already offered him a General Motors academic scholarship. The big schools were just now getting around to him, which he figured meant he was either way down on their list of prospects or was just recently put on it.

"The boy is right," Jim Lee said. "They just want to keep him on the string in case they lose their first choices."

The Conquering Heroes

"If I was Cotton Nash," Pat said, "those letters would have been hand delivered."

"Who is Cotton Nash?"

"Mom, he's just the best high-school player in the country."

"Just don't forget"—Jim Lee drained his glass and clunked it down hard on the table—"college is about education. If basketball can get you that education, fine. But it's that sheepskin you want, not your name in some program that will be worthless in two hours."

"I know, dad . . . I just love to play . . ."

"Last I heard, they had a team in Kalamazoo." His father picked up his cigarette from the ashtray. "*And* they're giving you an academic scholarship."

"Nobody's *giving* him anything, Jim. He's always earned whatever he got."

"Well, I'm going to bed," Pat announced, "before somebody calls and takes something away."

"Don't forget to say your prayers," his mother called after him as he climbed the stairs. She'd been saying it all his life.

Right.

Detroit Flesh

"It's nonnegotiable," Coach O.K. Free said. Free, a tall, thin black man in his mid-forties, had played basketball at Michigan State in the late sixties.

"That's a lot of money." The heavyset black man stared across Free's desk at the Medgar Evers High School basketball coach. "Nobody'll pay that. We sure won't."

"Then Jamail Jenks won't be playing for you." Free returned the stare. "I've already got two schools more than willing to pay."

"One hundred thousand dollars a year? Bull-shit!" The recruiter shook his head. "Plus fifty K to you? I don't believe it."

"I don't care what you believe," Free said. "Do

116

you have the talking authority? That's all that matters. Money talks."

"Listen, brother, how can you just sell one of your players? You're doin' nothin' but selling the kid into slavery."

"I ain't your fucking brother," Free snapped. "And I'm looking out for the kid. Your program will make millions off him and you expect me to tell him to play for nothin'? You're the one buying slaves for scholarships and pin money."

"I resent that, he'll get his diploma and our program is—"

"Resent it all you want. And fuck your program. It don't graduate forty percent. You just don't like my pricing. Well, my boys aren't going to college to be brain surgeons. If you ain't gonna talk straight, get your narrow nigger ass out of my office."

"I ought to report you to the NCAA," the recruiter said as he stood.

"Go right ahead. You'll end up out of a job. Your school will never get another player out of Detroit and I'll still be sitting right here. Now get the fuck outta here. You're wasting my time."

Ten minutes later Jamail Jenks, the subject of the recent discussion, walked into O.K. Free's office, slumped down in the recently vacated chair and put his feet up on Free's desk. He was wearing a new pair of size 16 $200 basketball shoes and a $400 designer sweatsuit. His neck was layered in heavy gold chain and his fingers were adorned with gold rings, one of which covered his whole left hand, spelling out JAMAIL in 22-carat gold.

"How'd it go, coach?"

"We're in the serious negotiation phase," Free said. "Don't worry, I got it handled."

"But I need some money now. I got expenses. I got to eat. I got no ride and my girl needs an abortion."

"I told you," Free said, raising his voice, "I got it handled. You'll have more money than you can spend. Look, I'll loan you another couple thousand. Get that girl fixed, then lose her. And *don't* go buying no car. We don't need the attention."

Free then unlocked a desk drawer and took out a wad of hundred dollar bills, counted out twenty and handed them to Jenks.

"If I hear that you're doin' any more coke I'll kill you myself. Now, first thing you do is buy some rubbers. AIDS ain't no joke."

"Thanks, coach." Jamail uncoiled his lanky frame and stood, jamming the wad of bills into his pocket, his rings making the process difficult.

"Jamail?" Free studied Jenks.

"Yeah, coach?"

"You got a great future. Don't fuck up. I didn't spend all that time teaching you the game to see you end up a street nigger. You follow me?"

Jamail nodded, anxious to be on his way with his pocket full of cash.

The Conquering Heroes

"Promise me, Jamail. The street is full of million-dollar talents with ten-cent heads. Look me in the eye and *promise* me."

Slowly Jenks's dark eyes directly confronted Free. "I promise."

"All right, get out of here and try to respect yourself. You're a child of the gods."

Free watched anxiously as Jamail Jenks ambled out of his office and headed for the streets.

The motherfucking streets! Free worried about all his players. They had to deal with the streets every day. He did his best to get them out, hook them up, find them something to get them started. Was it wrong for him to get his players money? Hell, no, it wasn't wrong, Free was convinced of that. How else could they survive? It *wasn't* wrong, it was just against the rules. Rules put there by the rich white man to keep all the money in *his* pockets.

All that O.K. Free was trying to do, he would tell you, was liberate a few of the kids who had been born doomed in the projects. And, to do that, he had to get his hand into the rich man's pockets.

Television had made the colleges and their basketball coaches rich. Well, it was O.K. Free's duty to spread the wealth. "Redistribute the wealth?" Free remembered the wino quoted in the Detroit *Free Press*. "You bet they should redistribute the wealth. Every Monday."

119

Meanwhile, a distributee, Jamail Jenks hit the streets running and by the following Monday had spent all but $150 on cocaine. He never did get his girl an abortion. He did dump her.

And Jamail was still driving the rental car that Pat Lee had loaned him Tuesday night. He needed the wheels, didn't he? Was he supposed to *walk* all over Detroit?

Pat Lee drove directly from Chuck Small's apartment to his house near the campus, fixed himself a sandwich, drank a beer and paced around the house trying to calm himself and forget Chuck Small.

Finally he decided to call Rachael at her house in Houston, using his basketball department credit card. He *needed* to talk to Rachael, to have her say something decent to him, make plans to meet when he returned to Houston.

The phone rang six times before Rachael's attorney-husband Benjamin Pankin answered.

Pat paused, shocked for a moment that Ben was home, then plunged ahead, ignoring the old adage that if a man answers, hang up.

"Ben?" Pat spoke as if he was trying to reach him all along. "I've got another client for you. A kid from Country Day named Sanford . . . yeh . . . the big white kid. I told his mother you would do a good job . . . Anne Sanford . . . We'll pick up the tab. Okay? Good. Thanks, Ben, always good to talk to you. Give my regards to Rachael."

Pat hung up, more frustrated than ever.

"Hi, daddy," his daughter Jennie said as she breezed through the door. She usually stopped off at his house on her way home from her senior year at University High. Pat had been divorced from her mother Sara since Jennie was in fourth grade.

She stood next to his chair now and smiled her beautiful smile at him. Jennie Lee was simply a doll. She had her mother's looks without Sara's personality, which was, as Pat saw it, a major plus. It was Jennie who had made the misery of marriage and divorce from Sara bearable.

"Hi, darlin'." Pat leaned up and she kissed him on the cheek. "How was school?"

Jennie plopped down on the couch, eyed him. "I got my acceptance to Yale while you were away. I'm really excited."

"I *knew* you could do it, baby," Pat said, hiding the dismay from his voice that was in his heart. He had no idea in the world where he was going to get the money to pay her way through Yale. He was barely scraping by with Ray at Southwestern and living at home with his mother. And now James was back home, allegedly on vacation from his job at Paramount, but, Pat suspected, he was really out of work again.

The nineties had become an economic twilight zone in America, just as they were to Pat. What had happened to all those dreams and plans of the sixties? Had they really died with the Kennedys and Martin Luther King? Or were they always just political and social fantasy? The so-called Reagan Revolution had resulted in a huge transfer of wealth from the middle and lower classes up to the rich while burying the American economy in a four trillion dollar debt.

"It's going to be lonely here with you gone," Pat said, not having the heart to tell her what the financial facts of life were.

"Oh, daddy," she laughed, "how would you know? You're hardly ever home." It was not a rebuke, just a simple observation the way she said it.

His chest suddenly ached. "Now, honey, there won't be anything to come home to."

"Please, daddy, don't start on that again."

"Sorry. The old man is feeling real sorry for himself. Forget it."

"Did you get that kid from Detroit?" Jennie was a big basketball fan and followed her father's recruiting efforts with more interest than anyone else in the family. She knew how frustrated he could get.

"I think so," Pat hedged, still not able to remember exactly what had happened in Detroit. "He's interested enough to have kept my rental car."

"Isn't that illegal?"

"I forgot I let him drive it. I've got to call his

coach and get it turned in today."

"How'd you do in Houston?" Jennie leaned forward, her knees together.

"Better there than I expected." Which was the truth. "I met with Eddie Sanford and I finally met his mother. She's okay. The father, though, is something else."

"I better go home and get cleaned up," Jennie said. "I've got a date with Sammy. We're going to the Nirvana concert."

"Oh? What kind of kid is Sam, anyway? I hope he's not like his old man."

"He's real nice, dad. Treats me like a lady. I don't even have to worry about a backseat wrestling match."

"Good, I'm happy for you. But keep your powder dry . . . he's still Sam Watts's kid. He may have a bad time-release gene in his DNA."

"Daddy, *please.*" Jennie hopped to her feet and leaned over to kiss him again on the cheek. Her cool lips against his hot skin were soothing, comforting. Somebody loved him, he needed to know that. He listened to her climb the stairs and rummage around in her old room. Just the sound of her in the house made him happy. He had no idea what would happen to his life when she went east. She'd go, too . . . somehow he'd swing it, even if he had to steal the money.

Reluctantly he picked up the phone and placed a call to O.K. Free in Detroit. He would ask about the car and probe around, try to get a handle on what the hell he had promised Jamail Jenks.

"Free!" The Medgar Evers High School coach picked up the phone on the first ring. "Whattaya want?"

"Coach?" Pat began. "This is Pat Lee in Dallas."

"Sure, Coach Lee, my man." Free seemed really happy to hear from him. "What can I do for you?"

"Well"—Pat, at first taken aback by Free's ebullient mood, decided to roll the dice—"get Jamail to sign our letter of intent today. You do that, I might get some sleep tonight."

"I don't think I can promise you a good night's sleep just yet." Free's tone was still friendly. "Anything else?"

"Yeah, coach." Pat forced a laugh. "Actually, I called about my rental car. I forgot that I left it with Jamail."

"I don't doubt it. The shape you were in when you left here. Hey, we had us quite a celebration, didn't we?"

"We sure did, coach. I'd hate to have it spoiled by . . . an oversight. I mean, if the NCAA got wind that he was using my rental car it would be trouble for all of us. Rules. I'm sorry to have to bother you—"

"No trouble at all, Pat." It was the first time Lee could recall Free using his first name. "I'll get right on it. Don't you worry. I'll get the car turned in."

The Conquering Heroes

"Thanks a *lot,* coach." Pat said. "Sorry about the trouble."

"Hey, we made a deal. We're playing on the same side. You just get those numbers nice and finalized."

Pat hung up. His hands were cold and clammy. He was sweating profusely.

What numbers?

His head really began to hurt.

The man and woman sprawled naked on the bed were covered with sweat as they went at one another. The motel radio was tuned to the Oldies station, appropriate when one had a couple of Oldies fucking. Carly Simon was singing "You're So Vain."

The woman growled as her orgasm began and Carly sang about a hat and an apricot scarf. Rumor was the song was about Warren Beatty. They *were* an item years ago.

"Fuck me harder!" she moaned as the man hurled his hips against hers.

"*Harder,*" Pat Lee's ex-wife Sara screamed as she came.

Barry Sand began to pound himself into her, trying to match her action. He howled and thrust into her, feeling the tightening beginning in his stomach and groin. He convulsed against Sara Jacobs Lee, ex-wife of his assistant coach and supposedly lifelong friend Pat Lee.

Barry Sand's betrayals of Pat Lee had continued and grown as the years passed, just as Pat had feared they would that long ago spring day on the Harbor City pier.

They continued to thrust and twist long after they were finished, sliding over one another's sweat-soaked bodies. Barry pinched the nipples of Sara's breasts. She slipped free of him and turned to take his flaccid penis in her mouth.

"You want *more?*" Barry said.

"Mmm," she said, her mouth full of soft flesh that she sucked and saw begin to grow and harden.

"I'll be damned." Barry groaned and thrust his hips against her face, tangling his hands in her hair.

"Whoa, *wait.*" He was surprised by the quickness of his response. "You better stop."

"I want it." Sara's lips released him long enough to make her demand, then she began sucking, bobbing her head and masturbating him with both hands.

He came quickly and she still kept sucking. She had always been a great lay, Barry thought. He wondered if Pat knew just how good a fuck his ex-wife was. Probably not. He'd kept Pat on the road so much. She gave an angry fuck, probably still sore at her ex for never being home. Who the hell did she think sent Pat on the road?

Barry always considered Sara one screwed-up

lady. Sexy, exciting, sure. Maybe that's what originally attracted Pat. Barry didn't lose sleep over that. He used the situation presented to him. And he liked a lot the idea that the one-time hotshot was now his boy, traveling over hell and gone to help make Barry Sand the "Dean of the Dixie Conference." And screwing his woman in the bargain.

Barry used his clout to sleep with friends' and associates' wives and fiancées. And even the occasional student.

In fact, at the moment, he was wondering what Cathy Sullivan would be like. If, that is, Chuck Small hadn't ruined her.

When the AIDS scare cut down his number of partners to those he had known he could trust to stay clean and quiet, Sara Jacobs Lee had always been at the top of the list.

"Did Pat finally get back?" Sara asked.

They were side by side, sharing a cigarette.

"Yeah, I've got some messes for him to clean up on campus before I can put him back on the road."

Barry took a long drag on the cigarette.

"The point guard we signed from Oak Cliff is supposed to take his SAT. Pat has to set up DeFor Clark to take the test for him."

Barry stretched and yawned. "And Jax Morrow isn't working out. Pat needs to convince Jax to quit the team and give up his scholarship. Hey, we need it for a kid who can contribute this coming year, get us back in the Big Dance. It's for the good of the team." He said it with a straight face.

"You really are a son of a bitch," Sara said, kissing his nipples.

"I surely hope so, darlin', I surely do . . ."

Did Pat know about his carrying on with Sara? Barry had once asked himself. He must have, at least for sure since they were divorced. Did he care? Probably not, not anymore. But what about when they were still married, all those lonely nights for Sara while he had Pat on the road turning up the talent for the greater glory of SWS and in particular head coach Barry Sand? He'd even thought about asking Pat, and then told himself not to push his luck. Why make the guy steamed over what he couldn't change, or maybe didn't want to change.

Sara had been a handful from the first for Boy Scout Pat Lee. And Pat was a strange one about the girls, even before Sara. Going back to those days in high school and Geena Keats, who was all over Pat and he wouldn't give her a tumble. Responsibility, Pat used to say. He wasn't ready for it, crap like that. During the state tournaments, Barry especially remembered, it was Pat that was driving Geena crazy with his stuff about responsibility and respect. Hey, Barry figured then, just as now, he would have been a fool not to take advantage of the situation.

The Districts

1960

Wood drew Colins in the first round of 1960 district play. Colins, a poor, mostly black community located near Wood on Lake Michigan, would be tough to beat. They were big and fast and loved to run.

Midwest Utilities was negotiating with the village of Colins to build a nuclear power plant along the Lake Michigan shoreline. Colins's poverty and access to the massive amounts of Lake Michigan water necessary for the nuclear plant's cooling towers made it the perfect location for the power company. In the short run, at least, it meant money and jobs. Later it would bring the highest rate of cancer and respiratory disease in the state.

Even though Wood was ten miles downwind from Colins, Midwest Utilities didn't have to give the Wood school district a dime. Fucking the downwinders turned out to be a policy of the nuclear industry, its politicians, lobbyists and investors. All the electricity generated in the Colins nuclear plant would go to Detroit on the other side of the state.

The district tournaments were held in Benton Harbor, thirty miles south of Colins, at a time when Benton Harbor was still a prosperous city with one of the newest gymnasiums in the area with a seating capacity of 3,000. The Wood-Colins rivalry was an old one, going back to the twenties. On Tuesday night, an hour before the game started, the Benton Harbor gymnasium was filled to the rafters.

"These guys are bigger than us, they may even be faster," Wood coach Roger Starr was saying to his players. "But," and Starr wiped the blackboard clean, "that doesn't make them better. I've said it before, I say it again, basketball is a head game. Keep your *heads*. Make good decisions, *don't* think about winning or losing. Stay within striking distance until the last half of the fourth quarter, *then* start concentrating on winning."

Pat stared at the floor and thought about the

infinite possibilities that would spiral out from the opening tip-off.

"Ron, they like to run," the coach continued. "So lay back. If Ron goes underneath, Steve, make sure you get back. Pat, Big Man Burns is six-seven, position him on offense and defense." Roger Starr clapped his hands. "*Everybody*, block out on the boards. Let's go!"

Pat controlled the tip. Even though he gave up four inches in height, Pat's jump was over forty inches. Losing the tip seemed to infuriate Colins's Big Man Burns and he proceeded to play angry all night. Pat took him to the baseline and embarrassed him, working on his anger, keeping him physically and emotionally off-balance.

The Colins coach tried several defenses to stop Wood and Pat Lee. But if they tried to drop off and double- or triple- team Pat, his teammates would hurt them somewhere else.

With the score close in the last half of the fourth quarter, Pat tied up Burns coming off the boards. Boiling by now, Burns threw an elbow into Pat's face, knocking him to the floor, splattering his blood on the hardwood.

Pat had suffered another dislocation of his nose. Burns was thrown out of the game. Pat finished the game with thirty-two points, a remarkable twenty-eight rebounds, and his nose packed with gauze.

Five guys ended in double figures for Wood and Chuck was four for four from the field.

Wood beat Colins going away.

"That looks painful," Geena was saying.

"It hurts a lot worse than it looks." Pat touched the fresh packing in his nose, and his fingers came away stained with blood. "Damn it, it's still bleeding."

They were standing next to the players' bus in the Benton Harbor High School parking lot.

"I'll pick you up back at school," Geena said, and tiptoed up to kiss him.

Instinctively Pat pulled his head back, protecting his tender nose. Her eyes went wide. Another rejection.

"Whoa," Pat said, "it's just that my whole face hurts." He scrambled to smooth over the awkward moment. "Besides, I'll get blood all over your coat."

"I don't *care*. It's an old coat—"

"Well, it's my blood." He immediately regretted that one.

"Sometimes, Pat Lee, you can be such a *jerk*." Geena turned and bumped into Barry Sand, who stumbled back as Geena strode off.

"Was it something I said?" Barry watched Geena until she reached the white-on-blue '57 Chevy convertible, then glanced up at Pat.

"I wouldn't bleed on her."

132

"Well," and Barry stepped onto the bus, "you're just not with it, Pat boy."

"What does that mean?" Pat followed him onto the bus.

"Ask your brother. He'll leave his body fluids anywhere."

"Hey, color me strange, I don't like bleeding on people, including the Homecoming Queen. Can you imagine what her father would say if she came home covered with blood? My blood?"

"From the way she acted," Barry sat down, "you couldn't have done worse if you shit on her."

"*Jesus*, Barry!" Pat took the seat directly behind Barry Sand. Steve climbed aboard and walked down the aisle, stopping next to his brother.

"Well," Steve said as he stood there, holding his duffel bag, "what the hell happened? Barb said you did something to Geena."

"Nothing happened." Pat looked out the bus window and saw the cheerleaders gathered around Geena's car.

"You shoulda bled on her, Pat," Ron Waters said from the rear seat.

Pat turned around, the unconscious frown making his nose hurt more. "How come you guys are so free with my blood?" Pat stared at Waters.

"Because . . ." Chuck Stanislawski was sitting across from Waters . . . "we're a team, buddy. When you bleed we're hurt."

"That's the deal, brother," Steve chimed in.

"Everything's the goddamn deal with you, little brother."

"Is everybody aboard?" Coach Starr stood at the front of the bus. "Pat, how's your nose?"

"Fine, coach."

"Well, son . . ." the coach pursed his lips . . . "it might have been a good idea to bleed on her." Said with a straight face.

They all laughed, except Pat. He didn't get it. Not then, not thirty years later. Of course by then nobody would think it was so funny . . .

Pat had to play the second-round game of the districts with his nose packed full of gauze.

Wood faced Richards, a tough sawmill town located on the St. Joseph River outside Benton Harbor. It was obvious from the start that the Richards game plan included going after Pat's damaged nose. By the second quarter he had been slapped in the face a dozen times and as he walked to the free-throw line for the tenth time blood was clearly seeping through the packing.

The referee called an official time out while Dr. Grant, the Frog's father, changed the gauze in his nose. Out of the corner of his eye Pat could see the two referees talking to the Richards coach, one official shaking his finger in the coach's face.

"You okay, son?" he asked as he handed Pat the ball at the line.

Pat nodded and sank both shots. He already had

twenty points and the first half hadn't yet ended. His whole head hurt but the pain just made him focus and concentrate harder. It seemed that as the blows kept coming Pat had finally removed feeling from his body.

He felt nothing. The crowd was a dull roar somewhere in the distance. His consciousness was encased by the sidelines and the baselines. Inside that rectangle he heard and saw everything with special clarity.

His teammates were sharp too.

Anticipation.

Position.

Movement.

They formed an unstoppable force. Richards was out of the game by halftime, and by the end of the third quarter Coach Starr began clearing the bench.

Chuck Stanislawski was the first to sit down. He had fourteen points on seven out of eight from the field. Barry Sand and Steve Lee each sat down with ten points. The Frog came out with eight. Pat followed him with twenty-eight points and twenty-six rebounds. Ron Waters stayed in the game to run the offense.

The coach immediately sent Pat to the locker room with Dr. Grant. When he saw himself in the mirror Pat realized why the doctor had followed him. He looked like his throat had been cut. The front of the jersey was soaked in blood that dripped from the soggy gauze in his nose.

"You see those guys from Richards?" Dr. Grant said, smiling. "You bled all over them. Put your head back."

He did, and the doctor put a cold towel on the back of his neck and a small ice pack on the bridge of his nose.

Geena was nowhere to be seen when the players' bus pulled into the Wood High School parking lot.

Pat listened to "Endless Sleep" as he rode home with Barb and Steve.

Nobody said anything.

The second round of the districts had ended.

Barry Sand was singing "Yakety Yak" as Pat walked beside him toward the old three-story red-brick schoolhouse.

It was Friday morning. Barry was singing about bringing in the dog and putting out the cat.

Wood was playing Lake Valley in the district finals that night.

Lake Valley was a wealthy suburb of Benton Harbor–St. Joseph. It was the only school in the district with a swimming team and a brand new indoor pool. They poured money into their athletic programs and built powerful teams with statewide reputations. And they had only lost one game.

"You look terrible with all that shit in your

nose." Barry had stopped singing and was studying Pat's face. "Geena speaking to you?"

"Not lately." Pat touched his nose like he was exploring foreign territory. "She's still mad, it seems, but lost track of exactly what she's mad about. I thought she'd cheer up after Kennedy won the New Hampshire primary."

Barry just looked at him, smirked and shook his head.

The chemistry lab was the second door on the right as Barry and Pat entered from the north. It was their first class.

Geena Keats was waiting outside the lab. As Barry stepped past Geena he said, "Hi, Geena, you sure look nice," and the burly forward disappeared into the lab.

Barry was right, Pat thought. No question about it, Geena looked great. Why didn't *he* say it instead of Barry?

"We have to talk," she began, her eyes cold. Clearly her mood hadn't improved with the New Hampshire primary.

"I tried to call you last night," Pat said, "your mother said you were busy—"

"I was."

"I didn't say you weren't, for God's sake." And Pat was reminded of the exchange outside the Harbor City theater. It seemed he wasn't about to do or say anything right, at least as far as she was concerned.

"I had a long talk with my parents last night," she said. "I think we ought to start seeing other people."

"Okay. I mean, if you want to—"

"It's not that I *want* to. It's just that I think we should . . ."

"Whatever you want to do." Pat looked down at his shoes, thinking what a damned fool he was but not able to handle it any other way. Also, he didn't need this at 8:15 in the morning on the day of the district finals.

"I'm not sure what brought this on, Geena . . ." Except, of course, he did.

"Don't act dumb. You *know* what the problem is. You know it's all over town . . . I mean, I throw myself at you and you're afraid to . . . to . . . well, you know damn well what I'm talking about. How do you *expect* me to feel?"

Which struck him as all wrong—he was holding off out of *respect* for her. If it was all over town, it was her doing. And he blurted that out, realizing it was a mistake the minute he did.

"Now it's *my* fault?" Geena turned and stomped off down the hall.

Lake Valley led by twelve at halftime.

"Okay, don't worry, plenty of time left. We just want to be in striking distance by the last half of the fourth quarter. Don't focus on winning or losing right now. Focus on executing." Wisdom words from Roger Starr. "We're going to the diamond-and-one full-court press. Ron at the point. Steve and Barry at the wings. Pat midcourt. Frog, you check in for Chuck and take the safety."

Pat began pulling the packing from his nose. He was going to need all the oxygen he could get before this game was over.

"We'll give them the inbounds pass, then trap the ball," Coach Starr continued. "Pat, you have to cut off passes to the midcourt. Now, there's plenty of time left, keep your cool, we'll be all right."

Pat controlled the opening jump and tipped the ball forward to Waters. Ron flipped the ball behind his back to Steve Lee already on his way to the basket. He laid the ball up, gently.

Lake Valley by ten.

The press caught Lake Valley sleeping and Sand stole the ball, dropped it off to Waters at the free-throw line and Ron buried the jumper.

Lake Valley by eight.

Pat intercepted the next inbounds pass when the Lake Valley guard tried to throw the ball to half-court, then drove the middle. As three defenders tried to close the lane Pat dumped off to brother Steve sliding down the baseline, and Steve made a reverse layup off the board.

Lake Valley by six.

Lake Valley time-out.

"All *right*," Coach Starr said, clapping his hands, "now fall back and let them come to midcourt. Once the ball is across the ten-second line trap it again in the half-court press."

They proceeded to drop back and confused the Lake Valley team that had used its time-out to diagram plays that would beat a full-court press and now there was no press.

Crossing midcourt, the Lake Valley guard relaxed. Steve and Ron closed and trapped the guard between the midcourt and the sideline. He forced a cross-court pass. Sand lunged out, intercepted the ball and went the length of the court alone.

Lake Valley by four.

The next time down, the guard panicked and dribbled the ball off his foot. Steve snatched up the ball and let the referee touch it. While the Lake Valley players stood around in flat-footed shock, Steve drilled a floor-length pass to the Frog all alone under the basket.

Lake Valley by two.

The next possession, Lake Valley was able to penetrate. The Frog's man took the ball into the middle and sprang into the air. But he never saw Pat, and was stunned when his jump shot came right back, bounced off his forehead into Ron Water's hands. Ron took the ball to the middle and led Steve and Sand in the three-on-one fast break. The Lake Valley defender wouldn't commit and the break penetrated as the ball went from Ron to Barry to Steve to Ron back to Steve, who laid it up on the right side. The defender, spun completely around trying to keep up with the passing, was flat on his back when the ball slid through the net and bounced off his chest.

The score was tied.

Now Roger Starr called a time-out and replaced the Frog with Chuck Stanislawski for offense.

"Keep the pressure on and take good percentage shots," Starr said. "Don't give them anything cheap and let them back in this game."

Chuck Stanislawski hit the first three shots after the time-out while Lake Valley only got off one shot and that fell short.

Pat posted up on the high corner of the key and hit four straight jump shots, and when Lake Valley came out to shut him down Pat dumped off to his brother and Barry, taking the backdoor to the baseline for another eight points.

The game was out of reach for Lake Valley.

Afterward Pat sat in the locker room still in his uniform while the rest of the team was showering.

"Come on, Pat," Coach Starr stood over him, clutching the district trophy, "we got a bus to catch."

Pat nodded and began to roll down his wet socks.

"The only way to keep playing is to keep winning. We've got regionals in Kalamazoo next week."

Pat pulled the soggy jersey off over his head and stood to take off his shorts.

"We have to win them *all*." The coach turned back. "There was a scout from Michigan State in the crowd. He came to see you, Pat."

"It's a little late."

"Better late than never." Starr smiled.

Geena Keats's '57 Chevrolet convertible was sitting in the Wood High School parking lot when the bus came back from Benton Harbor. Pat was surprised.

Wilbur Harrison was moaning "Kansas City" out of the Chevy's radio.

"Everybody's going to Cap's," Geena said. "I told Barb we'd meet her and Steve out there." She paused. "Okay?"

"Why wouldn't it be okay?" Pat didn't get it. One day she was through with him, wasn't going to see him. Now here she was. What the hell was he supposed to do, how grateful was he supposed to be?

"What's that supposed to mean? I thought you'd be glad to see me," Geena said.

"I'm sorry. I'm just tired. I . . ."

"That's okay." She smiled. "I've been kind of moody myself lately. I guess you've noticed."

142

He nodded, half-smiled. She smiled back. Damn, he loved her smile.

"My dad said there was a scout at the game. He was there watching you, wasn't he?"

"So the coach said." Pat shrugged. "I don't really know."

"Do you think they'll offer you a scholarship?" Geena knew that Pat, like his teammates, could only afford college on scholarship.

"It's kind of late in the recruiting season." Pat stretched, yawned, to relieve the tension.

He knew his college decision was important to Geena. She, of course, could afford to go anywhere and was leaning toward the University of Michigan. No athlete from Wood had ever gotten a full ride scholarship to a Division-I school. Pat didn't expect to be the first.

"Have you heard anything from U of M?" Geena asked.

The question wasn't going to disappear.

"Not since football season when they came to see Barry play." He still hadn't opened the mail that had come the previous week, so he wasn't really lying.

The Chevy bumped gently into the gravel parking lot of Cap's restaurant and stopped between Jim Lee's Volkswagen and Barry Sand's old Model-A Ford.

As they crossed the lot Geena slipped her soft hand against his palm, and he gently closed his fingers, her hand disappearing, swallowed up by his.

Geena pulled Pat gently behind her, weaving through the happy throng in Cap's Place toward the big round table in the corner where the team and the cheerleaders always congregated. Their place in Cap's Place.

Stan Marion and Rick Cane, two of Pat's football teammates, grabbed hold of him.

"Great game, man." Marion, an all-State guard, hugged him until Pat gasped for air. Cane pounded him on the back, making his nose hurt.

"All the way to State!" Stan yelled, and finally turned Pat loose.

Geena stood by, not too patiently waiting to move on to join the others already at the table.

"One game at a time, big man." Pat smiled at Marion and ruffled his long greased-back hair, messing up his carefully built ducktail.

"You guys'll do it," Rick said, giving Pat one more whack on the back.

Pat and Geena arrived in the middle of Ron Waters's and Barry Sand's endless argument over Jerry Lucas and Oscar Robertson.

"The Big O is twice the ballplayer," Ron said, and slammed his palm down on the table. Waters himself had a lot of floor sense and was a good technical ballplayer.

"Lucas is the best," Barry countered. "Ohio

State will run the NCAA tournament."

"Lucas has a better *team*," Ron came back. "That don't make him a better ballplayer than Robertson."

"Lucas is only a sophomore."

Whatever that meant, Pat thought, as he slid into the booth next to Geena, leaned back and closed his eyes. He didn't need to listen to the argument between Ron and Barry; they'd been having the same one for a year.

He let his mind wander to the coming week, and began dealing with permutations of the regional tournaments. That was the world he knew and could figure out. Geena? College? The world? Forget it, if you can.

Helping Jax

The car radio was tuned in to an Oldies station and Carly Simon was singing about Warren Beatty when Pat pulled into his parking space outside the Greg Dunne Memorial Field House. Apparently, Warren went to watch the races at Saratoga without Carly. Warren's horse won. Then Warren flew his Lear Jet to Nova Scotia and watched a total eclipse of the sun. It really pissed Carly off.

In his office on the second floor he put his feet on his desk and stared out the window, reminiscing about his high-school days.

Jan walked in with her hands full of mail. "Welcome back. You look awful."

"Thanks. I left my heart in Detroit and my liver in Houston. What you got for me?"

146

The Conquering Heroes

His secretary dumped the mail on his desk in two large piles, then pointed to the first one.

"These are all replies to your letters. There's one in there from a sixth grade kid in Chicago. Are we recruiting in elementary school now?"

Pat looked back out the window. "The kid is eleven and he's already six foot six. The doctors say he could grow another foot."

"He'll need his own medical and psychiatric attendant by then," Jan said. "But then, I suppose we all will." She pointed to the second pile. "Sign these and I'll get them out today."

"What else?" Pat was trying to recall *what year* that total eclipse had been visible from Nova Scotia.

"Jax Morrow is outside. He's supposed to escort D.J. Johnson around on his campus visit this weekend."

"How's Jax feeling?"

"Says his knee's okay. You know, he's a pretty good kid."

"Yeah. He's my one real success. A real student athlete. Send him in."

As she left, Pat began to sign the recruiting letters.

Six-foot-eight Jax Morrow ducked through the open doorway with a slight limp from recent orthoscopic surgery.

"Say, coach, where you at?" Jax was a good-looking young black man, a hard worker with

147

discipline and dedication and brains.

Pat had plans for Jax Morrow. They had been put on hold because of Jax's injuries but now he was healing and would soon be playing to the potential that Pat thought would make him the best shooting guard in the nation.

"Jax! Good to see you. How's the wheel?"

"Fine," Jax said, slapping the leg. "How was your trip?"

"Successful, I think. What I can remember of it. I got shitfaced in Detroit and woke up in Houston."

"You got to cut back on the whiskey and wild women, coach. How does it look for Jamail Jenks and Eddie Sanford?"

"Between us chickens," Pat said and lowered his voice, "I don't remember what I said in Detroit. I could have offered Jamail's coach Barry's job."

Jax laughed. "If only you could."

Pat nodded. "I got along fine with Eddie Sanford. I kind of mishandled his parents but I think we'll get him. He wants to play with you."

"I hope we get him. He always gave us hell whenever we played Country Day."

"Do me a favor and give him a call when you get a chance. Come in here and use my phone. Invite him to visit you. That way we can get an unofficial campus visit."

"Sure, no problem, but I need a favor. Get somebody else to squire Johnson around this weekend. Watts and Sand have got limos and hookers and hotel suites lined up. I don't want to get involved in all that."

"Okay, I understand. I'll get LeJune Hampton. He loves that shit."

"Thanks." Jax stood and stretched, started to leave, then stalled. "Ah . . . look, coach, I don't know how much you know about what happened with Chuck Small when you were gone."

"I know too much. Small's an animal."

"Well . . . Cathy Sullivan is a friend of mine and what they're doing to her is a crime."

"I know . . ."

"She came to see me after she got out of the hospital and I told her to talk to you. I hope that was all right."

"Sure, I'll certainly talk with her . . ."

"I knew I could count on you." Jax smiled. "Thanks. And thanks for cutting me loose from Johnson."

"LeJune'll probably take Johnson on a five-state crime spree," Pat said.

Jax walked out, laughing.

I wish it was all really that funny, Pat thought as he picked up his intercom phone. "Jan, get LeJune Hampton over here and tell him to come unarmed."

Athletic Director Brick Williams, Coach Barry Sand and President of the Board of Trustees and discount store mogul Sam Watts were sitting around the athletic director's comfortably appointed office.

DeFor Clark, Sand's graduate assistant, a tall black man, stood beside Sam Watts's chair.

Pat walked into the office just as Sam Watts was handing DeFor Clark a thick Southwestern Basketball Department envelope.

"The money's in there," Watts said to Clark. "Don't lose it. Let me know how everything goes."

Pat stood behind Clark and looked over his shoulder as he opened the envelope to check the contents. Inside Pat could see a bundle of hundred dollar bills wrapped in a piece of notepaper with FROM THE DESK OF SAM WATTS printed across the top.

"Meet me in my office in about twenty minutes," Sand told Clark. "We'll discuss DeWayne Barkely's SAT test."

"You got that handled?" Watts asked Barry.

"I've got Pat here on top of Barkely, and DeFor knows what to do." Barry nodded. "That's right, isn't it, Pat?"

Pat half-nodded. Of course, it wasn't "right."

The cash-filled envelope in hand, DeFor Clark left the meeting, closing the door behind him.

"Well, down to the nut-cutting." Watts wasted no time. "I just don't get it. Small shows no respect." He looked across the room, his hard gaze demanding comments.

The Conquering Heroes

Pat looked out the window. He wished he weren't here; he damn well didn't want to contribute to this meeting. It also occurred to him that if anyone in the room found out he and Jax Morrow had discussed Cathy Sullivan they would have all gone ballistic.

"We give him a hundred thousand to come here," Barry said, "plus another hundred thousand if he stays four years."

Pat noted that Barry had the numbers wrong but said nothing. Barry generally had his facts wrong. But he knew the way to survive on other people's backs. He did that right.

Barry paused to see if anyone else would carry the ball.

Pat watched two girls ride by on bicycles and silently sang the lyrics of Carly's alleged song to Warren.

Finally Barry spoke again. "Now the ungrateful asshole wants to jump to the NBA."

Watts shook his head. "I just don't understand these nigger boys. I guess I never will."

"Don't put your humanity way out on a limb there, Sam," Pat said, violating his rarely observed code of silence. He was still watching the girls on the bicycles and thinking about Cathy Sullivan's rape and Carly's and Warren's ill-starred love.

"It could be something as simple as the $12.5 million they're offering him," Pat went on.

Watts gave Pat a look, but when he failed to

catch Pat's eyes he gave it up.

"And now *this*." Watts slammed the flat of his hand against the table.

"The guy's been a problem ever since he got here," Barry said, and turned to Pat. "I warned you we might have trouble with him."

Pat turned slowly from the window. "Now it's my fault?" He looked back out the window. God, he hated these guys. He lived to find a way to beat them. It was at least part of the reason he was still around.

"We played hell getting him off last year after that cocaine . . . incident," Brick Williams was saying.

"They never proved it was his cocaine." Barry automatically spun out the defense.

"It was his nose they found it in," Pat said quietly to the window.

They ignored him.

"After everything we've done for him," Barry said.

"Like what?" Pat asked without turning from the window. "Except bribe him to come to school here and make you guys a fortune in basketball revenues."

Trustee President Sam Watts looked up, startled.

"What's Lee's problem?" Watts said to Barry, as though Pat weren't there.

"He woke up this morning with a goddamn

moral code. Mr. Lee here is a very moral fellow."

"Did anybody think to mention to *Mr.* Lee that he is hardly in a high enough tax bracket to afford a qualm?" Watts said. "Leave alone a whole moral code." He turned to Pat. "If you don't have anything helpful to say, just please shut the fuck up."

Pat turned now from the window. "This *is* something helpful. You guys are still running this program like a plantation."

"Not again!" from Brick Williams.

"Yeah. Again," Pat said. "It's nearly twenty-five years since the Terry Dixon disaster and you haven't learned a thing. The majority of the blacks on campus are still on athletic scholarships."

"You ought to know," Barry said, "you recruited 'em."

"And you keep them segregated in the athletic dorm or in off-campus apartments."

Brick Williams took off his gold-rimmed glasses and set them on his desk. "You can't very well solve social issues *or* academic problems and run a major college sports program."

"Well, you better do something," Pat said. "Christ! LeJune Hampton was caught carrying a nine-millimeter Beretta."

"A misunderstanding," Barry shot back.

"By who? Not him. He understands exactly what he plans to do with that pistol and he'll get pissed one day and shoot somebody."

"That's ridiculous."

"As I recall," Brick Williams said, "it was you, Pat, who was always so anxious to get the Dixie League ban against black athletes dropped."

"That was thirty years ago. What decade are you living in, Brick."

"Well, all I'm saying is now we got 'em and you still aren't happy."

"Their situation has hardly improved since we recruited Terry Dixon."

"We all remember what a mess that was," Williams said.

"It wasn't Dixon's fault. It was ours. It's still our fault. They're supposedly student-athletes, but they're still enrolled in useless courses without a prayer of getting a degree."

Barry shrugged. "They're here to play basketball, not be Rhodes scholars."

"You took them out of the inner city, you treat them like aliens in a world of rich white kids."

"We set up social programs for them," Sam Watts protested.

Pat told himself not to lose it. "Excuse me, I don't think hiring hookers to escort them during recruiting visits and setting up a phony black fraternity qualify as social programs."

"Oh, just shut up, Pat," Williams told him. "There are priorities. Barry got to the Final Four two years ago. A priority. It takes sacrifice and

154

compromise and . . . funding to run a winning Division-I program."

"We treat these kids damn good," Watts added. "They live a damn sight better than they do at home. What more do you want?"

"Well, remember that they aren't home. We need to help them adjust or Chuck Small will be a petty criminal compared to the monsters we create down the line."

"I think the Chuck Small situation is under control," Barry said. "Unfortunate, sure, but no big deal."

"Not to you. The Sullivan girl feels a little different about it."

"What do you know about the Sullivan girl?" Barry stared at Pat.

"Nothing."

"Good. Right. Then shut up about her. She's been taken care of."

"Look," Pat said, going back to safer ground, "we promised them degrees—"

"*I* never promised them anything," Barry said. "You did."

"Pat, I warned you that we had to take this integration business slowly," Watts said, "but you had all the answers—"

"Slowly? You've taken thirty years and what we've got are black athletes with no future beyond their next game."

"Speaking of no future," Barry said, "I want

you to hunt down Jax Morrow. That boy doesn't have one."

"What?"

"Dr. Knight says he's never gonna be a hundred percent on that knee. You've got to convince him to leave."

"Absolutely *not.* Jax is the only player making any progress toward a degree—"

"He isn't on an academic scholarship, for Christ's sake."

"Jax Morrow is just about the best shooting guard I've ever seen," Pat argued. "Besides, Eddie Sanford says he wants to play with Jax."

"We'll give Eddie somebody else to play with. I gave Jax his chance. Now I want him to give me his scholarship." Barry folded his arms across his chest and stared at Pat.

"No! I'll quit if you take Morrow's scholarship. And another thing, I'm not gonna lie for Chuck Small. You're crazy if you think you can cover up this rape."

"Your noble stand is duly noted," Watts said. "Now, you just keep your mouth shut and let us handle the girl—"

"I'm warning you—"

"No, Pat," Watts said, cutting him off, "you're threatening us. If you think you can threaten me, you best remember you're just a bug on the windshield of life." He smiled, pleased with his turn of phrase, and walked out of the office.

The Conquering Heroes

Sand and Williams followed, leaving Pat alone to look out the window. What he saw was the prone body of a portly history professor he recognized who had just collapsed alongside the jogging path. A small crowd had gathered and just stared down at the outstretched figure. Finally a blond kid in a Fiji jacket moved closer and poked the professor in the ribs with the toe of his new Nike Air Mowabb cross-training shoe.

The body did not move.

The Fiji shrugged and walked away, having exhausted his resources in CPR, lifesaving and just plain giving a shit.

Pat watched the scene. This latest generation was something to behold. Not that some of the older one was any bargain, he reminded himself.

In the silence of the athletic director's office Pat could hear the music on the office intercom from the Oldies station.

He was still staring out the window when Jan Dayton walked in.

"I got the recruiting letters off your desk." She was holding the signed letters. "Anything in here for kindergarteners?" No answer. "Something wrong?" She studied Pat's face.

"I think that guy just dropped dead out there." Pat pointed out the window toward the jogging path.

Jan studied the crumpled figure in the sweat-shirt.

"Fitness freaks," she said, shaking her head.

"That's it?"

"You want me to give a shit? Okay, I give a shit. Just don't tell anybody."

She looked back out the window, then returned her blue-eyed gaze to Pat's face. At thirty-five Jan was slender, athletic and attractive. She and Pat had been in and out of bed several times over the past two years. Jan was married to the golf coach.

"So?" She slipped her hand inside his shirt and scratched his chest lightly. "What's really bothering you?"

"I'm still working in this shithole, ain't I?"

"Good. I heard you threatened to quit . . . Oh, some girl called you, wouldn't leave her name. She said Jax Morrow recommended she talk to you. Also, DeWayne Barkely called about his SAT test. He wants to know what he's supposed to do."

Pat stopped on his way out the door. "Tell him to be here an hour before the test in a white button-down shirt and jeans."

"DeFor Clark going to take it for him? I hear he can predict his scores within twenty points."

"So they say."

"Well, the kid will be a major resource in our never-ending trek around the NCAA rules." She took in Pat's sour face. "Hey, relax, life's not *that* grim." And as if to prove it she kissed him lightly before slipping by him out of the office.

The Conquering Heroes

*   *   *

Pat picked up DeWayne Barkely in front of the Greg Dunne Memorial Field House at 7:30 A.M., as Barry Sand had arranged.

DeFor Clark was already in the car. DeFor had graduated with a 3.8 average in humanities. He and DeWayne wore the same kind of mustaches and were approximately the same size and height. They were also now dressed in the same clothes.

Pat Lee was driving them to Baker Hall for the SAT scam. What the hell, hadn't a famous U.S. senator once paid somebody to take a test for him at college? Pat shook his head, telling himself it was a rationalization, not an excuse. He did way too much of that to try to justify what he had to do to stick around here. Watts had a point about him riding a high horse into the ground . . .

DeWayne Barkely was a high-school senior. To play for SWS as a freshman under the rules of Prop 48 Barkely would have to take the SAT test and score at least 1,000. Sand didn't figure he was up to it. He had a point there. DeWayne had taken the SAT once before and scored 500.

"They give you 400 just for signing your name," Sam Watts had said when he had heard Barkely's score.

Pat now dropped Barkely and Clark off at Baker Hall and waited as the two young men separated and went through different entrances. DeFor proceeded to the bathroom and a commode stall. DeWayne went to the test room, showed his driver's license and sat down.

The proctors passed the answer sheets down the rows of desks. When DeWayne got his, he quickly signed his name and raised a hand.

"Yes?"

"I need to use the bathroom."

"All right," the proctor said reluctantly, "but hurry. Once we pass out the test you won't be allowed in or out of the room until you turn in your answer sheet."

DeWayne left his signed answer sheet on the desk and hurried to the bathroom, knocked on the stall and changed places at the commode with DeFor Clark, handing Clark his driver's license and telling him where his seat was located.

Clark went to the testing room and took DeWayne's place.

DeWayne waited fifteen minutes, then strolled out the side door of Baker Hall and got back into the car.

DeFor would be careful to score just high enough to qualify DeWayne to play as a freshman under the rules of Prop 48 but not so high as to arouse suspicion.

Barry Sand ordered the routine more than a few times. And it was only done with black players.

"They all look alike," Barry had laughed when he first devised the scheme.

The Conquering Heroes

*   *   *

"All right, let's go down the list," Barry ordered. He had called a coaches' meeting in his office. They now pulled out the blue-chip list.

"Dicky Moore from Chicago?" Barry asked ritually, already knowing the answer.

"Signed," DeFor Clark reported.

Clark acted as if he had signed Moore instead of Pat, who had spent two years talking to the kid, his parents, his coach.

Pat kept silent. Everybody knew the truth, not that that signified at the athletics department.

"Duron Jones?" Barry continued.

"Signed!" DeFor Clark piped up again.

Pat looked at the tall graduate assistant who had never played college basketball and was only a fair high-school player. He had brains, though, and they belonged to his mentor Barry Sand. Pat never kidded himself that just being black made you an automatic candidate for sainthood. It was just that he'd seen too many treated like less than humans. Jax Morrow and DeFor Clark were opposite ends of the spectrum.

Clark had gotten his job starting out as a ballboy gofer for Barry during his freshman year at Southwestern. He'd advanced his career by laughing at Barry's jokes and shrugging off insult and indignity at the hands of the head coach. Barry took it for a show of proper respect, and

Peter Gent

Barry would take that any way and from anyone he could get it.

Clark secured his place with SWS basketball by taking a petty larceny-shoplifting rap for Chuck Small when he had gone with him to a department store. Barry promised Clark a job would be waiting as soon as he finished serving his sixty-day sentence. Clark walked into jail like a character out of a vintage Jimmy Cagney movie.

Now, if the earlier meeting in the athletic director's office was any indication, DeFor Clark had been promoted to bagman. The envelope Sam Watts had given him appeared to have several thousand dollars in it. Pat had been wondering for what or whom that money was intended. He assumed it had to do with Chuck Small's rape of Cathy Sullivan . . .

"Jamail Jenks?" Barry was asking.

The room went silent. Finally Pat spoke. "I think he's ready to sign. I'll need one more trip to work out the noodles with Coach Free."

"It's getting late in the recruiting season to be saying 'I think,' Pat." Barry didn't look up from the sheet. "You lose this guy, you better just stay in Michigan."

"Don't threaten me, Barry."

Barry just looked at him. He knew damn well he needed Pat as much as anybody. And not, if he were able to face it, not just for recruiting but for his coaching smarts, which Barry congratulated himself for being smart enough to take advantage of. Pat loved to play a part with "his boys," loved it enough, so far anyway, to have stayed with a situation he obviously hated.

"Eddie Sanford?" Barry continued to read as if he didn't know the list and the answers by heart.

"One, maybe two more trips," Pat said. "I made contact with the mother and put her in touch with Ben Pankin."

"You've taken a long time with this kid," Barry said. "You wouldn't be going to Houston to take shots at Pankin's wife, our old friend Rachael, on university money?" Barry laughed at that one, and the other coaches followed suit as they figured it was an inside joke.

"The kid has verbally committed," Pat said, ignoring the provocation. "I just have to maneuver around his father. The guy could be big trouble. He could bring the roof and the NCAA down on us." The way I'd like to do, and one day . . . he thought but didn't say.

"Okay, so much for the list." Barry set the paper aside. "Now, we've got to make sure this Chuck Small thing is dead and buried and the girl keeps her mouth shut. Nothing about it leaves this office. Don't even tell your wives."

"How about other people's wives?" Pat put in.

Barry turned on him, said nothing, turned away at Pat's refusal to be stared down.

"I think that goes without saying."

"That's what I would have thought," Pat said, still staring at Barry.

Pat was walking to his car outside the Greg Dunne Memorial Arena when a girl with a battered face approached him.

"Coach Lee?"

"Yes?" Pat immediately knew who she was. He wanted to run. "What can I do for you?"

"My name is Cathy Sullivan. Jax Morrow suggested I talk to you. He said you were the only one in the basketball department he trusted."

"Good man, Jax," Pat stalled. "I recruited him out of Houston, always liked him, a terrific three-point shooter and a great player . . ." Jesus, he realized he was on the verge of babbling.

"Well, Jax said . . . I mean, he thought that maybe you could . . ."

She was struggling to hold herself together. "Jax said that you would listen to me."

"Sure." He didn't trust himself to let his true feelings for her show. He took in her pretty face, badly bruised, blue-yellow, scratched and cut. She had purple and blue-black marks on her arms and neck.

She hugged her arms up against her breasts. Her fists were clenched.

"It's about one of your players. Chuck Small . . . he beat me up, he . . . he *raped* me."

She seemed about to collapse and Pat held her.

164

The Conquering Heroes

He could feel how frail she was, smaller than his Jennie and only a couple of years older. This girl could easily have been his own daughter.

Finally she regained some control. "Will you help me? I can't tell my father. My boyfriend is so upset he won't talk to me. The police won't believe me and call *me* terrible names. And I keep getting these awful phone calls."

"Sure, sure, I'll help you," Pat said, without the faintest idea what exactly he could do. He hugged her gently. Her bone structure was fine and thin, there really wasn't much to her. It was a minor miracle that Small hadn't just smashed her like a china doll.

Maybe he had, and all that held the pieces in place were her guts and spirit, which obviously had their limits.

"You call me at this number, anytime," Pat said, and dug a card out of his shirt pocket. "It's my private line and if I'm not in it rings through to my answering service. They can find me."

Cathy Sullivan managed a smile for the first time since the rape.

"Thank you . . . you don't know what this means to me."

Pat held her by both shoulders at arm's length and looked into her inflamed eyes. "Now, you've got to promise me that you'll at least try to put this behind you. Talk to a counselor . . ." Big help, Pat, he thought. What would really help would be to put Chuck Small behind bars and give him Barry and company for roommates . . .

She sighed, as though trying to reorganize her breathing. "Thank you, Jax said you were a good man. I think you just saved my life."

She turned and walked away with a new bounce in her step. About halfway across the lot, she spun back on her toes and waved.

Underneath the brutal, mindless damage done by Chuck Small, Barry Sand, Dr. Knight and the campus cops she was still a pretty young girl with her whole life in front of her, Pat thought, or hoped, as he waved back.

One thing he knew, deep down, that in spite of the risks, the cost, he somehow had to help Cathy Sullivan, directly or indirectly, by bringing down Barry Sand and Sam Watts. Hell, he might even help save himself in the process.

In bed that night Pat kept going over scenarios that didn't add up. Finally he fell asleep, and his dreams again carried him back to earlier days when sweet victory first mixed with the taste of defeat. And put him on the road to SWS.

Playing the Game

1960

Pat took the ball off the defensive board, looking down the floor while he was still in the air.

Barry Sand was on the far sideline just past midcourt, with three steps on the Catholic Central defense.

Clearing the ball, Pat took one step and laid the pass out in front of Barry, who took it on the run and laid the ball off the board and into the hoop, but the defender caught up just in time to cut his legs out from under him.

Barry came down hard on his head and shoulder, fraying the ulnar nerve and leaving his right hand temporarily paralyzed.

The only excuse the Catholic Central player had was that Wood was beating them by twenty-two points and in less than a minute of playing time would be crowned regional champions.

Barry wasn't buying. He got to his feet, right arm hanging useless at his side, and proceeded to beat the Catholic Central player senseless with his big left fist. Before the referees could pull Barry away he had knocked out four teeth and broken the kid's nose. He didn't even remember the game until it all came back in a flash halfway through the summer.

For Wood, it was a disastrous victory. Barry's nerve damage put him out for the rest of the state tournament.

For Barry, the injury was a lifetime blow. At the time he had football scholarship offers from MIAA and Mid-America Conference colleges. When they learned of his injury the offers were quickly withdrawn—along with Barry's chance of going to college.

On March 10, 1960, Southwestern State University head basketball coach Greg Dunne woke up with a hangover. His wife, Joan, snored lightly beside him.

The previous night they had gotten drunk, and Dunne had stayed drunk every night since word came that the star player Cotton Nash was going to the University of Kentucky. His wife drank with him out of desperation. At least so she told herself.

Since the Dixie Conference season began, Dunne's basketball team had taken a nosedive. And now Cotton Nash was gone, along with any hope of turning the program around quickly. Dunne downed two double Bloody Marys before he showered, drank a third double after he dressed. By the time he walked out of the house into the morning cold, carrying his fourth in a Styrofoam cup, the coach felt almost human. He parked in his assigned spot behind the old field house and drained the cup. Now there was a pleasant buzzing in his head as he prepared to face the new young athletic director, Brick Williams.

Dunne walked through the locker room entrance. He would take another shower, shave, put on a fresh sweat outfit and basketball shoes, then go up to his office. Two nights earlier Texas State had beaten Southwestern State by three points. It was the eighth game Dunne had lost by four points or less.

"We heard about him from one of our alumni in Michigan," assistant coach Frank Wolfe was saying to Dunne in the basketball offices. "We still got that scholarship we were holding for Cotton Nash. We should check this kid out. Who knows? His team is still in the Michigan State tournaments."

"Yeah. Sure, sure . . ." Dunne just nodded and thought about his bottle stashed in his locker.

He stood, started for the door. "I'll be back in a little while," and was out of the office.

"Don't forget, his name's *Lee*," Wolfe called after the slamming door. "Pat Lee."

Barry Sand had been seriously sick to his stomach from unaccustomed booze ever since he lost yet another football scholarship. "The word about his nerve injury traveled fast," Pat was saying to his parents as they tried to comfort Barry.

"Is his injury really that bad?" Katherine Lee asked.

"Dr. Grant sent him to a specialist," Pat told her. "He doesn't think so, but nerve damage tends to scare off recruiters and head coaches."

"It's just easier for them not to honor their word than to take a chance on an injury," his father put in. By now Barry had headed for the bathroom.

"Where's Geena?" Pat's mother asked her son. "I haven't seen her in a while. You two fighting again?"

"You'll have to ask her. She's the one keeping score." Pat shook his head. "Between the quarter and semifinal games and trying to keep Barry here sober and in school, my dance card has been pretty full. My guess is she's furious at me but I don't even have time to go take my raps."

The Conquering Heroes

"Well, it'll be all over by Saturday," Jim Lee said, listening to Barry be sick in the bathroom. "Drinking for oblivion. This boy has got big problems. He's a buddy, Pat, we've got to do something for him."

"Unless we can make sure he gets and keeps a scholarship I can't think of a thing that'll kill what's eating him."

In the quarterfinals Wood had squeaked by Detroit Archangel Michael, a Romanian Orthodox parochial school, 65-64 on a twenty-foot shot at the buzzer by Chuck Stanislawski. They had come from eight points back with a minute to play. Two nights later they had played Fenn, the best team in the Upper Peninsula, to a 66-66 tie. Then in overtime Pat and Steve Lee found the range and outscored Fenn sixteen to two.

The following Saturday at Michigan State, Wood took the Jenison Fieldhouse floor at 4:00 P.M. against West Lansing Christian, the number-one team in the state, for the state championship.

Christian's starting guards were six feet three. Their forwards topped out at six feet five and six feet six. Their all-American center was six feet eight.

In the thirty-two minutes of game time Wood's smaller, highly disciplined, technically proficient and execution-oriented offense and defense were matched against the raw talent of the bigger, deeper, high-powered West Lansing team.

On offense, Wood moved confidently, opened the passing and driving lines, looking for the open man or the percentage shot. They moved without the ball, slipping their defenders on the weak side, using picks and breaks for easy layups—the passer always anticipating, the pass anticipated.

If West Lansing collapsed back to clog the lanes, Wood shot over them. When West Lansing moved out to stop the jump shots, Wood passed and drove by them.

When West Lansing had the ball, Wood played tight man-to-man and closed off the lanes. Whenever a shot went up they blocked out the bigger, taller West Lansing five, allowing them only one shot at the basket each time down the floor.

By the third quarter Christian was forcing its shots. They fouled trying to drive the lane or rebound over the Wood player blocking them out. They hacked. They shoved. They traveled. They threw the ball in the stands.

Wood slowly began to build on its lead and at the end of the third they were winning by ten. By the middle of the fourth quarter they were ahead by fifteen and building.

Pat had been so focused that when the final buzzer sounded, the roar of the crowd made him flinch. He'd forgotten they were even there.

Wood had won the state championship.

172

The Conquering Heroes

* * *

Pat was electric with mixed feelings. They had won the state championship and he was elated. At the same time he was oddly depressed because he had played his last game. He was facing the final comedown.

As he moved slowly toward the locker room, he heard someone say, "Don't take it too seriously, Pat." A short, stout man was suddenly walking beside him. Pat could smell the liquor on his breath. "Just remember, they're going to do the whole thing over again next year, without you." The man slipped a business card into Pat's hand. "You're a great player. I flew here all the way from Texas to see you play. I want you to play for me next year. A full-ride scholarship in the Dixie Conference."

Pat stared at him for a long moment, then thought of what had happened to his friend and teammate Barry Sand. Sure Barry could be a pain, overbearing, sometimes not exactly above taking advantage of you, but like his father had said, Barry was one of them, an old friend . . . you didn't desert a friend. At least he didn't . . .

"I won't go alone," Pat said suddenly, without real thought. "You'll have to agree to take one of my teammates. He missed the finals but he's a helluva ballplayer. His name is Barry Sand." Well, so he was exaggerating a little.

"I'll call you, Pat, I'm sure we can find a way to

bring your buddy to Southwestern." And the man moved away, trailing an alcoholic aroma.

Pat looked down at the card in his hand. It was wrinkled, dirty and sweaty. It read:

GREG DUNNE, Head Basketball Coach
Southwestern State University
Dallas, Texas

In April of 1960, on the heels of Wood winning the Michigan state championship, Pat Lee received a call from Southwestern State assistant coach Frank Wolfe, followed up with a written letter inviting him to visit the SWS campus and meet Coach Dunne at 11:00 A.M. to talk about a full-ride scholarship.

Pat had flown from Chicago to Dallas and taken a cab to the campus and arrived at Coach Dunne's office at 10:55. It was now 11:30 and Coach Dunne had still not arrived.

"I'll try him at home," the secretary said, picking up the phone and dialing. She let it ring a long time. "Coach? It's me, Sally. I'm calling from your office, there's a boy . . . coach? Coach? No. I called *you*." She paused and smiled at Pat. "Yes, coach, that's right. Well, there's a boy here that says he has an appointment with you." Pause. "I'll ask him." She covered the mouthpiece. "Is your name Pat Lee?" Pat nodded. "Yes, sir, it's him." The secretary winked at Pat, then sat upright. "Are you sure you want me to do that?" She looked at Pat, then spoke into the mouthpiece. "Still got that ol' stomach flu? Well, I can try."

Sally hung up and dug into one of her desk drawers and extracted a National Letter of Intent.

"I know this must seem strange—"

"Maybe I should—"

"You really won't catch him at a better time. He's been sort of under the weather, doesn't get to the office much."

"When we talked," Pat said, "he promised he would arrange something for a teammate of mine."

The secretary studied the papers in her desk. "There's nothing here . . ."

"Pat Lee!" Assistant coach Frank Wolfe walked into the office. "Goddamn, boy, glad you could make it." Wolfe stuck out his hand and grabbed Pat's. "Sorry Greg couldn't make it but I've taken care of everything. Right, Sally?"

Sally held up the papers. "He says there's supposed to be something here for one of his teammates. This is the last letter of intent I've got."

"Don't worry about it, your friend Barry Sand will be taken care of, Pat. We promised you that and we don't renege on our promises. Sand will be brought down here as . . . as a student assistant, and if he shows promise we'll get him on scholarship. Hey, until he plays we can set him up better than we can you. The NCAA and its rules really screws the players."

"Thanks," Pat said, "I appreciate that."

"We can get money and plane tickets and clothes to you through your pal Barry Sand. We already have an apartment rented for both of you."

The talk about money and the implication that maybe they were skirting NCAA rules made Pat uneasy, but he reminded himself it wasn't just for him. Barry Sand's last chance to go to college depended on this. He owed Barry that chance. Still . . .

"Well, I don't want to break any rules," Pat said.

"That's just the point," Wolfe came back. "We aren't breaking the rules. It's just a beautiful deal. If you want to go to school here you might as well sign now."

"Well, I haven't seen the campus—"

"Believe me, it's one of the most beautiful in the nation. Right here by the X, Pat."

Sally handed Pat the pen and, pushing aside his reservations, he signed.

Later, in his darker moments, he would recall the moment as signing on for a life's sentence.

And at other times he would try to look on the brighter side—after all, SWS *was* a good college, and drunk or sober, Greg Dunne knew basketball

The Conquering Heroes

like no other coach in the nation. As for helping out his "old friend" Barry Sand, well, that was another story. But, like they said, hindsight was 20/20, and at the time it had seemed like the thing to do. And he had been able to recruit blacks and help build a basketball power . . .

Players

On September 23, 1960, the SWS university basketball team was called to an unofficial practice because the NCAA didn't allow official practice to begin until October 15.

The team was lined up on the upstairs practice floor and Coach Dunne went down the row of freshman scholarship players, greeting each one by name. When he got to Pat Lee he squinted, ignoring Pat's outstretched hand, looked back at assistant Frank Wolfe, then back at Pat.

"Who the *fuck* is this guy?"

"Pat Lee," said Wolfe. "You were down with the, uh, stomach flu when he visited the campus and signed."

"What?" Dunne had no recollection of his

drunken trip to recruit Pat Lee at the state finals in East Lansing.

"Don't worry," Pat said. "You'll like me, I can grow on you."

"Grow on me five fucking inches by tomorrow and we'll talk. Well, that's it, I need some refreshment," and he turned abruptly and walked away.

After ten days of "unofficial" practice Pat made it clear he was probably the most fundamentally solid and talented player on the team.

Wood High School coach Roger Starr had taught the Greg Dunne system to Pat all through high school. And the system was ingenious, no question. But like many geniusy types, Greg Dunne had long ago crossed over the line into a kind of madness.

Southwestern State University had no great players with the raw, undisciplined talent that Pat had seen displayed by the great black high-school teams from Detroit, Flint, Jackson and Benton Harbor. In fact, Dixie League rules excluded black players.

He watched white forwards gun twenty-five-foot jump shots without success, then never follow the ball to the basket. He watched guards give up their dribble before knowing what they were going to do next. Pat himself could outjump the seven-foot white centers and slip by them into the open lanes they left to the basket for shots and rebounds.

Some of them had good skills but they all played scared. The veteran players suffered the most, having already gone through at least one losing season. Fear was etched in their game. There was a desperation to their play, driven by a fear of losing. During scrimmages they melted under the pressure of trying to win from the opening tip-off, and collapsed under the weight, the *fear* of spending entire games in front of thousands of people playing not to lose.

Basketball, Pat had learned, was a game of the mind, a high-speed chess game. The good players were always thinking three or four moves ahead. It didn't matter if you were ahead or behind for thirty-nine minutes. What mattered most was that you got the lead and kept it by the fortieth minute. Take your time and enjoy it, make the other team work, just do your job—every time.

Pat was taught to play the fundamental game, not forcing, taking his time. Look first for the pass, then for the shot, then for the drive, finally for the outlet, and moving without the ball, begin all over. If you got doubled, look for the open man. With these guys, too often the open man couldn't handle the quick pass, didn't even expect it.

If they laid off him, he shot over them. If his man moved up close, he drove past him. He blocked off the boards, picked for his teammates, followed up his shots and moved without the ball.

The Conquering Heroes

When Pat would snap a return pass, catching the defensive man still reacting to the first pass, his teammate with a clear move to the basket often would mishandle the pass.

Pat tried to know where everyone was on the floor and figured the ever changing geometry that would open up a shot, a passing or driving lane. He had played with people of greater skill, who knew how to anticipate each other. The sheer quickness of the game seemed to elude his Southwestern teammates.

No question, he felt, basketball was definitely a stepchild in Dixie Conference sports, and would remain one until blacks were allowed to play.

Official practice began on October 15, and from then on the coaches were there every day and Pat stared the greatest source of everyone's fear straight in the face—head coach Greg Dunne. His mood swings were a mile wide. Alcohol and losing had blown holes in his psyche. His own fear was contagious and his need to win was frightening.

Dunne pretty much left Pat alone, because Pat knew his system and played such a sound fundamental game. But his treatment of teammates left Pat certain they couldn't compete against the big NCAA schools with players so beaten down.

He held his tongue. Freshmen couldn't play varsity sports in 1960. But if by his sophomore year things hadn't changed, he would be facing a crisis . . .

*　　*　　*

Back in Detroit, the brand-new, 1.6-million-square-foot $54 million Cobo Hall hosted the first National Automobile Show for nine days in October of 1960. Detroit was really flexing its muscles. In November the 310,000-square-foot $34 million McCormick Place opened on the South Chicago lakefront. America needed space to show her wares. The world was her marketplace. It was, after all, the American Century.

And on basketball courts around Detroit and Chicago hundreds of talented black kids were taking basketball to a new level. It was becoming more and more a wide open, run-and-gun game.

The answer to Southwestern's basketball problems was to somehow find access to this mass of "untouchable" black talent.

"How was practice today?" Laude VanMeer asked as Pat and Barry walked into the apartment.

"Like being tied in a sack with a bunch of rabid squirrels," Pat told him. "Dunne is driving those guys nuts. They're only fair players and he's got them scared and confused."

Pat Lee and Barry Sand had known Laude VanMeer since high school, when Laude was a senior at Grand Rapids Calvin and Pat and Barry were sophomores at Wood. They had faced each other in the regionals. Wood had beaten Calvin but lost the next game. Every summer since then Laude had always come down to Harbor City for a couple weekends and he, Pat and Barry had hung out together.

Laude planned a career in politics. Being the only Democrat in his family, he had decided to move to Texas. Still a yellow-dog Democratic state in 1960, Texas congressmen controlled the U.S. House and Senate and headed all the major committees.

When Pat and Barry accepted the deal at Southwestern, Laude VanMeer arranged for them all to be roommates. They had a big three-bedroom apartment within walking distance of the field house and the new police school across the common.

"Rachael called from Chicago," Laude said. "She's gonna try to get down here right after the eighth."

"Why the eighth?" Pat asked.

"The presidential election," Laude said. "You must have heard, it's in all the papers."

Rachael had written and phoned Pat regularly after deciding to continue her campaign work for Kennedy right up to the November elections. And she had made and broken plans for several visits.

Now with the election Tuesday, Pat was hopeful she would keep the date. Marine Biology had obviously lost out to her love of politics and especially JFK.

"Your girl will be hanging out with the Bundy kids, McGeorge and Bill. I'll bet they end up in Kennedy's administration. You know how it works—Groton, Harvard, Wall Street, Washington," Laude said. "Their dad is a shirttail relative of mine."

"Your family is part of the Eastern establishment?" Pat was surprised.

"Hell, no. My father drinks martinis and plays golf with Gerry Ford. It's just that Harvey Bundy was from Grand Rapids."

"Guys from Grand Rapids start hanging around the White House and it's the end of the world," Pat said.

"Who the hell is Gerry Ford?" Barry asked. "One of Henry's kids?"

VanMeer and Pat looked at one another and back at Barry Sand. "Yeah, Barry," Laude said straight-faced, "he's one of Henry's kids. They exiled him to Grand Rapids for thinking up the Edsel."

"Really?" Barry filed the misinformation for later misapplication, like when Ford became president, Barry insisted he was part of old Henry's family tree. Facts rarely bothered Barry.

On November 8, 1960, John F. Kennedy was elected the thirty-fifth president of the United

The Conquering Heroes

States. As a reward, Rachael, with other campaign workers, was invited to meet the president-elect. Rachael, of course, canceled out on coming to Southwestern to be with Pat.

"This is just too big an opportunity to miss," she said excitedly over the phone.

"I guess that's Kennedy's appeal," Pat said. "With him in the White House, life will be just one big opportunity after another."

"You'd understand if you were a part of it."

"More exciting than real life? Tell your hero that down here blacks still can't play basketball in the Dixie Conference. I'll look for you when I see you." He hung up.

"She's not coming?" Laude said.

Pat shook his head.

"According to JFK we're at the beginning of a new day," VanMeer said.

Pat gave him a sour look. "Maybe, but in Dixie Conference towns the movie theaters still have 'Colored' entrances and drinking fountains. Down here it's still 1949. If my mother was here I could finally win an old argument."

"What argument?" Barry asked.

"That it's always 1949."

"Well, the Harvard boys will get around to fixing that," Laude said. "These guys compete with each other for the hell of it."

Pat shook his head. There seemed something

dangerous about competition for drill. These people played in order to win. Pat won in order to play. There *was* a difference. It had to do with the quality of love for the game.

The freshman team went home for Christmas while Coach Dunne took the varsity on a disastrous swing to the Christmas Classic Tournament in San Francisco. By the time winter term started and the freshmen returned, the team had a 1–7 record. The Dixie Conference season started the following week.

"Well, Barry," Pat said, "we've got to go to practice and see just how crazy seventeen days on the road have made Greg Dunne."

Before they reached the door, the phone rang and Pat answered.

"I've decided to move to D.C.," Rachael told him. "It just makes sense, Pat. I've got a part-time job with the Kennedy administration and . . . well, it's where I want to be."

"So this is the end of your rebellion? You're joining up."

"You're acting like a boy—"

"Well, your president," Pat cut her off, "has scared the shit out of us *boys* with his draft quota of 150,000."

"I was afraid you wouldn't understand. I believe in what he stands for."

Not much made sense to Pat. Then *or* later.

186

The Conquering Heroes

* * *

"He's in his office," Sally said uneasily as Pat Lee and Barry Sand walked into the basketball department. Greg Dunne had called and in an especially agitated voice ordered them to meet him *right away*. It was March 1962.

Pushing the door open, they did not see the coach sitting behind his desk. Where was he?

"Close the goddamn door! The bastards have been in and out of here all morning."

Pat and Barry searched for the coach.

"Down here. Get down and come over here."

"Wait a minute," Pat said, "what the hell is going on?"

"Just get *down*." Dunne was under his desk. "They're up in the light fixtures, I've got every other entrance plugged . . ."

Pat looked around the room. The electrical outlets were covered with athletic tape. The shades were pulled on the windows. The ceiling light provided the only illumination. He started toward the coach's desk.

"Wait! If you can reach that light switch and turn off the overhead light I think we'll be safe . . ."

"Coach, I don't think . . ." Barry began.

"Don't *think!* Just get that fucking light *off*."

"It'll be pitch black in here—"

"Good, then they can't see."

"Who can't see?" Barry said.

"If I knew who they were I wouldn't need you."

Dunne's voice was now small and scared. "I saw them on the team plane coming back last night . . ."

Texas State had beaten, as one of the players said, the dog shit out of Southwestern the night before to end the 1962 season. Pat had scored twenty-six points and pulled down eighteen rebounds, but his teammates still played scared. Greg Dunne arriving roaring drunk didn't help. He screamed and cursed them as they missed lay-ups, threw the ball away and played zero defense.

Pat felt a cold chill now. He stood in the middle of the room, then sat down on the overstuffed couch that ran along the inside wall.

"What are you doing?"

"Just checking, coach," Pat stalled. "I don't see them, I think they're gone. You probably scared 'em away."

"Get over here."

Head Coach Greg Dunne was huddled underneath the desk with the telephone.

"Well," Pat said quietly, "they're gone. They must have heard you on the phone."

"They're hiding in the damn thing." He kept his hand on the receiver. "Goddamn little green sonsabitches."

"Come on out of there." Barry stuck out his hand. "They're gone."

Coach Dunne's hand was soaking wet as Barry

pulled him from beneath the desk and sat him in his swivel chair.

Raising the shades, Pat got a good look at Dunne's alcohol-battered face. The man was clearly hallucinating. His eyes followed imaginary things on the wall. It was terrifying to see him.

Pat pried the phone out of the coach's hand and called the team doctor at the university health center. He was in the office in five minutes.

"I don't know why he called us," Pat said.

"In his fashion he must trust you." Dr. Smith was preparing an injection.

Apparently no longer chased by "them," Coach Dunne seemed to be in a trance. He just sat in his chair, staring out the window.

"You better stick around until this takes effect." The doctor held up the needle. "Then maybe the three of us can get him quietly over to the health center." Dr. Smith administered the injection. "Now, we might be able to salvage something if we can get him out of here without a scene. The man has nearly destroyed himself for this school. It's the least we can do. If the trustees or Sam Watts find out, he's finished. Even Brick Williams won't be able to save him."

The doctor was right. By 1962 Greg Dunne's behavior had become so bizarre that the staff was immune to anything short of a grand mal psychotic episode. And even though Barry was still an undergrad, Frank Wolfe moved him up on full-time staff. It then followed that Barry's participation in the rescue of Greg Dunne made it necessary to keep him close, and happy. A full-time job as an assistant on the SWS basketball staff kept Barry close and happier than "a pig in shit," Pat noted.

"And this is just the beginning, Pat," Barry said. "We're going to have it all, old buddy."

Pat continued pushing Greg Dunne to recruit black players, which didn't get results, but at least heated up the dialogue, much to Brick Williams's displeasure.

"If I were head coach, sir, I think I'd be able to handle such a sensitive issue," Barry had told Williams. Naturally, Barry and Brick Williams became friends, commiserating over Coach Dunne's drinking and his buddy Pat Lee's inability to understand the *delicacy* of the racial problem on the basketball team. Even then Barry understood that if he were ever going to succeed Dunne, he would need Brick Williams in his corner.

He also agreed with Pat about needing black players, and his plan called for Pat being the front man recruiting them.

Barry would win the games. Pat would be a race traitor.

Perfect . . .

The next fall Geena Keats enrolled at Southwestern, and by spring term she and Barry would set their wedding for right after Barry's graduation in 1964. Just the way she had told Pat she would do way back that day in Wood when she had all tearfully said she and Barry were alike and they were good together. Well, she was right about the first part . . .

On Christmas Day, 1963, the Southwestern basketball team took a MATS flight from San Francisco to Honolulu on the island of Oahu. Except for the players, Greg Dunne and Barry Sand, the plane was filled with military personnel.

Outside the terminal Dunne and Sand slid into a brand new '64 red and white Cadillac convertible while Pat and the rest of the team climbed aboard a standard-issue navy bus. Dunne and Sand zoomed down to Waikiki Beach and checked into a two-bedroom suite at the Royal Hawaiian hotel. The team chugged on the bus, in the heat, all the way out to Pearl Harbor and climbed three flights of stairs into the SUBPAC open-bay barracks, the bunks there stacked three and four high designed for "lunatic midgets," as Mark Anders, a guard, observed.

"Are we going to put up with this shit?" Jackie Jefferson, a forward from Houston, asked Pat. "You're the captain, do something."

"If I could do something I guess I would have hopped into the Caddy with Sand and Dunne. If

I had any brains I would have let the Little Green Men take care of Dunne last year."

"We're stuck here?" Ted Williams, a center from Lufkin, said. "We're miles from the beach. What the hell are we going to do?"

"I'm open to suggestions," Pat said.

"Let's refuse to play until we get a decent place to stay," Jackie Jefferson said.

Everybody agreed except Pat. Still, it was his responsibility to hunt down Greg Dunne and present him with the team's ultimatum. Everybody kicked in money for a cab; it cost a fortune to take a taxi from Pearl Harbor to Waikiki Beach . . .

"You've got to do something, coach," Pat told Greg Dunne as they sat in the airy two-bedroom suite overlooking the ocean. "We're stuck out at Pearl Harbor, you promised the team a trip to Hawaii, not a holiday with drunken sailors."

Barry sat on the overstuffed couch and said nothing.

"Pat," Dunne said, "we'll have to talk about this later. Barry and I have some military and political people coming up here for a reception."

Barry nodded in agreement, which made Pat crazy. "*Barry*, I'm in the middle of this. The team expected me to do something. I'm telling you, they won't play."

Dunne laughed. "They'll play or they'll swim home."

"Coach," Pat said, trying to reason with Dunne,

"you can't treat your players like this. They'll stay pissed all season. We won't win a game. Get us rooms somewhere off the base—"

"This is the Christmas season here, Pat." Dunne poured himself a plain tonic, his eyes lingering on a bottle of vodka. "We were lucky to get this suite and the two connecting ones for Brick."

"Dr. Williams is coming?"

"A last minute hurry-up decision. He's flying on to Tokyo after Christmas. He's got Olympic business to settle with the Japs." The coach sipped his tonic, clearly not relishing it.

"You people have six bedrooms." Pat walked over to the drink table and poured himself a tonic. "You owe me, coach."

"Even if I did, which I most certainly don't, what the hell can I do? *It's out of the question.*" He was clearly getting agitated.

Pat opened a bottle of vodka and poured several ounces into the tonic bottle Dunne was using.

Barry watched, said nothing. Greg Dunne's fall could mean his rise.

"You're sure there's nothing you can do?"

"I wouldn't try even if there was. Goddamn you, get off my back. You guys are lucky to be here. I'm the coach, I'm the boss . . ."

Pat approached with the tonic bottle laced with vodka. Dunne was losing it. He was also asking for it.

193

"This is my *vacation*." Dunne took a drink of the tonic. He had mostly been on the wagon since his visit from the Little Green Men. "These games don't mean anything—"

"They do to us." Pat refilled the coach's glass.

Dunne took a drink, looked at his glass. "I need some more ice."

"I'll get it. You enjoy the view and relax. You've got important people to entertain."

Pat dropped in a couple of cubes, and Dunne emptied the spiked glass . . .

Coach Greg Dunne stayed drunk for four days. He never got to entertain all the military brass and political big shots.

Meanwhile Southwestern had beaten the Air Force champions by thirty-five and CINCPAC's champs by twenty-five.

Barry Sand struck a pose as coach while Coach Greg Dunne was in a straitjacket being hosed down every few hours with cold water.

They beat all the military teams, Pat averaging nearly forty points a game.

Barry Sand modestly allowed the press *and* Dr. Brick Williams to assume that the team's unexpectedly good performance should be credited to Barry Sand's substituting for Greg Dunne at the helm.

Pat wanted to be sick, but in a crazy way he was responsible, he reminded himself, both ways. In the middle again. Still.

The Conquering Heroes

* * *

"We're going to send a lot more troops to Vietnam, son." The square-jawed navy commander stood next to the locker as Pat rolled down his knee socks. "The Joint Chiefs have had a war plan ready for months, the draft calls are going way up. You'll be drafted as soon as you graduate from college."

Pat was drained. They had just beaten the Army champs and he had scored fifty points for the first time in his life.

"You'll be lucky if they let you finish school. After the stunt you pulled."

"What are you talking about?"

"You put your coach in the hospital, is what I'm talking about."

"Who says so?" Feeling uneasy.

"I do," the commander said, "and in the navy that's enough."

"I'm not in the navy, you are."

"Okay, son, have it your way. But if you don't want to get your ass blown off you better listen to me. This is my offer." The commander leaned down close to Pat's face. "You enlist in the navy and we'll get you here playing basketball for CINCPAC. I guarantee you good duty for your full tour."

"Or," Pat said, "until a better player joins the navy."

"You've got my guarantee. Besides, I don't see

a player from any branch of the service out there better than you. You're going to have to go in the service. LBJ won't back out of Vietnam, not after Kennedy got Khrushchev to pull the missiles out of Cuba."

"I've got a 2S deferment."

"Son, I'm here to tell you that by '65 or '66 Selective Service will be taking every warm body. There's a major buildup coming. We're gonna call the Commie bluff in Southeast Asia." The commander put his hand on Pat's shoulder. "Now, listen up. You enlist and go to boot camp—"

"Boot camp?"

"Everybody has to go to boot camp. You apply for officer candidate school. We have people, they'll send you to OCS, you'll get a commission and we'll get you stationed here. You can play basketball in Hawaii until your tour is up."

"How long is that?"

"Six years. I know that seems like a long—"

"Six years! Fuck that!"

"Look, pal, a lot of guys would crawl across broken bottles to get a shot at what I just offered you." He looked at the clipboard he'd been carrying. "First thing tomorrow, I'll be sending a letter to Harbor City, Michigan. Does that make the hair stand up on your pencil neck?"

It did.

Pat's draft board was in Harbor City.

The Conquering Heroes

And J.D. Mazurski of the feuding Mazurskis was the clerk.

Pat was walking alone from the basketball arena back to the SUBPAC barracks, his mind occupied with the threat the commander had made to notify the Harbor City draft board. Would he have been worried if it was Nazis to go fight against? He thought not. But Vietnam, just like his father had predicted, it was spooky and it made no sense . . . Suddenly he saw a dark shape moving straight for him. His heel caught in the curb and he fell flat on his back in the dirt. Someone was coming after him.

Pat found himself looking into the grinning face of Barry Sand.

"Jesus H. Christ, you scared the living shit out of me, Barry."

Sand kept grinning as he smoothed Pat's shirt.

"What are you doing around here, Barry?"

"I just wanted to thank you. You played some fantastic games and Brick Williams thinks the wins are all due to my coaching."

"You didn't do any coaching, you walked up and down the sidelines."

"I know, but Williams doesn't need to know. This is a big career break for me, *and* you . . ."

"Bullshit—"

"Don't get your nuts in an uproar. You don't have to say anything good about me, just don't say anything bad. Remember, we're buddies, we came here together. You won't look good badmouthing me. Besides, the higher I go, the more I can do for you, old buddy. Let's find us a bar, this place gives me the creeps."

"Let's get away from here. That guard post is just up the road. I hate those Marines."

Pat, angry, went along . . . but just for now, he told himself. "I don't want to go to the International Marketplace. If I never hear Don Ho sing 'Tiny Bubbles' again it'll be way too soon."

Barry turned back. "He's gonna be a big star—"

"Yeah, and I'm gonna be the admiral in the Turkish navy."

"If you don't figure something out on the draft you just may have to be."

"You heard about my fight with the sailor?"

"By now the Harbor City draft board has heard. The guy came up yelling at Williams. He was really pissed."

"I don't believe this," Pat was saying over the strains of "Tiny Bubbles." "You had two hundred songs to pick off that jukebox and you play Don Ho?"

They were in a small roadside bar halfway between Pearl Harbor and Honolulu. The chances they would run into anybody they knew were slim.

"We got bigger things to worry about than

music. Williams is ready to help me get a start in coaching."

"Well, Frank Wolfe is leaving for Duke and—"

"I'm too young, I need experience," Barry said. "I know that. Williams wants me to go to Tokyo for the summer games. He can get me a job. No money but good experience."

Not to mention PR exposure, Pat thought. "How's he gonna manage that?"

"He'll be the U.S. embassy Olympic attaché at the Tokyo Olympics. Later I'd have to coach basketball in Europe and Latin America for the Peace Corps. Ain't that something? The Peace Corps . . ."

"There'll be no stopping you short of a well-placed bullet."

"Hey, why would you say that?"

"I don't know . . . maybe to remind you that nobody's bulletproof," Pat said. "You have a tendency to betray people, old buddy. It could be fatal."

Back from the Pearl Harbor military basketball tournament in January of 1964, Pat had to go to Dr. Brick Williams for help. He hated asking Williams for favors but the Harbor City draft board was still after him. It was two days after he had received notice from Clerk J.D. Mazurski that the Harbor City draft board had revoked his 2S deferment and reclassified him 1A. He was still five months from graduation.

The accompanying letter from the draft board said:

"The aforementioned Patrick Lee, duly identified and named by a senior officer at CINCPAC, is adjudged to be guilty of public behavior damaging to American policy goals in the Pacific Theater . . . disgracing The Flag while a guest of The Navy at Pearl Harbor . . . heard to make seditious public statements criticizing the United States military effort in The Republic of Vietnam . . . 2S deferment is hereby revoked . . . Lee is ordered to report to Fort Wayne in Detroit for immediate induction. By order of General Lewis B. Hershey."

Translation: Get with the program or get the shit stomped out of you.

The letter was signed by the clerk of the Harbor City draft board, J.D. Mazurski. The infamous Tommy Mazurski's uncle. This was a blood feud, as Pat had known it would be.

It took three months, the intervention of Dr. Williams, including two trips by Williams to Washington, to get Pat reclassified. J.D. Mazurski fought them every step of the way, but Williams and his contacts prevailed. Which didn't mean the feud was over. There was still Steve Lee, Ron

The Conquering Heroes

Waters and Chuck Stanislawski to use as fodder.

Brick Williams, of course, didn't help Pat for nothing. He was a silent partner with Sam Watts in the new professional basketball team, the Dallas Ponies, and Pat Lee figured prominently in their plans.

Meanwhile, Geena Keats and Barry Sand, as promised, were married. She was pregnant, not as promised. Pat, standing up for Barry, didn't find that out until later. They had all come a long way from the sock hop and Saturday mornings at Sharpe's drugstore in Wood.

In October of 1964, just as Pat and the Dallas Ponies opened their first season, the XVIII Olympiad was held in Tokyo, the first Olympics ever held in the Orient.

Pete Newell coached the United States basketball team to the gold medal. He had invited Pat to try out but Watts and Williams vetoed that, telling Pat to report to the Dallas Ponies training camp in July for workouts three days a week. Pay-back. They practiced at Southwestern and wore old Southwestern practice uniforms. In 1964 the Dallas Ponies played in virtual anonymity and for very little money.

In August of 1964 Dr. Brick Williams was assigned to the U.S. embassy in Tokyo as Olympic cultural attaché, and brought along Barry Sand as his assistant. All through the basketball competition Barry Sand was prominent sitting at the farthest end of the bench and wearing the U.S.A. Olympic colors. Nobody ever figured out what Barry's job actually was, but Barry carried the eight by ten photo of himself with the U.S.A. team everywhere, then and thereafter.

The next year Brick Williams asked discount-store mogul and his Dallas Ponies partner Sam Watts to resign his presidency of the SWS alumni rebel brigade to head up the board of trustees and help him begin a search for a new coach.

The first thing they did was land Barry Sand a job coaching international basketball on a Peace Corps grant. Another step in Barry's image-building.

Barry arrived in Guatemala in 1966 to begin organizing and coaching the Guatemalan national basketball team for the 1968 Mexico City Olympics. Funds had been supplied by the United States embassy's cultural exchange program.

Barry was met on the ground floor of the embassy building by Susan Penny, secretary to the assistant cultural attaché.

She looked familiar.

"You've been assigned living quarters, Barry." She smiled and shoved a thick manila envelope into his hands. "Welcome to Guatemala."

"Do I know you?" Barry asked.

"You don't remember me?"

"You look familiar but—"

The Conquering Heroes

"I dated Laude VanMeer a couple times."

"Sure, I remember. So, has Laude begun his run for whatever office it was he wanted?"

"Not yet. He took a job with the State Department and is here as assistant cultural attaché. He's still got plans for a political career back in Texas. He figured this would give him some seasoning and help him make connections what with LBJ in D.C."

"It'll be good to see a familiar face," Barry said.

"Laude says you can't begin networking too soon if you expect to be successful . . . By the way, we have great embassy parties."

"You'll get uniforms and equipment through the diplomatic pouch," Laude VanMeer was saying to Barry Sand. "Right now, Barry, we want you to get over to the country club and mingle."

Barry looked puzzled.

"Hang around and listen to what's being said. If anybody asks, tell them practice will start later, then come back here and tell me what you've heard."

"About the basketball team?"

"*No*, about politics, gossip, the United States. What's being said and who is saying it. We want to know what they think about us. This country is too close to the Panama Canal to be allowed to go red."

Ambition, it seemed, had bent Laude VanMeer into strange shapes.

"We've still got trouble with the leftists in the Dominican Republic. And in El Salvador, we can't let the Communists subvert next year's elections."

Barry smiled and nodded. "Sure thing, Laude, just as long as it looks like I've been coaching basketball on my résumé."

"No problem . . . these people believe their kids can go to the Olympics. So *don't* say anything to disabuse them of that notion. Sports fatalities are common in Latin America."

Barry didn't have the faintest idea what VanMeer was talking about. He didn't exactly understand international basketball. He had less of a grasp on international politics.

"I'll do what it takes . . ." Barry said, not at all sure what that was.

Laude nodded. "We're at the sharp end here. Revolution could spread like wildfire."

"Yeah? These people look too tired to piss standing up, leave alone play basketball or make a revolution. Besides, I haven't seen anybody in this whole country over five-ten. The basketball team will suck."

"We've got to worry about outsiders, Barry. The Cubans . . ."

"You got Cubans here? Any tall enough to play the pivot?" Barry thought that was pretty funny.

The Conquering Heroes

"Shape up, Barry," VanMeer said. "You'll end up missing or dead. These people down here don't joke around."

Barry pulled on his game face and nodded. "Okay, Laude. But I didn't sign up to spread the gospel. I know this is political and not *just* about basketball—"

"It's not about basketball at all," VanMeer said.

"Well, I came here for the basketball exposure. You came for political credentials. You and Uncle Sam got your agendas and I have mine. I'll play your games, on the court and off, just as long as we understand each other. Hell, I guess I can always fix up my win-loss record. Who they gonna believe? Me or a bunch of greasers who probably can't hit the backboard with a shotgun from the free-throw line."

"We understand each other, Barry," VanMeer said, apparently pleased. "Let's just do our jobs. After all, we're all on the same team."

Barry stayed six months in Guatemala and was just beginning to get his team more or less organized when three players were arrested and shot as terrorists.

"Shit," he said when Laude VanMeer told him about the arrests and firing squads. "I wish they'd been that aggressive on the court." He laughed. "I guess they finally understood the meaning of good execution."

VanMeer just stared at Barry.

When two more of his players were arrested, Barry was ordered to Italy, where he was active in setting up the pipeline carrying U.S. talent to the Italian national basketball team. His success at bringing American basketball talent to Italy and Europe was building him a reputation that he worked hard to enhance. But after a year he was forced to return to the States when a splinter Maoist terror group targeted him as a CIA agent and put him on a death list.

"Christ!" Barry said as he was taken to the airport in an armored car. "I could understand this if I hadn't won any games."

Soon after his return, Barry, with his wife, the former Geena Keats, was dispatched to South America and again Europe, spending a final year in Germany. It was obvious Brick Williams had been grooming Barry Sand to replace Greg Dunne, who had returned to the bottle with a vengeance. It was only a matter of time before they would retire Dunne, naming a building after him, and hire Barry Sand.

As planned, after Barry returned from his coaching job in Germany, Brick Williams succeeded in getting him named head coach at SWS. Greg Dunne was retired with a watch and the blueprints for the Greg Dunne Memorial Field House.

The Conquering Heroes

*   *   *

Pat Lee, meanwhile, was having his fill of pay-back to Brick Williams by playing on his so-called professional basketball team that excelled not in the skill of its play or players but in the low pay and long miserable road trips that robbed a man of sleep and a sound sacroiliac. When Barry, as they'd discussed earlier, now as head coach offered his old teammate the head recruiting job, Pat took it. He'd had a couple of feelers from the NBA but they weren't really serious and he was already pretty old for top competition. He understood the game, loved it, still, and felt he could contribute best by working with the young guys, especially young talented blacks. He had his misgivings about Barry, the same ones he'd always had, but they were, as Barry liked to say, "old buddies," and this time in this imperfect world it seemed that what was good for Barry Sand could also be good for Pat Lee.

Barry had kept his promise to let Pat get the jump on the other Dixie Conference schools and scour the Northern inner cities for black players. So far, so good.

It was less than a year later, though, that it became clear appearances weren't reality, and that playing black athletes in the Dixie Conference was not going to be a day at the beach, no matter how good they were or how many games they won. And Barry Sand's true colors would fly as never before.

Meanwhile some 12,000 miles away, others of the old Michigan gang had been trying to cope with something closer to life and death than SWS basketball.

Boys at War

Chuck Stanislawski sat in the Recon Bar on the road from Quang Tri to Da Nang, cursing his bad luck.

The South Vietnamese were fighting again among themselves over who was going to pretend to govern the people. Premier Ky had ousted General Thi from the government leadership committee and that pissed off Buddhists and troops loyal to Thi. So Thi's troops fought Ky's troops, and when Ky finally won, Buddhists torched themselves for the Western television news while other losers torched the American consular and U.S.I.S. offices in Hue.

But what really pissed Chuck off was the sonsabitches that decided to drop mortar rounds on Da Nang and blew his ass clean out of bed and ruptured his left eardrum.

Westmoreland had requested another 200,000 troops to be added to the 200,000 already in the country, then announced that a Communist victory in South Vietnam was impossible. "Tell it to the poor bastards in the Ashau," Chuck said into his warm beer. A whole camp of Special Forces had been wiped out in the Ashau, and Chuck had met one of them in Saigon.

Chuck had picked up shrapnel in his back in Bong Son, where they had shipped him as soon as he arrived in-country. Three days later a mine blew up the guy next to him and drove dozens of needle-sized pieces of metal into Chuck's back. He was medevac'd out and got two weeks in Saigon. The Special Forces sergeant from the Ashau was in the next bed and headed back two days before Chuck was reassigned.

Chuck was still picking shrapnel out of his back, but it was the reassignment he was still cursing. "Over two hundred thousand GIs in-country and I'm put in the same fucking squad with the Mazurski brothers." Chuck drained the beer and clunked his bottle on the table.

Two days after his reassignment they had gone out on a search-and-destroy mission. The Mazurski brothers searched until they found a couple dozen women and children bathing upriver, set up the mortar and took bets on what body parts would float by first.

All bets in and a round out.

At first Chuck thought they were all fucking with him, but when the round went out and the body parts floated by, Chuck lost it and opened up on both Mazurski brothers and the rest with his M-14.

Somehow, he had emptied a clip without hitting anybody.

The whole squad was assholes and elbows trying to find cover. One guy tore all his fingernails off trying to dig an instant hole in the ground with his bare hands.

"I know better than to shoot at the whole covey," Chuck muttered as he started his next beer. "I should have picked my targets—Joe and Sam."

When they returned to base, nobody said anything to Chuck. But within an hour a slick dropped out of the sky to take Chuck to Quang Tri to wait for his next assignment.

So he sat quietly every day now in the Recon Bar, waiting.

Chuck figured he wouldn't have too much longer to wait. The rumor was that a big move was planned in the Ia Drang Valley. If his bad luck held, they'd sure as hell send him there—

It felt like a baseball hitting his leg.

Whatever it was banged to the floor under his chair.

He looked down. His bad luck hadn't held. It had gotten worse.

A fused fragmentation grenade lay next to his right foot.

Before the explosion, Chuck heard several more of them hitting the floor, coming into the roomful of GIs through the windows and the door.

The blast flipped him wrongside-up and he seemed to be flying ever-so-slowly through the air.

Chuck Stanislawski never hit the ground.

They shipped the bag home to his mother marked BODY PARTS MISSING.

Mrs. Stanislawski had survived WW II, the Nazis, the Communists in Poland, the Iron Guard in the DP camps. She was devastated.

The Mazurski clan was delighted.

Ron Waters won his Congressional Medal of Honor in Tay Ninh province during Operation Attleboro, the biggest operation up to that time in Vietnam.

Waters was the best natural soldier in his outfit. Just like he had been the best natural athlete at Wood High School. He watched and listened to the bush veterans, learning everything as fast as he could.

Westmoreland had been sure, since the first battle of the Ia Drang Valley, that a war of attrition was winnable. Air mobility, enemy "pain thresholds" and body counts convinced the general.

To Ron, the war was about survival—his.

He learned strategy and tactics according to his own pain threshold and body count. The strategy was not to get killed. The tactics were anything he could learn to prolong his life one more day. He was a good learner.

The black humor of that winning day was not lost on Ron, nor was the fact that he risked his life countless times that day to do it. He never tried to explain to anyone how simple the decision was to him.

It was an easy choice: live or die. He could wait to die in the trap that his idiot West Point captain had led them into, or he could do what was necessary to live another day. To do that, he needed to get as many others out of the trap as possible. He couldn't fight a VC battalion alone.

The captain had read his map wrong, humping them into a narrow valley dead up against an unfordable river. The VC sprang the ambush and poured a murderous fire down on them from the low hills on both sides.

Waters was trapped in a bomb crater with a black kid from Cleveland named Reed, the lieutenant, an E6 from Los Angeles and the radioman.

They had been up near the front of the column when the point man stepped on a mine, had his shit blown into the trees, and the VC sprang the trap. Only Waters and Reed were still alive, some fifty yards from the river. Slugs were kicking up dirt everywhere. The VC began lobbing mortar rounds into the valley.

"Reed!" Ron yelled as he hugged the ground. "How many grenades you got?" He quickly shucked his pack.

"Four!" Reed screamed straight into the ground.

"Grab everybody's frags," Ron ordered. "I'll get the sergeant's shotgun; then we make a run for the river."

"I ain't leavin' my piece." Reed buried his face deeper in the dirt.

"Grab a .45, these M14s'll be useless when we get out of the river."

"You mean *if*, motherfucker."

"Christ, Reed, I played ball in high school with a pessimist like you."

When Ron crawled in between the dead sergeant and the radioman, the VC saw him move and poured fire into the crater. The dead bodies jumped as the slugs pounded into flesh. Ron managed to recover five grenades, the sergeant's .45, his shotgun and a bandolier full of 00 buckshot.

Reed was digging in the lieutenant's holster when a VC gunner found the range and put three rounds through his stomach and chest.

When the slugs hit him, Reed coughed up parts of his lungs and glared at Ron—a look-what-you-made-me-do look. Then he died.

The Conquering Heroes

Ron never forgot the look in the kid's eyes. He was only nineteen, just out of high school.

Now Ron lay between the dead E6 and the dead radioman and waited until the intensity of the fight seemed to move toward the rear of the column. He had stuffed the pistol in his belt, the frags in his cargo pockets and slipped the bandolier over his shoulder. He took hold of the cut-down twelve gauge, took five deep breaths, then jumped to his feet and ran for the river. He couldn't hear the firing, but the sound of lead was in the air all around him. Slugs were knocking chunks off trees, chopping up branches and leaves, kicking up the dirt at his feet. He just kept running for the river.

Forty yards . . .

Now he could hear the firing, a cacophony of different weapons. The air hummed, alive with rounds that sounded like giant insects circling his head.

He kept running . . .

Suddenly a small figure, a VC in a UCLA sweatshirt, stepped from behind a tree directly in front of him. The VC soldier was swinging up his AK-47 from less than five feet away.

Ron lunged, swinging the shotgun like a baseball bat. He missed the man but knocked the AK flying. He dropped his shoulder and ran over the guy like he was a tackler from Kalamazoo Catholic Central High School. As he did, his shoulder caught the VC in the UCLA sweatshirt on the point of the chin and sent him flying backward ass over elbows.

"I was educated in your country at U.C.R.A." The old Kingston Trio joke jumped into Ron's fried mind from the ozone.

Five more strides and Ron dove headlong into the river, clawing for the bottom, letting the current pull him along. His lungs were already bursting but he wasn't coming up anytime soon.

When he did surface he had pulled himself against the near shore and saw that the river had dug out a high bluff overgrown with vegetation. He hid there and listened to the sounds of the fight.

Finally, he moved downriver about a half-mile and eased up onto the bank beneath the cover of the heavy undergrowth. He could hear voices and the unmistakable thump of mortar tubes. Peeking out, he found himself within twenty yards of the VC heavy mortar battery. There were nine men and three tubes lobbing rounds over the low hill in front of them onto the Americans on the other side.

Ron studied the terrain, looking for more VC and a place to set himself up. Most of the VC seemed to be up on the hills bracketing the valley. He positioned himself behind a downed tree, checked his shotgun and stacked his grenades beside him.

He took out the first two mortar tubes with his first two grenades. The second mortar blew just as a man dropped a round in the tube, and in the confusion of the secondary explosion Ron took out the third tube, then lay back down behind the tree trunk.

They never knew he was there.

Lying there and planning how to stay alive the rest of the day, Ron heard yelling to his left. He eased up over the trunk and saw two men standing about fifty yards behind what remained of the mortars. Then a third moved out of what appeared to be a hummock; he was a VC colonel and the hummock was his TOC. The two men ran up to the mortar battery to assess damage and give aid while the colonel went back into his command bunker.

Ron worked downriver along the bank until he was behind the TOC, then moved inland, expecting at any time to step on a mine or into a shitload of Viet Cong.

The command bunker was blind from the rear, providing Ron cover from the several soldiers who had now converged on the destroyed mortar battery to try to sort out of the bloody confusion what had happened. He took his ritual deep breaths and then ran, crouched over, right up to the back of the TOC. Terrified the sound of his heavy breathing could be heard inside, Ron stopped a moment, forcing himself to calm down and inspect the layout of the bunker. As he studied the entrance the colonel had used, Ron found a gap about a foot square where he could look right inside the TOC. The colonel was standing next to a map table; a VC major was talking into a large field radio. There were four other soldiers inside. The whole TOC wasn't more than six-feet square.

Ron dropped the two frags through the hole, then took off, running straight back from the bunker and diving into a shell hole just as the grenades destroyed the bunker and everyone inside.

The VC still had no idea what was happening. For that matter, beyond that moment, neither did Ron Waters.

As he watched the confused men mill around what remained of the bunker and their two top commanders, Ron realized the only way back was right through the middle of them.

The small-arms fire from the hills and the valley was still heavy, but the hard, deadly crump of mortar rounds exploding among the Americans had stopped.

Now came the whooshing scream of artillery as the Americans were finally calling in fire support. He damn well had to get out of there . . . before long would come the gunships, then the jets with their napalm.

As soon as the artillery rounds started landing on the hills and behind, Ron jumped up and started running. The VC around the destroyed command bunker were hitting the ground as Ron ran right past them. One man raised and pointed his assault rifle at Ron, and got a chest full of 00 buck.

Racing up the backside of the hill, shells landing all around him, Ron dropped into the first hole he saw. Unfortunately, the hole already had an occupant. Fortunately for Ron, he landed on the guy's back with both knees, snapping his spine.

Now the artillery barrage let up, and along the hilltop the VC resumed the murderous fire down on the trapped Americans.

Ron studied his situation. He was on the enemy's right flank. Less than ten feet away three men were pouring fire from a Russian-made heavy machine gun.

Ron's first round nearly took off the gunner's head and mortally wounded the man on the gunner's left. As the third man turned, Ron's second load of 00 buckshot hit him in the face.

Scuttling over and dropping into the hole, Ron shot the wounded man a second time, then turned the heavy machine gun left and began spraying the entrenched positions from the right flank that he had exposed. Firing point-blank into the VC, Ron began yelling and waving down at the GIs, trying to get someone's attention, praying someone was left alive down there. He hadn't overlooked the fact that for Ron Waters to survive he needed as much of his unit as possible to survive with him.

The VC redirected some of their fire from the valley onto Ron's position. He fired back, wondering if the guys down in the valley would figure out what was happening.

The sound of lead buzzing and thumping around him increased; he kept firing, hoping the gun wouldn't jam or overheat . . . suddenly someone dropped into the hole with him.

Turning and digging for the .45, knowing he was too late, Ron looked into the face of his top sergeant, a black guy from New York City nicknamed Eyes.

"You handle the belt!" Eyes moved in behind the gun. "I've got a squad coming up behind me."

Ron nodded and fed the ammunition belt into the Russian weapon, glancing behind him to see GIs working their way up the right side of the hill.

"How the hell did you get here, Waters?" Eyes raked the VC as the other GIs began dropping into holes and behind trees around them.

"A long story, Top," Ron said. "This seemed like a better place to be than down there."

Fire from the valley increased, and soon GIs crawled from holes and behind trees and began to assault the now confused and demoralized VC survivors on the hill . . .

When the captain eventually wrote Ron up for the Congressional Medal of Honor he doubled the size of the enemy force as well as the number of mortars Ron had knocked out and VC officers and men he had killed. It was standard practice in Vietnam to halve the casualties and double the body count. By following such Standard Operating Procedures the captain also covered his own ass for walking his command straight into an ambush.

LBJ would award Pvt. Ronald Waters the Congressional Medal of Honor in the White House Rose Garden.

Ron was then ordered back to Saigon and spent two weeks at the Hung Dao Hotel on Tu Do Street trying to forget what he had seen while riding in the convoy on the way to becoming a hero.

It was called "The Candy Game."

The rules were simple.

As the trucks roared through the villages, the soldiers threw candy out of the backs into the middle of the road. Then they took bets on whether the Vietnamese kids lining the road could run out, grab the candy and get away safely before the next truck ran right over them.

They even gave odds. Eight-to-two against the kids and for the trucks.

As far as Ron could tell, the odds seemed about right.

The trucks won a lot more than the kids did.

Ron Waters lost part of his mind and all of his taste for sweets.

The Candy Game.

*   *   *

The military bus taking the inductees from Harbor City to Fort Wayne in Detroit headed south along Lake Michigan; then when it reached I-94 it headed east.

Steve Lee heard familiar last names as they were called aboard the bus, but he recognized none of the faces. He had been avoiding the draft for so long he figured these had to be the younger brothers of the guys he had played high-school ball against.

The young men Steve had known had already gone to Vietnam and returned, or not returned.

He was the oldest by several years.

Chuck Stanislawski had gone and not returned.

Ron Waters had gone, won the Congressional Medal of Honor, and returned. He didn't talk very much or show off his medal.

Steve stared out the window, studying the passing landscape, wondering if he would see it again. Everything seemed so visceral, the colors brighter, the images sharper. Steve thought about Israel fighting and winning the Six Day War. Why couldn't he go to a Six Day War?

He figured he would spend a year in-country and get killed catching his plane back to the world. The grapevine was full of stories about Short Timers and Fucking New Guys.

The bus slowed. Steve looked up front and could see two State police cars with their flashers going. The bus driver climbed down and talked to one of the State policemen, then climbed back aboard and talked to the lieutenant in charge.

"Attention! Attention!" the lieutenant called out. "Because of the riots in Detroit we cannot safely proceed to Fort Wayne. You are to return to Harbor City and wait to be recontacted for processing."

So Steve went back to Wood and waited.

With Detroit still in flames and the death toll climbing toward forty-three, President and Mrs. Johnson led a nation-wide day of prayer for civil and racial peace.

That night rioting broke out in Milwaukee.

Four days later President Johnson announced plans to send 50,000 more troops to Vietnam.

The man wasn't listening to his own prayers. What did he expect God to do?

Steve waited and waited and waited.

Not one man on that bus was ever contacted again by the Harbor City Selective Service Board. None was ever inducted into the military.

What was impervious to prayer, political pressure, public demonstrations and pleas for mercy was swallowed and lost forever in the bureaucracy.

Eventually Vietnamization, Nixon and the draft lottery would send them slipping quietly back into mainstream life. They would sell insurance, stocks and bonds. They would become journalists, politicians, talk show hosts and movie actors. They would become lawyers, land developers and bank embezzlers.

They would forget about the mistakes, the lies, the body counts, the murders, and the murderers. Life would return to normal.

The Plantation

Pat Lee came back to Wood and his old high-school coach Roger Starr told him about Terry Dixon from Flint Northern.

Dixon was the perfect choice to be the first black player to break into Dixie Conference basketball. A straight-A student, he had been all-state four years running and was being heavily recruited by Michigan State, the University of Michigan and Notre Dame. Six foot five, he averaged thirty-one points and eighteen rebounds a game.

Michigan State seemed to have the inside track when Pat Lee learned that Terry Dixon's natural father, Claud, lived in South Dallas. Claud Dixon had been a star player at Eastern Michigan, where he met and married Wanda Jeter. Terry was born

225

during Claud's senior year, and the couple divorced when Terry was eight.

Terry Dixon worshipped his father; he was devastated by the divorce. His home situation deteriorated further when his mother Wanda married Donny Russell from Flint and he was moved away from his father in Ypsilanti. Stepfather Donny Russell was an unemployed auto worker given to fits of drunken rage that he took out on Wanda and Terry. Soon Terry learned to stay away from home, finding a friend in the Flint Northern basketball coach and a refuge on the basketball floor. Terry lived with the coach, who insisted he work on his academic skills with the same dedication he polished his basketball game.

Meanwhile, Terry's natural father Claud had moved to Dallas and found a job at the Ford assembly plant in Arlington. When Pat first contacted Claud Dixon, he laid out what he had in mind for Terry.

"This will be a difficult situation for Terry," Pat said, "but he's the right choice to break the color barrier in the lily-white Dixie Conference. He'll be the centerpiece of our offense. There's not a player in the conference that can touch him."

"I want him to get an education," Claud Dixon, a bright articulate man, said. "Hey, I never finished college and I don't want my son to go the same route."

"I've seen Terry's transcripts," Pat said. "He'll get a degree from SWS, I guarantee it."

"Well, I'd sure like to spend some time with Terry," Claud Dixon said. "I've always regretted leaving him at the mercy of that sonofabitch that married Wanda."

"The boy seems to have made the best of a bad situation," Pat pressed. "Help me put him in a good situation and, believe me, the sky's the limit."

And Pat absolutely believed it when he said it.

"All right," Claud Dixon said, "I'll call him."

So Pat landed the very first recruit he went after. He was truly delighted. He was making a difference, building a new and better program at SWS just as he'd promised.

Or so he thought.

Terry Dixon had been practicing with the freshman team since October 15. His teammates liked and respected him . . . there was no culture gap on the team because Pat had surrounded Terry with talented white kids from Michigan, Wisconsin and northern Indiana.

The first major "incident" occurred just before Thanksgiving during the first varsity-freshman scrimmage. It was open to the public at no charge and a couple thousand people came to see Terry Dixon, some out of a desire to watch someone play skilled basketball, many more to taunt and torment.

Barry Sand was coaching the varsity, Pat the freshmen. Pat knew he could outcoach Barry and Terry Dixon could outplay anybody on the varsity. When he would look back, Pat realized that he had to accept at least some of the blame for what happened. He was so carried away by what he *hoped* would happen that he didn't consider the reality. But what was he supposed to do, tell Terry not to play his best? He couldn't do that.

When the boos started and the racial epithets began, Pat called time-out to calm his players and tell them to ignore the fans. He still believed that at least in the game there could be some justice.

"We've been over and over this, boys," Pat said. "We knew this might happen." But had he really faced it head-on? he wondered.

"I been called a nigger before, coach," Terry said. "Don't worry."

Pat welcomed that, even let it reassure him.

The freshmen, led by Terry Dixon's forty-five points and twenty-two rebounds, walloped the varsity.

Pat Lee had been right about his recruiting.

He was dead wrong about the Southwestern fans. They were furious that some "nigger" and a "bunch of Yankees" had humiliated the SWS varsity.

The game ended in a near-riot.

The Conquering Heroes

In the locker room Pat was apologizing to Terry and the other freshmen when Barry and Brick Williams stormed in, pulling Pat into the coach's office.

"You dumb sonofabitch," Williams said. "What the hell did you think you were doing out there?"

"I was coaching. Did you see those kids!"

"Yes, I *saw* them. And so did a couple thousand other people. None of them came to watch your nigger embarrass the varsity—"

"The varsity embarrassed themselves. Dixon just played basketball." Pat decided to go on the offensive. "What the hell's the matter with you two? Do you realize how good that freshman team is? You'll blow away everybody in the conference next year—"

"*Fuck* next year," Williams said. "There won't be a next year if you keep letting Dixon show up all the white players."

"What—"

"I've tried to tell you," Williams cut him off. "But you're Mister know-it-all Yankee meddler."

"I don't believe this . . ."

"Well, believe *this* . . . we have exactly one black on campus, Terry Dixon. All our fans, our trustees, our alumni and faculty are white. They don't like it that a black kid shows up the white kids."

"What do you expect me to do, tell him not to play as well as he can?"

"*Yes.* At least not in public against our own players. Next year on the varsity, he can do his stuff against the enemy."

"But you agreed—"

"I *agreed,* because I want a nationally ranked team and you two convinced me we need black basketball players to win at a national level. I did *not* agree to let them act like they belong here."

"What the hell is he talking about?" Pat turned to Barry.

"Just a little indiscretion, Pat," Barry said. "It's the better part of valor, you ever hear that?"

Dixon showed up for practice the next day with a black eye and a split lip.

"What happened?" Pat said, able to guess.

"I was walking across the campus to math class and three football guys jumped me."

"Go have the trainer patch you up." Pat went looking for a telephone.

"I've already heard the whole story," Brick Williams said on the phone.

"Well, what are you going to do about it?"

"Nothing. The Dixon kid has been asking for trouble all term."

"What are you *talking* about? Terry never looks for trouble."

"Then what the hell was he doing strutting around on the campus?"

The Conquering Heroes

"He was going to his math class, for Christ's sake."

"I told Barry I didn't want black players wandering around the campus with the rest of the students—"

"How the hell do you expect him to go to class if he doesn't walk on the campus?"

"I don't expect him to go to class. Barry signed on to that as part of our deal. I'll make sure he stays eligible—"

"If he doesn't go to class how will he ever graduate?"

"He didn't come here to graduate, he came to play basketball. Look, I'm busy. Talk to Barry about it. This was all settled before you were even hired."

Pat confronted Barry in his office.

"Pat"—Barry held up his hands—"it was the only way I could get Williams to agree to let us go after inner-city players. He'll let 'em play. He just don't want to see them on campus."

"*Goddamn*, how could you agree to that and then not tell me? You let me go out recruiting with my head in a bag. I promised this kid and his father stuff I now can't deliver."

"Pat, relax, this is just the beginning. When we start winning nobody will care if Terry Dixon takes a crap in War Memorial Fountain. But right now we have to make some sacrifices—"

"Terry Dixon's education being one of them?"

"It'll only be for a while."

Brick Williams and Sam Watts would continue to insist the black players be discouraged from walking around the campus and not even attend class. Dr. Brick Williams would take care of their transcripts and maintaining their eligibility.

Pat didn't give up. He scouted and recruited the best black players he could find in Detroit, Chicago, Gary and the Northeastern cities. But at the same time the practice of segregating the black players was a cancer affecting the whole basketball program and recruiting process. It soured Pat's soul, but it never quite convinced him to give up.

By the time black athletes could walk relatively freely on the campus to attend classes Pat found himself recruiting players who had little interest in attending classes. They thought they were just stopping at SWS on their way to the NBA. Few ever got their degrees and even fewer made it to the NBA.

And so, without anyone quite recognizing it, began Southwestern State Plantation Basketball.

In its first year the team would go twenty and two and win the Dixie Conference title. After that, despite opponents' complaints about "nigger basketball" there would be no stopping them.

They dominated the Dixie Conference, and by the early eighties began taking NCAA tournament bids for granted. The SWS basketball program had become a money machine that would net an average of $2 million a year by the end of the eighties. By the nineties the profit was skyrocketing even higher. And all this success was seldom shared by the players, black or white.

Inner-city blacks being plucked out of their world and dropped into the middle of a nearly all-white campus resulted in major cases of culture shock. It was Pat's job, as usual, to deal with the problems. He often told himself he at least could do something to help these people, justify his still being there. He was, in a way, at least partly responsible.

By the mid-eighties there were skeletons in every closet and dirt swept under every rug in the Greg Dunne Memorial Field House. And Pat Lee spent too much time pacifying the police and the courts over the behavior of his players. But didn't he at least owe them that much? It was a Catch-22. And, eventually, it created a Chuck Small.

Eddie Sanford's Visit

"Small raped the girl," Jax Morrow was saying. "Sand put out the word to cover it up."

"She was a friend of yours?" Eddie Sanford said, shaking his head.

"Cathy Sullivan, yeah. Coach Lee and I are trying to get some action on this. It's not making us too popular."

Eddie Sanford and Jax were alone in Morrow's room in the SWS athletic dorm.

"Lee is really pissed," Jax said.

"Why do you stay *here?*"

"Eddie, it's a fair question. Well, the answer is I want a shot at the NBA, and that means I need TV exposure and to play on an NCAA contender. SWS has been in the NCAA playoffs more than any other team in the last ten years. I've worked for this all my life. So has my family. Everybody's sacrificed." His fists clenched now. "Eddie, I'll tell you the truth . . . I'd do damn near anything to have my chance. For myself, for my family . . . Look, if you want to play major college basketball you'll have a hard time finding a squeaky clean program. There's no way to *know*. Just because they don't announce it on TV doesn't mean the school's all pure and clean. I looked at a lot of schools before picking SWS. This place isn't the exception, but it sure isn't the worst."

"That story about Chuck Small blows my mind."

"Get used to it. Small ain't the only one. Last year they brought in a kid from Chicago. Good player. But he'd give up his gold and his girl before he'd give up the ball."

Eddie had to laugh.

"One night he gets drunk and sticks up a convenience store. Well, the kid was having a great year. His picture was in the paper every week. The clerk knew the guy. He gets back to his room, the police are waiting. But they didn't take him to jail. They take him to Coach Sand's house. Sand starts bitching . . . not 'how could you commit armed robbery' but how could he betray Barry Sand. You know what the kid says?"

Eddie waited.

"He told Sand that he wasn't getting enough money. The guy has just committed a crime and he's got the balls to stand there with about twelve pounds of gold chain around his neck and say he had to resort to armed robbery to make ends meet. He was nineteen years old."

Eddie just looked and listened. What else could he do?

"So," Jax said, "first Sand gets the charges dropped and covered up; then he gives the kid another thousand a month. Now the kid wears so much gold he sounds like Marley's ghost walking into the locker room."

"That's pretty . . . funny, I guess, but I'm wondering if I want to come here," Eddie said.

"Hey, that's up to you, but I wish I was the Great White Hope on the Southwestern campus."

"What?"

"I like it here but I'm *black*. We black players are encouraged to remember that we were brought here to play basketball. Never mind how different we are from each other, we all end up hanging out together. It's de facto segregation."

"Don't you go to class?"

"Sure I do," Jax said, "but I'm just about the only black player actually making progress toward a degree. I go to class, go to practice and come back here and study. I don't get into other campus activities."

"That's got to be tough," Eddie said. "I thought there was a black fraternity on campus."

"There is, but it doesn't have a national charter.

Coach Sand just created it for black athletes, and Sam Watts provided the funding for a house and expenses."

Jax went to his refrigerator and got out two Tecate beers. He tossed one red, black and gold can to Eddie.

"Believe it or not, it could be worse," Jax said. "I'll get an education and I'll graduate in spite of the basketball department."

"What about Coach Lee?"

"He makes the difference, Eddie. He's not like the rest of them, don't ask me why. Oh, he has to go out and hustle to get players. He feeds everybody the standard line about Southwestern being the fast track to the NBA. But Lee tries to keep his promises and encourages the players to get their degrees. He's backed me against Sand a couple times . . ."

"You ever think about going somewhere else?"

"Sure, but if I were to transfer I'd have to sit out a full year. I can't afford to lose that much time. Anyway, this *is* a good academic school. My degree will *mean* something."

"Jax, one reason I'd come here is because I want to play with you."

"Well, *tell* 'em that. They'll listen to you. You're seven foot and *white*. You can ask for the moon."

"All I'd ever take is a scholarship," Eddie said. "I don't want money."

"Good, that's good," Jax said. "That means they

got nothing on you. You think they help out guys like Small and LeJune Hampton because they like them? They do it to have something over them, to threaten them with. Lee, though, he really seems to like players. You'd like playing for him, he knows the game."

"What do you mean play for him? I thought he was the recruiting coach."

"He's damn near everything here," Jax said. "Sand spends all his time making television appearances, giving interviews."

The music in the next room boomed out as some rapper told his story about a girl with a big butt and a nine millimeter. Jax beat the wall. The rap faded.

"While Sand is off taping his TV and radio shows, hustling money from alumni or telling high-school kids not to do drugs for fifteen K a pop, Lee designs the offense and defense. He coaches us right up to the start of the season. Then Sand steps in long enough to sit on the bench and ream us out during the game. If the opposition throws something new at us and Lee is off somewhere recruiting, we are fucked. Sand couldn't make an adjustment in his belt, let alone a game plan."

"How does he get away with it?"

"Politics. Brick Williams, the athletic director, and Sand are long-time buddies. And Williams hates Lee."

The Conquering Heroes

"Why?"

"Apparently it goes back to when Lee was playing," Jax said. "The Dixie Conference was all white and Lee kept after Williams to get some good black players. He kept saying there were black high-school teams in Michigan that could win the Dixie Conference. Williams didn't much like hearing that. And Sand had Dr. Williams on his nuts. Williams got him a couple of political coaching jobs through the Peace Corps or the State Department."

The rapper music blasted out, and Jax slammed the flat of his hand against the wall.

"I hate that music. The dumb asses can only rhyme nine millimeter and suck my dick."

"I read that Sand coached in Italy and was important in organizing the European Basketball League."

"I'm sure Sand believes it. I heard he had to leave because the Red Brigade had him on a death list." Jax smiled. "Now those people *must* have known their basketball."

"You're making this up."

"No, I'm not. Sand is a politician, *not* a coach. Sand's even got a picture of himself sitting on the bench with the '64 Olympic basketball team. Nobody knows what he did. But there his big ass is, in color and in an Olympic outfit sitting next to Pete Newell."

"So politics explains how he got the job." Eddie

Sanford looked out the window at the darkened campus. "How does he keep his job? He can't keep fooling everybody all the time."

"The players aren't fooled. But the public still sees Sand as a winner. Hell, Sand has himself listed as a member of the '61 to '64 teams. He was never a player."

"Why doesn't somebody in the pressbox pick up on it?" Eddie asked. "Some of these guys have been covering the games since the sixties."

"What can they say? They need access. If anybody ever seriously criticized Sand's credentials they'd never get back into the press box . . . Eddie, have you ever been in a TV booth during a live broadcast?"

"No. But I've noticed that they don't always seem to be describing the game I'm watching."

"That's because there's so much broadcasting shit going down that analyzing the *game* is impossible. I did some color commentary last year after they scoped my knee." Jax leaned forward and rubbed the damaged joint. "In one ear a plug connects me to a guy in the truck screaming stuff he wants repeated over the air . . . stats, details, anecdotes." Jax smiled and shook his head. "At the same time he tells me my sound bites are too long, I'm talking like a field nigger and nobody can understand me."

"He said that? He said 'field nigger'?"

"A live TV broadcast prefers dead people to

dead air." Jax gave up a short burst of laughter, then continued his story. "Now in my other ear the announcer is screaming the play-by-play of the game. It was fascinating. Next to him on a huge cardboard sheet the guy had a long list of words and phrases like 'in the paint,' 'crashed the boards,' 'nothing but net,' 'dime, dish, dump' . . . And each time he used one he would put a little check mark by it to make sure he didn't keep repeating himself."

Eddie laughed as Jax bore on, using his big hands to paint pictures in the air.

"Now, with one eye I'm supposed to be watching the game, and with the other I'm checking the stat sheets, scouting reports and player profiles for tidbits for my color commentary. Remember, the guy in the truck has never stopped yelling in my ear. Then with my other two eyes I'm supposed to watch the benches, the coaches, the subs and the crowd."

Jax walked to the small refrigerator under his desk, opened it and took out two more Tecate beers.

"I had to process all the information and draw conclusions on strategies, weaknesses, mistakes, adjustments, great plays and, most of all, *coaching ability*."

Jax handed Eddie Sanford his beer.

"And that's how a guy like Barry Sand can end up as head coach of a winning NCAA team and nobody know any better." Jax took a deep swallow of beer. "And when he finally does get fired TV will pay him a fortune for his knowledgeable commentary."

A gunshot rang out in the hall. Eddie jumped from his seat, spinning to face the door. Jax Morrow never moved.

"That's our power forward from Newark announcing his return from a date."

Two more sharp bangs rattled the windows.

"He got laid twice."

Pat lay on his back in the bed. Rachael Golen-Pankin was astride his hips, thrusting him into her, whipping her thick black hair against his face and chest.

Her breasts hung down. He squeezed and massaged them. Leaning up to suck on one nipple, then the other, falling back against the pillow.

Rachael, the golden girl who had seemed prematurely a woman, had been raised the perfect daughter, had rebelled, but ultimately married her high-school sweetheart Benjamin Pankin and settled into the life of the Chicago Gold Coast, then on to the Texas rich of River Oaks with her successful, influential husband.

But that was only part of the résumé and not even a hint of what was inside. They could call her a Jewish-American Princess, a JAP—she even called herself that—but she only fit the cliché on the outside. The summer of 1960 that had been the end and the beginning for Pat and his crowd and millions of other young Americans was her summer of rebellion, of searching and believing. She and Pat had become close after Geena gave up on him and went to Barry, but when Kennedy was nominated she had gone off for service on the New Frontier in Camelot, in search of what she believed was a new justice and equality for America. It was the time when she had stood up Pat for a date at SWS because of Kennedy. And she held on to her dream until it was savaged by the assassination in Dallas.

Rachael still had something of the old fire, but for the past twenty years her spark of rebellion was kept alive mostly by the sexual interludes with Pat—not exactly what she envisioned for herself, but at least they confirmed and reconfirmed that something was still very much alive inside. . . .

Rachael

Harbor City
Summer—1960

"Barb says the Keatses moved to Dallas. Geena's old man has opened a Keats Metal and Coil Plant at Nuevo Laredo on the Mexican side of the border," Steve told his older brother.

"Well, I guess that's that," Pat said. But inside he felt a void he wasn't expressing. Geena had just been too much for him, and who could blame her for finally giving up . . . and moving toward Barry?

Steve was driving Jim Lee's VW Beetle along the Harbor City North Beach. It was July 4th, 1960. Independence Day.

"They ship sealed trucks to and from the Wood

plant. It's some sort of cheap-labor tax-dodge."

Pat was watching the Harbor City Public Works men using pitchforks, shovels and dump trucks to clear the beach of dead fish.

It was the beginning of what the locals referred to as the Jewish resort season that would run to Labor Day. The Lee brothers had come to watch the resorters cope with the biggest fish-kill in two years.

The little Lake Michigan town of Harbor City had been a quiet resort since before Al Capone had bought his lakeside mansion and 300 acres of lakefront. Scarface, in fact, had often come across by boat from Chicago to relax. Harbor City's quiet existence had only been interrupted once, when Agent Melvin Purvis, desperate to upstage "that little toad" J. Edgar Hoover, had acted on questionable information about the whereabouts of John Dillinger and his gang. Purvis and his G-men had surrounded and attacked the Lakeside Resort Cabins at daybreak, and the gun battle had spread into the streets, resulting in the deaths of an FBI agent and three innocent people taking the morning air. One of the victims was the mayor of the nearby town of Wood, Grant Waters, also Wood's leading businessman and Ron Waters's grandfather. No one *ever* saw John Dillinger in Harbor City. He was across the lake in Chicago thinking about going to the movies. After his conviction for tax evasion, Capone never returned to his property, which was remodeled into the Mado-lynn Resort, the finest in Harbor City, and it was from the bluffs of Lake Michigan to the Mado-lynn that the old bootlegger's tunnel was rumored to lead.

The north side of Harbor City had been considered a classic Jewish family-style resort area for over forty years. In the twenties and thirties excursion boats brought people across Lake Michigan from Chicago to this idyllic little lakeside town. Now industry, booming with Cold War prosperity, threatened to chase them all away.

The once-thriving resorts that were a few miles from the lakefront had already started to go down financially. The Victorian and Georgian-style mansions with their magnificent dining and ball rooms were being eaten away with dry rot. The carefully manicured acres of grass were overgrown with weeds.

Closer to Lake Michigan the resort owners held on to a faded grandeur, but each year they lost ground to the declining quality of the lake and the growing airline business that lured kids away from their families and off on excursions to Europe.

Still, in this summer of 1960, the place had its charm.

At night people walked from one sprawling resort to the next along the lake and listened to the bands and the Chicago comedians, watched the dance contests and the organized games. And like many young men from Harbor City and Wood, Pat and Steve cruised in the endless traffic jam on North Shore Drive looking for girls and adventures.

Sometimes, they even found them.

But every year another kosher delicatessen or butcher shop closed, the crowds on the sidewalks got smaller and the traffic jams were mostly cars with Michigan plates—kids from Harbor City, Kalamazoo, Holland, Grand Rapids and Wood. Last year always seemed to have been a better year.

"I see the Dunes didn't open their pool this year," Steve was saying as they passed one of the larger more modern resorts on North Shore Drive.

"Tate Davis told me that he had a hell of a time finding a lifeguard's job this summer."

Tate Davis, Harbor City's state diving champion, during the fifties used to put on two diving shows a night at the Dunes. Now the Dunes didn't even fill the pool for the guests.

It was getting dark when Steve turned off North Shore Drive down the alley between the Lakeside Resort cabins.

They had gone about halfway down the alley, where there were no street lights, when suddenly Steve slammed on the brakes. The VW's headlights had picked up a big black nosed-and-decked, chopped-and-channeled, '49 Mercury turned sideways in their path.

"What the fuck are they doing?" Steve said.

The Mercury's headlights were on a young kid the big car had cornered between a fence and a cottage wall. The guys in the car yelled at the kid, who stayed motionless, head down, face hidden.

"Come on, you little hebe, try to get away." The voice was familiar. "I'll squash you into kosher sausage."

A chill ran down Pat's spine. "The Mazurski brothers . . ."

Steve asked, "Can you see how many there are in the car?"

Pat shook his head, his stomach in knots, his mouth gone dry. Where was Barry Sand when you really needed him? Off sleeping with somebody else's girl. So he was still a little pissed at his buddy, not quite so forgiving as he pretended.

"Tate told me that Tommy is out of Jackson and back in town."

Tommy Mazurski had been sentenced to Jackson State Prison for felonious assault after beating up a Kalamazoo high-school football star, rupturing a kidney and putting out an eye.

"I thought he was doing three to five."

"Time off for good behavior," Steve said. "Hard to believe in Tommy's case."

The Conquering Heroes

"Well, there's nobody behind us. We could back up—"

"I don't back up for those pieces of dog shit!"

"The police will want to know if we tried not to get the shit beat out of us."

"You think we're going to be in any shape to give statements to the police if all five of those assholes are in that Merc?"

Pat nodded. "So, brother, what do we do?"

"We better get three of them before they get out of the car." Steve reached in the backseat. "Mom's Sears catalogue is back here somewhere."

At which point the driver stepped out of the Mercury and the interior light went on. All the Mazurski brothers were present and accounted for. Tommy, the driver, walked directly to Pat's side of the car and bent down. He hadn't recognized Pat and Steve; the Volkswagen's headlights had blinded him.

"You punks better back up unless—" Tommy's eyes showed recognition. He leaned forward for a better look.

"Let's go, Pat," Steve said softly as he lifted the Sears catalogue out of the backseat.

Tommy's look was hardening as Pat gently pulled the handle, releasing the door.

"Hey," Tommy began, "you're that shitbird from—"

Pat slammed the door into Tommy as hard as he could. The top of the frame smashed Tommy across the forehead and knocked him flat. Pat and Steve jumped out of the VW and crossed to the Merc, careful to stay out of their Volkswagen's headlights. It was no longer a question of honor; survival had become the issue.

They were after the four Mazurski brothers still in the car. Half-blinded by the VW's high beams, the Mazurskis had not seen what had happened to their older brother.

Steve slipped around the trunk to the passenger side while Pat moved up toward the open driver's door.

"Hey! Mazurski!" Steve was standing at the rear fender. As Sam, who was riding shotgun, started to turn, Steve moved toward him. Sam stuck his head out the window just in time to get it whacked by a five-pound catalogue; his head hit the bottom sill and he slumped over in the seat.

Joe Mazurski, sitting in the middle of the front seat, dove for the open driver's door. As his head came out, Pat aimed for his chin but missed and drove the punch into his throat. Joe fell out onto the ground, gagging. The two youngest Mazurskis, Dickie and Danny, fifteen and sixteen, were trapped in the backseat.

"Steve, watch them." Pat ran over and double-checked Tommy, still unconscious.

"I'll check on the kid they were hassling," Pat said, and walked over to the small figure with the dark hair. "Are you okay?"

The head turned and Pat caught a sideways glance of the face.

"Christ, Steve, he's a girl . . . I mean, she's a girl." He turned back to the small slender girl. "Did they hurt you?"

She shook her head.

"Do you live on the beach?"

"No." Her voice was deep, raspy. "I was just taking a walk . . ."

"Where do you live?"

"Out at the Mado-lynn." She was silhouetted in the head-lights and Pat could see her breasts straining the fabric of her shirt.

"That's a pretty long walk."

"I like long walks." She looked at Pat, full-faced, for the first time. Damn, he thought, she was beautiful, big brown eyes and full lips. Five foot, tops.

"We gotta go," Steve said, "I can't keep everybody under control. Joe's getting his breath and I think I can hear Tommy starting to groan."

"You better come with us," Pat told the girl. "We'll take you back to the Mado-lynn." He held out his hand, which she just stared at. "Come on, we're running on empty. We can't keep these guys down forever."

The girl seemed rooted to the pavement.

"What's your name?" Pat asked.

"Rachael." She studied his face.

"I'm Pat. That's my brother Steve." He reached

for her again, slowly. "And scattered around you are the Mazurski brothers."

"Come *on*," Steve was saying. Dickie tried now to get out of the backseat and Steve slapped him across the face with the catalogue. "Let's go," Steve called, "the natives are getting restless."

Pat now had the girl gently by the arm and was leading her to the Volkswagen. He put her in the front seat. Steve dove into the back through the driver's side, and Pat slid behind the wheel.

"Christ," Steve moaned, "they're going to hunt us down and kill us."

"Well, for now let's put some distance between us and them," Pat said, and backed the Volkswagen out of the alley as fast as he could. "So, Rachael, you from Chicago?"

"Yes." She looked straight ahead.

"Your family staying at the Mado-lynn?"

"My mother and I." She seemed to relax a little and leaned back in the seat. "My dad comes in from Chicago on the weekends. He's a lawyer. We've been coming here for summers since I was a little girl . . . This is our last summer."

They pulled into the long drive leading back to the Mado-lynn. It was still the finest resort along this part of the lake, with acres of carefully tended grass and shrubs, an indoor pool, tennis courts, a large main lodge built from the original Capone house and dozens of bungalows along the one mile of lake frontage.

The Conquering Heroes

"We're staying over there in bungalow seven."

"That's bigger than our house!" Steve said.

"Maybe I'll see you guys again," Rachael said, allowing a smile.

"How about me this weekend?" Pat asked, impressing himself, as he stopped the car in front of bungalow seven. Suddenly, he felt almost desperate to see her again. This wasn't like him, but there it was . . .

"I don't know . . . my father is coming, and Benji . . ."

"How about Friday night?" Pat pressed. "I'll take you to a lake with live fish and water you can actually swim in."

She looked at him, nodded. "What time?"

"Five o'clock?"

"I have to warn you," Rachael said, and looked straight into his eyes, "my parents are old-fashioned, they expect me to date Jewish boys. That's one reason we've always come here—"

"I'll wear a yarmulke."

"Get out of here." She laughed as she opened the door. "All right then, Friday night and please *don't* wear a yarmulke." She ran quickly to the front door of bungalow seven and disappeared inside.

"God, Steve, did you get a look at her? Did you see that face?" Pat was taking the back way out of Harbor City to avoid any chance encounter with the Mazurski boys.

"She had some serious tits, too," Steve said. "Well, considering her parents, it's a good thing you're circumcised."

"I'll show her old man my dick."

"Always play to your strength, brother. Forget romance, you better remember that we just started a major family feud tonight. Harbor City won't be a safe place for you to be romancing anybody. This is dangerous territory from now on."

Pat realized Steve was right. This was the Swamp. Feuding was in the Mazurski boys' blood. And a feud with them could be lifelong.

Harbor City had always been Indian country. Last year things got worse when J.D. Mazurski was appointed clerk of the Harbor City draft board. J.D. was from the uptown side of the Mazurski clan. He had made good money in construction and he employed his family, including his nephews—Tommy, Sam and Joe.

Bad news all around for Pat and Steve.

Pat had arrived at bungalow seven at exactly five o'clock Friday afternoon.

Rachael had stepped through the door, dressed all in white; loose-fitting cotton pants and pullover shirt, a white wide-brim Panama hat on the back of her black hair. The contrast of the white against her dark coloring, big eyes and black hair was stunning, Pat thought. Mrs. Golen, Rachael's mother, had been polite, but had looked at Pat as if his head were on backward . . .

"We'll go back through Sawmill," Pat said. "It's on the way to the lake." He was driving them out of Harbor City the back way, not wanting to tangle with the Mazurski boys.

Soon they were driving east on an empty country road through miles of orchards and blueberry patches until they got to the town of Sawmill. Set on a bluff at the headwaters of the Birch River, the town consisted of twelve blocks of empty buildings, an abandoned five-story red-brick hotel, an operating gas station, a small corner grocery store and a tavern called the Buzz Saw.

"During the lumber boom," Pat told Rachael, "Sawmill had sawmills, taverns, millionaires, and that hotel was full every night." His arm swept in a semicircle. "The downtown ran four blocks in every direction except south toward the river."

"What happened?"

"The lumber ran out."

"Just like that? I mean, didn't anybody notice that they were getting thin on trees?"

"The same way they notice Lake Michigan is getting thin on fish. They see it, they feel it, they hear it, but they still deny it."

"What happened to all the people?"

"A few stayed and tried to keep the town alive. Sawmill was their home. Like Mary Lou Jenkins, the mayor's daughter, she lived in that big white house next to the hotel." Pat pointed at the once-grand house, now abandoned and collapsing in on itself. "At eighteen Mary Lou was the belle of Sawmill. First the trees ran out, then her father and the town died. She was an old maid at twenty-five."

Pat paused to look at Rachael. She seemed fixed on the house.

"The last seventy years of her life no one ever saw her outside that house. They say she died staring out that top floor window."

"God, what a sad story."

Rachael, Pat could swear, had tears in her eyes. Most other girls would have shut him up long ago.

"It happened in a lot of the old boom-bust saw-mill towns. They called them Lumber Widows."

"Where did all the lumber go?"

"Well, Grand Rapids, it became the furniture capital. Schooners ran out of Muskegon and Harbor City to Chicago. They only cut the best trees, tore down whole forests to get at them and left what they didn't want to rot."

"It's hard to believe people would do that."

"That's what makes it so easy to get away with," Pat said. "Look around Harbor City. The game is make a profit, get out and leave the mess for somebody else to clean up." He looked at Rachael to see if she was still with him. "Old John Jacob Astor's American Fur Company trapped out all the rivers and took the money to New York. The big steel and car companies are gouging the Upper Peninsula for iron and copper ore and sending the money east. And now the big plastic and chemical companies are polluting the rivers and lakes and sending the money east. The St. Lawrence Seaway opens this all the way up to the ocean at Quebec. Who knows what kind of mess it will make." He looked back at Rachael. "The money goes and the garbage stays."

"Maybe you ought to go into the garbage business," Rachael said, her eyes still fixed on Mary Lou Jenkins's old white house. "It sounds like a growth industry."

"It's already spoken for," Pat said. "Hey, I'm sorry to be putting all this on you. I don't get a captive audience very often."

"It's okay, but let's go." She smiled at him.

Pat turned the VW south, crossing the Birch below Sawmill to the south, heading toward Wood. He drove slowly, passing the apple, peach and cherry orchards starting to get heavy with fruit. A rooster pheasant glided across the road and a small deer appeared in the corner of a cornfield. They took a graded gravel road that angled along the river bottom north of the Wilson's Hill drain, passing a tar-paper shack with two naked kids in the doorway. A poached deer hung, gutted and aging in a tree.

"People actually live there?" Rachael turned and watched as they drove by.

"This is hillbilly country, real poor people. Some classmates of mine just got indoor plumbing."

"So," Rachael said, "this is the boondocks. I'm really down in it."

She seemed animated, when most girls would have been bored silly. Pat turned, climbing the north side and dropping back off the east side of Wilson's Hill back into the bottom land heading into Wood. He crossed north of the Birch River on the steel bridge and came back south over a dam, passing the silt ponds and the millrace.

"We used to fish for rock bass under that old gristmill there," Pat said as he pointed to a red plank building. "You can still see the old waterwheel."

"That's really a great old mill," Rachael said.

"Yeah, well, we loved the place, and every now and then we'd see a big catfish or a pickerel."

"Any fish in there now?"

"Are you kidding? Even the trash fish are struggling. Pollution from Keats Metal and insecticides from the farms."

"Pat, is this sort of a crusade with you?"

"No, not really, but I've lived through some of it. It was a beautiful place . . ."

He pulled back out onto the road and drove through Wood, heading south toward Black Lake. "I just thought maybe you might be interested—"

"I *am*, really, but it seems to upset you so much."

"I guess it just makes me mad . . . I mean, all the people and the great places . . . nobody wants to tell the truth about it."

"Well, people lie to themselves all the time," she said. "Nobody wants bad news. They mind fuck themselves."

Pat was startled by her language, but kept quiet as he turned into the lane that led to the old farm on the east side of Black Lake, then went through the groves of trees his father had planted during the Depression. He drove through the vineyards to the farmhouse on the hill, then stopped the car and stared straight ahead.

"This is my grandmother's place. She mostly lives in town since my grandfather died. Black Lake is down the backside of the hill through the woods."

"It's beautiful, Pat."

"Did you say 'mind fuck'?" he asked finally.

Rachael looked at him, her dark eyes seeming to sting his flesh.

Suddenly he was embarrassed. His arms turned to gooseflesh. Who was this girl who seemed so . . . mature? He badly wanted to know but doubted he ever would.

"Mind fuck?" Rachael repeated. "Yes, Pat, I said it."

And this time her smile was very different as

she leaned forward and pressed her lips against his.

"Don't worry, I'm on the pill," she whispered into his ear as he cupped her breasts, then slid his hands over her taut body.

They were in the house on the sun-porch bed overlooking the woods and the lake beyond. Rachael was nude but still rakishly wearing her hat. Pat only had his shirt and shoes off. He couldn't remember how they got from the car to the house, or how they got her pullover shirt off over that Panama hat.

There was an extravagance about her sexuality that was overwhelming. Straining to match her, Pat suddenly forced a previously unknown door, letting his passions flow unchecked.

Now she pushed him flat on the bed and straddled his chest, Panama hat cocked to the side of her head. She ran her fingers across his face, tracing his jawline. The touch made him shiver. She slid down and kissed him hard on the mouth, licking the insides of his cheeks, the roof of his mouth.

They clutched at each other, her lips pressed to the hollow in his throat, her nails raking his bare chest. She slid farther down, licking and kissing while she unbuckled his belt. Her tongue was on his stomach, and she had found him hard, clutching and stroking him.

The Conquering Heroes

She stood, stripped him, then knelt down and bent forward. All that he could see was the top of that Panama hat and some loose wisps of hair as she slowly slipped him into her mouth. He could feel the inside of her mouth, the warm breath from her nose. She tried to swallow him, then held him tight with her lips. Her tongue caressed the length of him.

Suddenly she stopped, released him, then ran her tongue from bottom to top and looked up at him.

"Is this your first time?" she asked, her moist lips red, a blush glowing through her perfect dark-hued skin.

"*Yes . . .*"

"That's nice." She bent down and started again.

Her lips and mouth were stronger on him than before. Her tongue seemed to have a life of its own. Finally, holding him tight between her lips, she pulled away and he came free with a tiny pop. She planted a small kiss on the very top.

Crawling up the length of the bed, she pulled him over and into her with delicate movement, wrapped her strong lean legs around his waist, and smiled.

"Now"—she took off her hat—"let's us make love."

She was lying across him, her hair wet with perspiration. He had no idea how long they had been like that. Sweat ran off his face and from his scalp line in rivulets. The bed was soaked.

He felt wonderful.

"Well," Rachael murmured, "what do you think?"

"Did I pass out or something?"

"You did a lot of or something." She slid off his chest and curled up next to him under his arm. "You're in good shape."

"Well, my coach says take care of your body and it takes care of you."

"It took very nice care of me," Rachael whispered. "Thank you."

Pat drifted off for a while, then felt himself being shaken and, for a scary moment, thought maybe it had all been a wonderful dream. But Rachael was kneeling next to him, pushing on his shoulder.

"Come on," she said, "let's go swimming."

They took the path through the woods, down the hill to the lake and jumped off the small dock. The lake was like bathwater.

"Hey, tell me about yourself," Pat said as he swam up beside her.

"What do you need to know?" Rachael said, and grabbed onto his shoulder and floated on her back. "Besides that I know how to fuck."

"Everything, anything," he said, sputtering and laughing.

"Well, you could say I am a Jewish-American

The Conquering Heroes

Princess recently gone bad. I was engaged to my high-school boyfriend and was going to go to Northwestern while he finished law school."

"What happened?"

"I didn't like the way my life was being laid out for me. I want to do some things. Anyway, I applied to Michigan to study marine biology."

They swam lazily back to shore and climbed the hill to the house.

"Okay," he said, "let's hear more about the JAP gone bad."

"Not much to tell." Her face flushed as she avoided his eyes. "Everybody wants me back with my fiancé. My father is already doing a slow burn, and I was not to see you under any circumstances. I wish he'd understand I'm eighteen years old." She sat on the bed and dried herself with a towel. "And I *don't* want to marry Benji."

"Benji?"

"Benjamin Pankin."

"Your married name would be Mrs. Benji Pankin?"

Pat hoped he hadn't offended, and tried a smile. At first she gave him a look, then began to laugh. And then before he could say anything more, she grabbed him by the hair, pulled him to her and kissed him hard, deep and long. She finished off by kissing both his eyes gently.

Rachael was beyond anything he'd ever known. They might not last the summer, but for as long as it lasted he'd damn well accept it and savor it. Not like with Geena . . .

In the distance a whistle blew—the ten o'clock passenger train from Chicago, its deep lonesome moan signaling it was still miles away, probably just clearing the crossing at Nero. It didn't stop at Nero anymore, just blew on through. Nero used to be a regular stop, the radish capital of Michigan. Somebody somewhere came up with a better radish or a better deal. Nobody in Nero ever found out.

Pat wondered if there had been any radish widows in Nero.

Well, to hell with that now. Nero was dead and gone. Rachael was here and now.

"I have to be in Lake Forest by the second week in August," Rachael announced.

They were lying in the pine grove on a quilt that covered a soft bed of evergreen needles.

"Why?"

"I'm going to work on Kennedy's presidential campaign in Chicago."

"You're kidding."

While they watched TV convention coverage she had never mentioned wanting to take an active part.

"I figure Jake Arvey and Richard Daley will deliver Chicago without much help," Pat said.

"Not the northern suburbs, and Illinois and

The Conquering Heroes

Michigan will be important states. Don't you want Kennedy elected?"

"I don't want Nixon."

"That's a pretty negative view."

"I figure Soapy Williams and Walter Reuther have already come out for Kennedy. A governor and head of the auto workers union should win him Michigan."

"Doesn't it excite you that such a young guy could be president?"

"Not as much as you, I guess."

Rachael sat up abruptly. She was wearing cut-off jeans and a white T-shirt that had THE BOBS— RIVERVIEW PARK stenciled across the front.

"I hear a car."

"Sure. From up here you can hear them all the way back into Wood." He was watching a fox squirrel jump from limb to limb. It was a hot day but on the hill a cool breeze rustled the trees.

"You want to go swimming—?"

"*Shush*. Listen." Rachael turned her head, trying to filter sound out of the wind in the trees. "I'm telling you, there's a car coming."

"If it was coming here," Pat said as he sat up and listened, "I would already have heard it."

"I just wish I knew what he was up to," Rachael said.

"Who?"

"My father."

"I thought he was back in Chicago. You just

talked to your mother on the phone this morning."

"He lies to her all the time. Oscar will never let anybody beat him, and I think he sees you as a threat to his darlin' daughter."

Pat looked at her, not knowing what to say, so he switched to safer ground. "That's a tractor you hear. It's about four miles away. My guess is that it's spraying or running a brush hog at the Maple Hill Farm."

"Are you sure?"

"I've spent a lot of summers right here with nothing to do but listen. I haven't even heard a car come this way out of Wood for the last hour."

"I'm sorry I got scared," Rachael said, and crawled on top of him and put her head on his chest. "Pat Lee, you make me feel safe. I like that."

Pat decided against telling her how in a way she scared him, at the same time she made him feel wonderful.

"What do they call a busload of lawyers going off a cliff?" he said as he stroked her hair.

"I give up," she sighed, and sprawled across him.

"A good start."

"Very funny."

Soon her even breathing told him she was asleep. He kept watching the trees and finally spotted a flying squirrel soar from one tree to the next. The five o'clock whistle blew from on top of the Wood Town Hall, and soon after he could hear cars traveling out of Wood in all directions, none even slowing at the lane leading to the farm.

Twenty minutes later Rachael woke up with a start. Then, finding herself in Pat's arms, relaxed into his chest, mumbled something and slipped back into sleep.

At 6:00 P.M. Pat heard Chuck Stanislawski's pickup pull away from the Black Lake Inn. Chuck always kept it in first gear too long, and the whine was nearly as familiar as his voice. Chuck was shifting down about a quarter mile from the lane; he was coming up to see them, Pat figured.

He kissed Rachael on the cheek and began rubbing her back. "Hey, wake up." He kissed her again. "Chuck is on his way up to see us."

"Huh?" Her face was wrinkled from sleep as she lifted her head. "What?"

Pat kissed her on the lips and pulled her up. She put her arms around his neck and held tight. She kissed him, leaned back and stretched.

"What did you say?"

"Chuck is on his way up."

"Why?"

"I don't know, we'll see when he gets here. He's

coming from the inn. My guess is he's bringing us dinner."

"Really? Hey, great. I'm starving." She paused, then stared at Pat. "How do you know all this?"

"I heard him leave the inn. He's coming up the lane right now. Listen."

They could hear the truck laboring up the hill.

"And you know all this just from the sound of the truck?"

"What can I say? I know my ground."

"My little woodsman." She kissed him again. "Come on, let's go get the food."

The pickup was pulling up to the house as they walked out of the woods.

Pat could smell the food. Now, if there was no bad news for dessert, his day would be complete. He didn't need conversation about what tough guys, especially the Mazurski brothers, might be hunting him all over the county . . .

"Does she eat like this all the time?" Chuck had hardly taken his eyes off Rachael since he'd arrived.

"I wouldn't advise getting too close," Pat said. "I almost lost a finger yesterday."

Rachael just frowned at him and kept eating.

"Any news?" Pat asked.

"Same old stuff in Harbor City," Chuck said as he watched Rachael finish off her second baked potato. "Joe and Sam Mazurski beat up some tourist kid and the judge told them to enlist in the army or get ready for jail."

"And?"

"They're going to keep the world safe for democracy."

"Great idea, good riddance. I'd figured with Uncle J.D. on the draft board they'd never have to serve . . . What about Tommy?"

"He's dropped out of sight." Chuck said. "The army wouldn't take him anyway, he's a convicted felon."

"Did you grow up around here?" Rachael asked Chuck, carefully licking her fingers clean. Like a cat, it seemed to Pat.

"I came here in the fifth grade as a Polish DP," Chuck said, his eyes on her. "After the war somebody knocked on the door and asked for my father. I remember seeing him go out the door. He had been on the town council, that was his crime."

"Did you ever see him again?"

Chuck shook his head. "We waited for him, until my brother Viktor was eighteen. Old enough for the army. We escaped through Germany and spent the next years in refugee camps."

"Didn't you have any friends or family, someone to stay with?"

"No"—Chuck took a drink of beer and smiled at Rachael— "all our relatives were still in Poland. Finally the Red Cross said this town in Michigan would sponsor six families of displaced persons.

We arrived in Wood in January of 1952, along with another Polish family, and two Latvian and two Lithuanian."

"Is that when you two guys met?"

"I saw this scrawny-looking kid on the playground during a recess," Pat said. "He could hardly speak any English. I figured him an easy mark. He beat the shit out of me in front of the whole school. I *had* to be his friend."

"It's funny," Chuck said, finishing his beer, "but it's those times that I'll always remember as the best times in school."

"For you," Pat said. "What about me?"

"You loved it and you've never had a better friend." Chuck leaned back and stretched. "You know, mostly school was boring, most of the teachers hated us, but we'll forget all that. All we'll remember will be the good times . . . the fight, the football games, the baseball team, the state championship. Remember the good, forget the bad . . ."

Chuck stood up then and took Rachael's hand. "It was nice meeting you. If you get tired of him I'll come and beat the shit out of him for you."

"It looks to me like you'll have to get in line." Rachael laughed.

"He's right, you know," Rachael said as they watched Chuck leave. "This summer . . . we'll remember what we want to remember. He's real smart. You must like him a lot."

The Conquering Heroes

"I'd trust him with my life, and damn near have more than once."

"What does his brother Viktor do?"

"Six months after they arrived in Wood, Viktor was riding his bike to school and was killed by a hit-and-run driver."

Rachael shook her head.

"You see why he works at remembering the good things."

It was a long, warm, wonderful summer.

Opportunity knocked, especially for Rachael. Pat didn't think that far ahead, and tried hard to block out the troubles on the horizon. Somehow he sensed this would be the last time he would be able to do that.

Rachael and Pat, Back to the Future

Rachael stiffened and bent back, digging her nails into Pat's thighs as he lunged into her. She moaned deeply and collapsed on his chest, spent and relieved.

"God!" she gasped, "drunk or sober you're still a great fuck."

She lit a cigarette and turned on the television.

"So? What are you doing in town? You still Southwestern's one-man meat market?"

He took a drag on her cigarette. "You always did know how to turn a phrase . . . Actually I came to Houston to see this terrific seven-foot kid only to find out that he had driven up to Dallas to visit one of my players for the weekend."

"That the kid you put on to Ben?"

The Conquering Heroes

"Yeah." Pat was watching the cigarette smoke curl to the ceiling. "I keep messing up with this kid but I still think I'll get him."

"Good for you. Barry should be proud."

"You're harder on me than usual tonight. Is this relationship headed for whips and chains?"

"You never can tell."

He watched her face outlined in the glow from the television. "You are still the most beautiful woman I have ever seen. Thirty years haven't changed that. It was a lucky thing for me that you moved to Houston when Ben left Justice."

Rachael allowed a half-smile of acknowledgement, then pointed to the television. "Look, your lifetime friend and nemesis."

Pat turned up the volume to go with Barry Sand's face.

"I stick with the basics . . ." Sand was earnestly saying to the sportscaster's beanbag question about Southwestern's dominance of the Dixie Conference.

"That lying sonofabitch. You know, I used to love basketball—"

"I used to love politics. Until they shot and killed about half the guys on my team. After Bobby hit the kitchen floor at the Ambassador Hotel I decided I didn't like politics. Talk about your contact sports . . ."

Pat couldn't stop watching Barry Sand. It was the same interview Barry had been giving since he first won the Dixie Conference. It was smooth and he had it down pat.

"It's dog eat dog. That's why I have to take a tough position on illegal recruiting. It would be easy to corrupt kids with cash and cars, especially the inner-city and ghetto kids. But I just won't allow it."

"Do you *believe* this guy?" Pat said.

"Today the market mix competing for the entertainment dollar is huge. We have to offer the best in the country and that's my job. I find, recruit and then try to mold this raw talent into a winning team, all within the NCAA regulations. I try to make certain these kids get their degrees. It puts us at a disadvantage against the pros."

"But, coach," the sportscaster nervously asked his only hardball question, "NCAA statistics show less than thirty percent of your players graduate."

"Why, that's just plain old poppycock." Barry shook his head. "I've got ex-players calling every day to thank me not just for playing on a winning team but for the extra effort I made to make certain they got their degrees."

The sportscaster looked relieved.

"Did he really say poppycock?" Pat said. "From student assistant to head coach on *poppycock*."

"We're talking over thirty years of hustling," Rachael said.

"But everything was set by the end of the six-ties," Pat argued. "Since then my life has been lived in an ever growing theme park."

"Oh, come on, Pat. Anyway, I was talking about politics."

"Sports in the nineties *is* politics, and money. Too much of both—"

"Please Pat, don't start on this again . . ."

Pat pointed at the television. "He makes over two million a year."

"Really?"

"When you add up the no-interest house loan, his TV and radio-show revenues, his product endorsements and sporting goods deals . . . His deal with Nike is worth a million. Barry Sand makes over two million, and that's not figuring in the stock he has in Watts Discount and Keats Industries, his father-in-law's company."

"He could have been your father-in-law if you hadn't fucked up."

"No, I don't think so. If I'd married Geena Keats I'd just have two ex-wives instead of one. You happen to be the only woman I've been able to maintain any relationship with—"

"You call this a relationship?" She saw his face go tight. "All right, sorry . . . it's *something*, no question. And I'm not complaining, except when you start carrying on about Barry. He's not exactly new news. Besides, he gives great interviews." She smiled, trying to relieve the tension, to divert him. It didn't work.

"Barry doesn't know any more about basketball

than he did in high school, and he didn't know that much in high school. I beat all the Dixie Conference schools to the inner-city street players. I was the first to get black players, I just went and got them . . ."

Rachael sighed, swung her feet off the bed and looked around for her underwear, found it and began dressing. Pat didn't seem to notice; he was staring at the television screen.

Rachael hooked up her bra and pulled on her half-slip. Pat continued to carry on. "There's a guy who's kept a room all year in this hotel just to recruit Eddie Sanford but *I'll* get Eddie . . ."

"That's wonderful, Pat." Rachael padded barefoot into the bathroom and closed the bathroom door with a bang.

Pat raised his voice as he heard the shower water begin to splatter. "Barry stands on the sidelines and yells nonsense for forty minutes. He doesn't even understand the game, he gets beaten by inferior teams and blames the players or recruiting or . . ."

The shower stopped and the bathroom door opened. Rachael walked out drying her hair, then proceeded to get dressed.

"He just doesn't know dick about basketball."

"I'm leaving, Pat," Rachael announced.

"What's the rush?"

She kissed him lightly, and headed for the door. "No rush, sport, I'm just calling time-out."

The Conquering Heroes

*   *   *

In the shower Pat understood too well why Rachael had left. Goddamn, when would he learn she hated hearing the old song about Barry? For that matter, as she'd told him more than once, she didn't want to hear about the old anything . . . including the good old days and the way they were. "Redford and Streisand, we aren't," she'd said. No argument there . . .

He finished dressing and headed up to the Derrick Lounge. If Eddie Sanford wasn't around he might as well spend some time with his mother.

"Eddie's in Dallas," Anne said as she set his vodka in front of him.

"I heard," Pat said. "I see I'm the only customer, again."

"You've become the rush hour."

"You know, from what I can gather, your Eddie really loves the game. I like that. I guess he reminds me a little of myself, at least the way I was."

"What happened?"

"Well, I came down here and played for Greg Dunne. He was drunk most of the time, turned games into nightmares, even though he was smart as hell. By the time I was a senior I just wanted out . . . The college system stinks."

"You told me the other night, remember? About the money, avoiding one-sided games . . . Why doesn't somebody raise hell?"

"Sports media isn't exactly filled with investigative journalists." Pat took a drink from her hand. "Besides, who wants to kill the cash cow? Everybody . . . the media, corporations, their news operations, stands to profit. Gamblers are getting nervous about carrying the book on college basketball. They know something is going on. It's not about who wins or loses, except for the players and coaches. It's how exciting the game is. Keep the audience interested to the last minutes."

"Telling all this to the mother of a player you're trying to recruit seems pretty dumb. You ain't exactly the brightest light on the Christmas tree, Pat Lee." She smiled when she said it.

"I'm trying to be honest with you, with Eddie. Maybe I'm exaggerating a little, I get carried away, but the point is there *can* be life even in this lousy system. Eddie's the best kid I've run across in years. I think he'll hold his own, on and off the court. And I'll try to help him if he needs help, I'm pretty good at that. Hell, who knows? Maybe he'll be the first of his generation to bring the game back where it used to be."

"What about your family? You said you had a daughter . . ."

"Yes, and I've got to get Jennie the hell out of here and away from her boyfriend, Sam Watts's kid. She wants to go to Yale, and I've got to see that she does."

"Can you afford it?"

"It's one big reason I hang in here."

"But what about you?"

"For me, it's the rare kid like Eddie and my own kids, that I don't see much."

"Well, buck up, Mr. Lee. No more sad songs. You think I like being a cocktail hostess? Maybe we both need to start finding what we lost." She looked at him.

"I can't get that son of a bitch Chuck Small to come to a meeting. I thought we were doing him a favor," Barry was saying to Pat in his office.

"Good deeds seldom go unpunished," Pat said, doubting that Barry caught his sarcasm. "Anyway, my guess is someone's told Small it's a felony to conspire about his rape of the Sullivan girl and to threaten him with criminal prosecution unless he blows off the NBA."

"*Who* do you think explained that to him?"

"The NBA has lawyers, too, Barry."

"What do you think?"

"I think maybe they got you." He wasn't really so sure. Small was scared of being exposed, maybe scared enough to give the NBA a pass.

"Well, we'll keep threatening him, but make sure it's done in private and he's not wearing a wire—"

"I told you, I won't have any more to do with this."

279

"Be careful, Pat. Don't push me—"

DeFor Clark walked into the office just then, holding a thick SOUTHWESTERN UNIVERSITY BASKETBALL envelope.

"Is it in there?" Barry asked him. Clark handed the envelope to Barry. They both ignored Pat.

Barry opened the envelope and extracted a bundle of $100 bills wrapped in notepaper with FROM THE DESK OF SAM WATTS printed across the top.

It was exactly like the envelope Watts had given Clark at the meeting in Brick Williams's office.

Barry thumbed through the thick wad of bills. "Okay." He handed the thick envelope back to Clark. "Make sure you do it right."

"I got it right before, didn't I?" Clark stuffed the money in his jacket pocket. "Anything else?"

"Just make sure it gets there."

Clark nodded and left. He never acknowledged Pat's presence.

"So what's the deal with Free and Jenks?" Barry asked quickly before Pat could say anything.

"I'll have to fly to Detroit once more, it needs a face-to-face."

"I'm getting real tired of your excuses on Jenks!"

It was Sand's favorite intimidation technique: a mood swing from calm to rage. He had learned it well from Greg Dunne. It had no effect on Pat. He had played for Greg Dunne and had endured his alcoholic mood swings and rages, sometimes carried out in the middle of a game.

"Well, Barry, I'm tired of you being tired. Fuck you, Barry. I'll deliver Jenks and Sanford."

Barry Sand was smart enough to let it pass. What he wanted most right now was what Pat had just promised him. With Pat it was a matter of honor to deliver. Good old honorable Pat Lee, the original and forever boy scout . . .

"So what was Clark's score on DeWayne Barkely's SAT test?" Pat was saying.

"A thousand ten combined," Barry said.

"Pretty good."

"Fuck good, it was perfect! Just high enough but not suspicious."

"Unless they look at his first test score."

"Why would they do that?"

"I didn't say they would . . ."

"Well, goddammit, quit being so fucking negative."

"It comes with the territory, coach."

The door to Sand's office swung open and his secretary Suzie stuck her head inside the room. "Coach, Jax Morrow is waiting. He said you sent for him."

"Oh, yeah. Tell him to wait."

Suzie closed the door.

"Listen to me . . ." Barry leaned toward Pat.

"*No*. Absolutely not. Give him a chance, damn it." Pat knew what was coming. "It's crazy to want to get rid of Jax, I won't do it—"

"We got to cut him. That knee surgery, back muscle tear, ankle sprains . . . shit, he's walking wounded."

"He's just starting to come around, I've been working out with him. He can be a great one, you know that." Pat didn't bother to add that it would damn near kill Jax to lose his scholarship. "Barry, this kid is as good a shooting guard as there is. You don't throw away talent like his—"

"He's gotta go. Damaged goods. I want his scholarship back, I found a kid in Louisiana—"

"Barry! Goddammit, you can't. Leave the talent to me and let DeFor Clark blow sunshine up your ass."

"Real funny, Pat. I've decided, Morrow's history. I want his scholarship."

"Don't *do* this."

"I'm not. You are."

"Fuck you." Pat swiped the playbooks, magazines, letters, loose papers and game plans off Sand's desk. "I'll quit before I'll do that. He goes, I go."

Pat turned and left the office, slamming the door behind him.

Jax Morrow glanced up at Pat as he stormed out and quickly guessed what was waiting for him.

"Don't let that asshole do it to you, Jax," Pat said. "If he does I'm getting the fuck out of here."

Jax watched Pat leave the basketball offices,

then got up slowly as Barry Sand called him into his office to give up what he would kill to keep.

Pat was well on his way to getting loaded when his ex-wife Sara came storming through the front door. She already knew that he had threatened to quit his job over Jax Morrow.

Barry, of course, had told her.

"You *can't* quit."

Pat poured himself another drink. "Tell you what, Sara. You stop fucking the coach, maybe I'll reconsider."

"Very funny . . . get serious, Pat. We've got Ray in college right here at SWS, and Jennie has been accepted at Yale. Where's the money going to come from?"

"Don't you worry about the money. I'll get the money." He had no good idea where but just now the alcohol and wishful thinking were putting up a good argument.

"Well, just don't expect my father to support us. It's your responsibility. The divorce decree was very specific. Where are you going to go? We're in a recession around here, if you hadn't noticed."

"I noticed that your father and his buddies caused the goddamn recession. What's he gonna do this time? Move all his plants to China?"

Pat was talking about Sara's father's computer business, a company that built relatively inexpensive clones of IBM personal computers in

Peter Gent

Mexico. He was a close friend and confidant of George Bush and had helped finance the Contras in Nicaragua and political attacks on Bill Clinton and Al Gore.

Sara was surprised. "Who told you that? They're just talking. It's world market now." Sara was suddenly defensive. "He has to compete by going where labor costs are lowest—"

"And union organizers are taken out back and shot. What's he taking to the party? Top secret technology and his pipeline to the Pentagon?"

"Don't you *dare* accuse my father of being a traitor—"

"He'll do 'til the real thing comes along."

"You bastard!"

"Fuck you *and* your close intimate personal friend Barry Sand. Hell, he might just as well have raped that Sullivan girl himself."

"Barry didn't do anything. I believe it was you who threatened Small with rape charges if he talked to the NBA. If there's an investigation you'll be the one they dip in shit and deep fry."

"Why, darling, you seem to know so much about Barry's future damage-control strategy, and you express it so well. Where have you been all afternoon, looking at the ceiling in his office and shining his leather couch with your back?"

"Fuck you."

"It wasn't me. You must have had your eyes closed."

The Conquering Heroes

"I don't need eyes to recognize your limp dick!"

"Genital slander? I guess we're down and dirty now. Fit for a schoolyard brawl." Pat took another swig of vodka. "What should I say? Lemme see . . . I got it . . . ready? You got a cunt the size of a number-two washtub." He smiled drunkenly at her. "How was that?"

Sara smashed a porcelain lamp across his forehead.

Pat fell back into his easy chair, seeing stars.

"Come on, daddy." Jennie was smiling brightly. "You can swallow your pride."

Jennie had come to see him every day, trying to get him to improve relations with her mother. She knew nothing, or at least believed nothing, about her mother's carryings-on with Barry Sand.

Sara and Pat's fight over Pat's threat to quit if Barry tried to drop Jax Morrow from the scholarship program had made things really ugly. Bad words, thrown table lamp . . . "Call her and apologize, I bet she'll forgive you," Jennie said.

"It's a little more complicated than that, honey." Pat touched the scab on his forehead where the lamp had impacted. "This was a long time coming. There are a lot of scars besides this one on my head. As for my pride, honey, it would fit in a thimble these days."

285

"But don't you see, daddy, that's just it. You two have too much you've shared to throw it away over an argument."

"This was more than just an argument, sweetheart. There are . . . a lot of things you just don't know about."

"I don't *want* to know the gory details." Jennie had tears in her eyes. "I just want to see you two together again."

Her father shook his head. "Jennie, when you live as long as your mother and I you make so many mistakes you can't even remember them all. I could apologize for a solid year and still not cover all the things I've done wrong. As for your mother—" He cut himself off.

"You could try."

Pat walked over and sat on the couch next to his daughter. He hugged her to him with his heavy arms. He kissed her forehead. "We aren't just fighting with each other. We're fighting with ourselves too."

Jennie shook her head violently. "I don't *care* . . . At least promise me you'll think about it." She hugged him and stood up.

"I'll do that, honey. Your mother and I may not be much but we sure lucked out with you."

Jennie waved off the compliment, her face serious. "Daddy, did Chuck Small really rape that Sullivan girl?"

The question caught Pat totally by surprise.

"Who told you about that? Your mom? Barry Sand?"

"I'm not stupid, dad. I hear things. Anyway, I heard the girl was just trying to make trouble for Coach Sand—"

"Jesus. Now I know where you heard it. Cathy Sullivan may well cause trouble for Barry, but *not* because she wants to. Small did rape her, Jennie, and now they're trying to blame her. Blame the victim."

"I heard the girl has been spending the night here . . ."

Pat frowned and shook his head. "She stayed here *one* night because she was afraid to stay by herself."

"Mom . . . I mean people . . . say that you're sleeping with her."

"What do you think, Jennie?"

"I think that you're my dad, and maybe the only man here with the nerve to stand up for her."

"I'm not the only one," Pat said. "If there were two more that would make an even four who give a damn."

"Well, I'm proud of you, dad. I gotta go." She rolled up on her tiptoes and Pat leaned down. She kissed his cheek. "You need a shave."

As soon as she was out of sight his heart sank like the *Bismarck*. He closed the door and the room was suddenly halved in size. The walls began their relentless moves in on him.

He poured himself a drink and turned on the television.

He would drink and let the images wash over him until the pain in his chest went away or he passed out, whichever came first.

Oblivion came first, along with dreams of better, different days . . . days when he and Barry and Geena, now Barry's wife, were different people, or seemed to be.

Friends

1960

It was a cold, clear early-spring day. Pat Lee and Barry Sand were at the end of the South Pier, sitting below the Harbor City lighthouse, studying the fish-kill that had to be miles square.

Across the channel and the breakwater the North Beach that fronted the old-style resorts was literally heaped with fish. The high northwest winds of the two previous nights had piled them in layers covering the white sand thirty yards back from the water line and out of sight to the north. The surface of the water was still covered as far as the eye could see. They kept rolling in.

"Can't imagine why people don't want to spend

a lot of money to vacation here."

Barry sipped on a quart of beer in a brown paper bag. "The government people say it's some kind of temperature inversion, whatever that is."

Pat stared at the fish that were jammed up against the breakwater and sluicing into the channel against the current of the Birch River, creating a jam that continued on south around and down the south pier. There were so many seagulls around that for the rest of his life Pat would think of death when he heard seagulls crying.

"Rats with wings," Barry said, taking another pull on his quart of beer.

"A temperature inversion, huh?" Pat said.

"That's what they said. It's the fifth big kill around here this year."

"What it couldn't be, of course, is all the fucking sewage every son of a bitch feels like dumping in the lake and the rivers."

"Well, it don't make shit to me." Barry took another swallow.

"That's what you're drinking, if that beer was brewed in Milwaukee."

Sand pulled the brown quart bottle out of the bag and squinted at the label. "Milwaukee," he announced. "Hey, what the fuck are we doing out here?"

"I'm not sure, it was your idea . . ."

Barry took another long drink. "Well, old buddy,

fact is, I wanted to thank you for setting me up at Southwestern. I got a letter from Frank Wolfe. I'm going to be his student assistant. I get tuition, fees, books, our apartment is paid for by some big alum named Watts, I get to eat at the basketball training table, plus I get five hundred a month!"

"That's better than my scholarship."

"Yeah, and since I'm not a player it's all legal. If my arm heals up and I can play, they'll cut me a new deal. We're in hog heaven and it's all on account of you."

"Well, I'm glad I could help," Pat said.

"You really did. And just remember, I owe you. I won't forget it."

Barry stared out at the water, his expression unaccustomedly solemn. He turned and looked at Pat.

"What?" Pat said.

Barry turned back to the water.

"Pat, I really like you and Geena, you know?" He took another long drink.

"Yeah, I know . . ."

"Geena tell you that we went out together?"

"No . . . but you two have been dancing around me like mice on a stove since March."

"Yeah . . . well, it was the night after the state championship game . . . it was my fault, I got drunk. I was feeling really sorry for myself because I got hurt and missed the championships."

291

Pat stared silently out at the blue gray lake. A giant ore-carrier was sliding along the horizon taking tons of rock to be smelted and made into pigs somewhere along the southern shore around Gary, Indiana. He'd been half-expecting this.

"She told me it was a big mistake and not to get any ideas about her." He finished his beer and pulled another quart from his coat pocket. "Hey, she told me she loves *you*."

"Just don't tell me *when* she told you that."

Pat watched the ore-carrier until it was out of sight. Down on the beach the gulls were feasting.

"Are you gonna tell her I told you?"

"Are you?"

"No."

"It's your secret, you guys deal with it."

"We still friends?"

"Geena and you is between Geena and you." What was he saying? He should have been screaming. But how could he? He'd been so damn proper when Geena came on with him . . . what right . . . ? He stuffed down his anger, got to his feet and helped Barry get himself upright.

The lake swells were getting bigger. The wind was up and frayed clouds began skating across the blue sky from the west. Behind them the sky looked threatening.

"It looks like Chicago's getting some rain," Pat said. "Let's get on home."

The Conquering Heroes

"We think you should stay awhile." The voice came from behind.

Two of the five Mazurski brothers were standing between Pat and Barry and the only way to the beach that didn't include swimming in freezing cold water and dead fish.

Joe Mazurski had a five-foot two-by-four and began stalking Pat to his right. Sam had a club-sized piece of driftwood and began moving to his left, looking for an open shot at Barry.

Suddenly Barry faked a charge at Sam and then cut between Pat and Joe, shoving Joe right off the side of the pier.

"Holy shit," Sam yelled, dropping his club and running to the spot where his brother disappeared off the pier. "He can't swim!"

Barry and Pat watched him, then walked up behind Sam and looked. And there was Joe, red-faced, lying flat out on top of a giant raft of dead fish.

Pat walked over to the catwalk where the donut life preservers were hanging. Two of them were snugged by long lifelines to the catwalk legs. Pat came back and tossed one to Joe.

Sam turned to Pat. "You two fucks were lucky this time . . ." He saw the second life preserver in Pat's hand, just as he felt Pat's other hand push him face first into the lake of dead fish. Pat dropped the other donut on Sam.

As they drove off the South Beach, Pat stopped

at the coast-guard station and pointed out the Mazurski boys.

"I'd like to let 'em drown," the seaman said.

A sentiment Pat and Barry shared.

Geena refused to talk to Pat in the hall after chem lab. She looked through him, eyes red and swollen. She turned and walked away without a word.

When he first tried to talk to her he had reached out to touch her and she had moved away so quickly the movement startled him. He didn't try to touch her again. During his last attempt at conversation Pat found himself standing out of reach.

Ron Waters walked up to Pat as Geena hurried away down the hall. They both watched her go.

"So?" Ron asked. "How'd it go this time?"

"You talking about Geena?" Steve Lee said as he walked up. "Barb says she cries a lot. Old man Keats is still hot on moving to Mexico. He's looking around for an assembly plant in some place called Nuevo Laredo. Geena ain't too happy about it."

The phone was ringing as Pat walked in the front door from school. The house was empty.

"Yeah?"

"Pat? This is Geena . . . Do you have time to take a ride? I'll pick you up in ten minutes." Click.

The Conquering Heroes

*   *   *

He was waiting on the porch steps when she drove up. Before she could change her mind he went quickly to the car and slid into the passenger seat.

She drove without speaking to the bluffs above Lake Michigan north of the Mado-lynn resort outside Harbor City. She stopped the Chevy a little too close to the edge of the bluffs for comfort, and Pat was reminded of the legends about a bootleggers' tunnel somewhere below the bluffs.

A freighter was cruising along the horizon taking tons of newsprint to Chicago from the paper mills along the Kalamazoo River. All the polychlorinated biphenyls from the mill waste, Pat had heard, were dumped into the river and drained into the lake. He watched the freighter until it was out of sight. Down on the beach the gulls were still feasting.

"So, Barry told you?" Geena looked out at the water.

"Yeah." Pat remembered his buddy Barry had told him he wasn't going to tell her that he'd told him. He kept his eyes on the ship. "I'm not mad, I'm . . ."

Geena started crying.

"Pat . . . I know this sounds crazy, but, well, I'm in love with Barry. We're going to get married right after we graduate from college. He's what

I want, he's, well, he's sort of like me . . . we're good together . . ."

Two months ago she was trying to get him into bed. Now she was in love with Barry and they had made wedding plans. Where the hell had he been? Winning the state championship, but it didn't seem enough of an answer. You were supposed to be *rewarded* for victory.

"Well, ah, congratulations to both of you."

"Pat, I *knew* you'd understand, I told Barry you would. God, you're one in a million . . ."

"Right, and I got a million things to do." Like what? he asked himself.

After graduation the Keatses closed up their house, put a FOR SALE sign in the front and moved to Dallas. David Keats was going to build coil and die-cast plants along the Texas-Mexican border to take advantage of the available cheap labor.

And David Keats's little girl Geena would become the coach's wife.

The Coach's Party

The Barry Sands were hosting their weekly party for Southwestern State University's assistant basketball coaches. The night was spent talking basketball, getting drunk and kissing ass, mostly Barry's.

Pat was making talk with Geena about the problems of their old hometown of Wood during the eighties and nineties.

"I'll tell you what *is* terrible," Geena said. "How ungrateful all your old friends in Wood are, suing my dad for supposedly polluting the Millpond and the Birch River."

"You grew up there, too, Geena."

She ignored that. "After all the jobs and money he brought to that town . . ."

"And took away," Pat said. "Not to mention

dumping mercury into the river. Even in Texas poisoning a well is a hanging offense."

Geena wondered why Barry had ever hired Pat. She couldn't stand him anymore. The righteous son of a bitch. She wanted him gone. But Barry said he needed him. Well, damn it, she didn't.

Lately she'd noticed she was gaining weight and she hated it. And she knew, of course, that Barry was cheating on her. It didn't occur to her that that was how they'd gotten together in the first place, only that time they'd done it together . . . cheating on Pat.

"You'll love this one, Pat," Barry said abruptly, stepping between Pat and Geena. "It's a world-class recruiting story."

Geena stared at her husband for a long moment, then walked into the other room to talk to the other wives about what assholes their husbands were. They had to agree with her; it was a perk of being the head coach's wife.

"That's my wife," Barry said as he glanced over his shoulder while she disappeared.

And welcome to her, Pat thought. "So what's the big story?"

"I heard it from an NCAA enforcement guy in Kansas City last year. It happened in New York. You remember that big kid that was playing AAU ball about six years ago. He was over seven foot and had all the scouts drooling at the Nike Tournament in Vegas."

The Conquering Heroes

Pat nodded. "He was a Muslim kid, got killed in a drug deal."

"That's the one. It seems like right after the Vegas tourney every school in the country was after him."

"Except us," Pat pointed out.

"Yeah, right, you didn't want to go after him."

"You and I and Sam Watts went round and round about it."

"That's right! Why didn't you go after him?"

"He had a street agent, I already told you."

"So why won't you deal with street agents?"

"Just tell the story, Barry."

"Oh, yeah, the story. It's amazing, it never made the papers but this NCAA guy swears it's true. So the street agent is fielding all these offers. The kid is buried in college sweatsuits, T-shirts, shoes, hats, and the mail is pouring in. The kid can't say no to anybody and the street agent, ah . . . you know that little guy that used to hang around Madison Square Garden and hustle for Syracuse . . ." Barry frowned and started snapping his fingers.

Pat let him suffer a little longer, then said, "Al Davis."

"Right. The same name as the Raiders guy. Anyway, this Davis starts to take money from other street agents who claim to be representing schools. Now, Davis can't say no either and the money and goodies are pouring in. Pretty soon

Davis is driving a Cadillac and the kid has a BMW, one of the cheaper models. Now, a lot of time has passed and a lot of money and merchandise has changed hands. This kid could have opened up a store."

"Suddenly the money men want commitments," Pat said.

"You got it. So Davis starts telling the kid that they've got to start making decisions. They can't keep leading on all these people. It's all right to take a little bit from a lot of people, but they've taken a lot from a lot and some of these people want answers."

"I take it that some of these people are serious men," Pat said.

"Some of them are major Wise Guys." Barry nodded. "Some are thugs and most are street hustlers hoping to ride this kid to the big time. So Davis keeps telling the kid that they've *got* to make a decision. But the kid is living like a Colombian drug lord. He don't want to just say no. The way the kid sees it, he earned this stuff, he didn't ask for it. These people just started sending it to him, starting with shoes and sweatshirts and ending with Fed Ex overnight letters stuffed with cash. If there's a problem, it's up to Davis to deal with it."

"So," Pat picked it up, "Davis tells everybody that the kid has narrowed his selection list down to, what, five schools?"

The Conquering Heroes

"Eight."

"Davis doesn't want to cut off the cash flow cold turkey," Pat said.

"Right. A couple Wise Guys get cut out and are pissed off, but Davis pays them off with money from the schools still in the running. Now he has to shorten the list some more. So he cuts it to three schools, all fronted by Wise Guys with plenty of money."

"The most money, would be my guess," Pat said.

"Probably." Barry narrowed his eyes. "Hey, you already heard this story?"

"No, not about your kid, but it sounds familiar."

"Well, you're not gonna believe how it ends. The three schools are really pouring it on. Money, tickets to Knicks games and the Giants, trips to Vegas."

"And along comes signing day," Pat said.

Barry nodded his head slowly. "The three schools sit and wait to hear which one he's chosen. They've accepted that only one of them can win, they buried this kid in money and favors with a one-in-three chance of winning but it's okay, that was the deal. What do you think happened?"

"The kid signed with a fourth school. One that Davis didn't even know he was considering."

"You already heard the story."

"No, I told you I hadn't, but now you know

why I won't deal with street agents. Your kid was no different than any eighteen-year-old. He'd tell whoever was with him at the moment what they wanted to hear. The fourth school was there at the right moment."

"If you're so goddamn smart, why didn't you do what the fourth school did?"

"Because of the part of the story you haven't told."

"You mean him getting killed over drugs?"

"No. What the guy from the NCAA told you."

"How do you know what the guy from the NCAA told me?"

"I don't, Barry, I'm waiting for you to finish the story."

"Well . . ." Barry eyed Pat suspiciously. "According to the NCAA, the kid wasn't killed over drugs. They had him whacked."

"The NCAA?" Pat said it with a straight face.

"Don't act stupid. One of the other street agents."

"Or all of them."

"No, that's crazy. The NCAA figures one of the agents was a poor loser."

"No," Pat said. "That's wrong; it was all of them."

"Why?"

"Because of what you already know. All three street agents and the schools they fronted had accepted the deal that only one of them could win and two of them were going to lose."

"Right. What's your point?"

"It wasn't the one sore loser," Pat said. "It was *three* very serious people sending a message."

"To the kid?"

"He was dead. You don't send messages to a dead kid. The dead kid was the message. If you're going to play the game with the big boys you better play by their rules, even if you're only an eighteen-year-old kid."

"I doubt—"

"Look"—Pat cut him off—"it wasn't that they lost the kid. It was that they lost the kid to a school that wasn't even in the game. They couldn't allow any more eighteen-year-olds to get away with changing the rules in the middle of the game."

"That's pretty farfetched," Barry said, "conspiring to kill a kid in order to keep winning."

"It wasn't about winning, it was about losing. They had accepted the deal that two of the schools would lose. Who won wasn't the point, who lost was. They couldn't allow all three schools to lose out on the kid. The deal was two losers, *not three*. Three losers could not be allowed."

"Come on, you don't know all that."

"No, but I'd bet on it. By the way, what happened to Davis?"

"The guy from the NCAA didn't say anything happened to Davis."

"That's because he's not around anymore, right?

He wasn't needed as a message. He just got whacked for fucking up. You ask around the gyms in New York. I'm betting they'll tell you Davis sleeps with the fishes."

"You really think so?"

"It's why I don't deal with street agents. They can't deliver and I don't want to be standing next to them when they don't."

"Jesus, it's hard to believe. Whacking a kid for signing the wrong letter of intent."

"But you do believe it."

"Well, the guy from the NCAA told me—"

"Horse shit. You don't believe NCAA enforcement about anything. Why would you believe this if it's so unbelievable?"

"Because—"

"It's not so fucking unbelievable."

"I sure hate telling stories to you."

"Well, old buddy, your wife's in the other room. Go convince her you're not fucking my ex-wife. See if she'll listen to *that* story."

The phone was ringing when Cathy walked into her dorm room.

"Hello." She was hoping it was her boyfriend Tim Brian calling. Finally.

"Your boyfriend gave me your number. So, do you fuck him too? He don't sound like he gets much. Said you got what you deserved."

"Yes, I probably did." Cathy slammed the

phone. She couldn't believe these people.

The phone rang again. "I'm just calling as a friend to tell you that if you make any trouble for a certain friend of mine I'm personally coming after you with a pair of pliers and I'm gonna rip your nipples off . . ."

Pat had just poured himself a drink when the doorbell rang.

He pulled the door open. Cathy Sullivan stood shivering on the porch. It was not a cold night.

"Can I come in?"

"Sure." Pat stepped back from the door. "Can I get you something to drink?"

"What are you drinking?"

"Vodka."

"Okay."

"You sure?"

Cathy nodded. Pat could see the bruises on her face. Her lip looked like it had cracked open again. Her eyes were red.

He poured the vodka and handed it to her.

She drank it down like water.

"Can I have another?" She held out her glass. Her voice was flat.

"How much have you had to drink already?"

"That was my first." She kept holding out the glass. "Another."

"Look, too much of this shit can kill you. I should know."

"I don't have that kind of luck." She looked at her empty glass. "Please."

"Okay, but don't you think we should talk about what's bothering you?" He poured a little more vodka into her glass.

"You know what's bothering me, everybody on campus knows."

"Well, maybe if we talk about it we can find some way to solve this—"

She drained her glass.

"What way, Mr. Lee? You got a way to unfuck me?"

"You got guts, Cathy," Pat said, taking her glass. "Guts can get you through damn near anything. Even this." Bullshit, of course.

"I don't care, right now I just want to get drunk. Do you have an extra bedroom?"

Pat nodded.

"Can I stay here tonight? I'm afraid to stay at the dorm."

"Sure."

"It's been so long since I slept." Cathy poured herself a third drink.

"Why don't you slow down a little?"

"Do you think I should just forget it and take the money?"

"What? Who's offering you money?" Pat figured he knew as he asked, seeing Sam Watts handing DeFor Clark the SOUTHWESTERN BASKETBALL DEPARTMENT envelope stuffed with cash.

"You know."

"You tell me."

"You know who," Cathy said, and swayed on her feet. "Where's that bedroom? I think I'll lay down . . ."

Pat led her back to the bedroom and she lay down. Pat covered her with a blanket.

"Don't tell anybody where I am. I don't want . . ." And she slipped into unconsciousness.

Several times during the night Pat walked to the bedroom and checked Cathy's pulse. It was strong. She *was* tough.

"Pat . . ." Jan was standing at the door of his office. "Barry wants you in his office. Sam Watts is there."

"What do they want?"

"They didn't say but they don't look too happy."

Pat walked into the office expecting the worst. He got it.

"Pat, what did you do after you left my house last night?" Barry was standing by his filing cabinet.

Sam Watts was sitting in Barry's chair behind his desk.

"What?"

"You heard him," Watts said. "What did you do last night?"

"I was at his house." Pat pointed at Barry. "Watching everybody take a turn kissing his ass."

"After that," Barry said, ignoring the remark. "After you left my house."

"I went home."

"And?"

"And nothing. I stayed home."

"Did you have any visitors?" Watts asked, looking down at his hands.

"None of your business."

"I'm afraid it is."

Pat turned to leave.

"You had a female student in your house all night."

"So?" Pat stopped and turned back.

"It was Cathy Sullivan," Barry said. "Wasn't it?"

"It's none of your fucking business."

"This is a girl who has falsely accused one of our top players of assault and rape." Sam Watts slammed his hand on the desk top. "This *is* our fucking business, mister. If you're conspiring with her against the university—"

"Hey! I'd be real careful about talking conspiracy around here. You guys are right on the edge of committing some major felonies."

"We haven't done anything," Barry said quickly.

"Barry? Dipshit?" Pat leaned forward and thumped himself on the chest with his index finger. "It's me, Pat, your old high-school buddy. I *know* what you've done."

"You might want to consider," Watts said, "that

your job is hanging in the balance."

"My job is about balance. I live on the high wire. So lay off that shit. What you need to decide is whether you want me on the inside pissing out or on the outside pissing in?"

"What do you think Jennie would say if she knew that Cathy Sullivan stayed all night with you?"

"I already know the answer to that. So knock off the threats."

"Maybe you ought to consider your son Ray," Watts put in. "His grades aren't all that good. It would take one phone call to the dean of students—"

"You guys are *unbelievable*." Pat just stared at Watts.

"It's you that's unbelievable." Watts met his gaze with his cold gray eyes. "Don't you think you ought to consider the welfare of your own children over this basketball groupie?"

"What did the girl want?" Barry asked, picking up the thread. "It's important to keep this thing contained."

"She just wanted to be left *alone*. And how do you know she was there? Are you having her watched? Or me?"

Sam Watts and Barry Sand said nothing.

"She told me that you've been offering her money."

"We've done no such thing," Barry said.

"Don't bullshit me, Barry. I saw DeFor Clark carry the envelopes full of cash out of here."

Watts looked up at Pat. "That's a lie. I've never given DeFor Clark any money."

"Christ, Sam"—Pat clenched his right fist—"you gave him money right in front of me the other day."

"Pat, what you see or don't see in these offices," Barry warned, "*stays* in these offices."

"Yeah. Right. Don't you see how out of control all this is getting?"

"Everything has been taken care of," Barry said, looking briefly at Sam Watts. "There's nothing to worry about. Chuck Small will announce his decision to finish his career at Southwestern any day."

"And," Pat shot back, "a piss ant can put a twelve-pound shot . . ."

One on One

The two of them had the whole field house floor to themselves.

Jax Morrow had the ball at the top of the key. Pat was defending. Jax took a long step toward Pat with his right leg, declaring his left foot as his pivot. He kept the ball low and extended in front of him, down by his right ankle and away from Pat's outstretched arm and upturned left hand.

If Jax got his right foot within twelve inches of Pat's left foot, he would just drop his left shoulder and drive to the basket. So Pat slid his left foot back and out to cut off the lane to the basket. Jax just rocked back to an upright position, holding the ball chest high.

Now Pat had to be careful how he reacted. If

he closed too fast to prevent the three-point shot, Jax would eye fake him up onto his toes and drive the armpit of whichever hand Pat put up to try to stop the shot. So Pat moved carefully up on Jax, keeping his stance wide and low, his arms spread with the palms up.

He was too slow.

Jax elevated quickly. The spring in his feet and calves was powerful and quick. He leaped at least three feet straight up and lofted the jump shot high over Pat's head. The ball rotated slowly, arching through the air and slashing through the net without touching the rim.

"Three points and game. Play again?" Jax trotted after the ball.

"I get to shoot first."

"Okay."

Pat took the ball and moved out just past the three-point line and bent to face Jax.

Jax lay back.

Pat drilled the three-point jump shot.

"You gotta play defense, buddy." Pat spun the ball in his hands.

"You gotta prove that wasn't a lucky shot before I risk giving you the drive."

Pat immediately put the ball up again. It dropped through the net with a loud snap.

Now Jax moved out on him and they went at each other hard. Pat rocked low toward Jax's right side, paused an instant to check Jax's foot position, then slipped by with a strong drive. As he put the ball up with his left hand, Jax sprang from behind and pinned the ball to the backboard.

"Son of a bitch!" Pat had been certain he had beaten him to the basket. "Nice block. Your legs have really come back."

"Just keep telling *that* to Barry." Jax palmed the ball and walked back to the top of the key, where he popped a three-pointer before Pat could get back on defense.

"Hey, you're supposed to check the ball to me."

"Learn to get back on defense, coach. Especially after somebody stuffs you like I did. Don't take anything for granted."

"Who told you that?"

"You did."

"I didn't think you were listening a lot of the time."

"Coach, I hang on your every word"—Jax dribbled the ball—"and I block most of your shots."

"In your dreams . . . Did Barry say anything to you about your scholarship the other day in his office?" Pat was crouched low, crowding Jax and handchecking him hard.

Jax started his dribble, moving the ball from hand to hand, behind his back and between his legs.

The ball-handling skill of the latest generation of players fascinated Pat. The ball seemed to be one with their thoughts.

"No," Jax said. "He seemed sort of shook up by the way you left." He twisted back and forth from side to side, all the time moving the ball around his body like a hula hoop. "He just asked me about Cathy, how she was doing and if I thought she was gonna file rape charges against Small. I told him I didn't know."

Jax took a hard step to his right, reversed his direction with a between-the-legs dribble and took Pat to the basket with his left hand, using the glass to make the shot.

Pat was two steps behind when the shot went up.

"Nice move." Pat grabbed the ball as it bounced off the floor. "Sand is talking like he wants your scholarship back. He tried to get me to talk you out of it. I told him to go fuck himself."

They were on the ride side of the key two steps behind the three-point line. Pat was defending. Jax just flicked up the shot with his wrist and dropped it from twenty-three feet.

"Christ! Give an old man a break. Nice shot."

"*Can* he take my scholarship?"

"He can try but I can't imagine even Barry Sand cutting a talent like you loose. He didn't mention your scholarship at all?"

"No." Jax trotted to the baseline and picked up the ball. "He just asked about Cathy. He acted real friendly."

"I'd like to think he's just fucking with me," Pat

said, "using you to keep me off-balance. He knows how much I like you, you're my real prize . . ."

Jax checked the ball to Pat. Pat flicked it back to him. This time Jax drove by him so fast that Pat was only half-turned when the slam dunk bounced off the floor.

"No," Pat said, "it's got to be . . ." He watched the ball bounce and thought about his meeting with Barry. "It's this mess with Small. He wants to drag me back into it and is using you as a lever. Fuck him, don't worry."

"That's real easy for you to say." Jax picked up the ball. "What I want to know is, if push comes to shove, do you think he'll try and take it?"

"I'll quit if he tries, I told him that," Pat said. "It would be a stupid move that would come back to haunt him."

"Fuck haunting *him*, it's haunting *me*." Jax slammed the ball to the floor, caught the hard rebound with his outsized hands. "Christ! Just because I got hurt . . . I'm playing good now. Did you tell him?"

Pat nodded. "I told him you were the best shooting guard in the country."

"He's got to give me a chance."

"That's what I told him, and Williams and Watts," Pat said. "I told them I'm gone if they fuck with you. I made it damn clear."

"I've got a three-five grade-point," Jax said.

"How can they take my scholarship?"

"They can't. The only thing they can do is try and get you to quit."

"I *need* that degree. It's why I came here. You promised they couldn't take my scholarship as long as I kept up my grades."

"I know, don't worry, it's all bullshit." Pat held out his hands for the ball. "He's up to something else and he's fucking with your head. Half this business is mind games, you know that. Just chill out."

Jax passed Pat the ball. "But if he's trying to fuck with me he'll fuck with me. They'll all fuck with me. They always have . . ."

"I told you, I threatened to quit. He'll back off," Pat said. "Now, about Chuck Small and the Sullivan girl . . ."

"Did she come to see you?"

"Yes. I told her I'd help. She's been getting obscene phone calls and people are harassing her on campus." Pat dribbled the ball but made no offensive effort. He just kept talking. "She was so scared the other night, she asked to stay at my house. Somebody found out and now Watts and Barry are giving me shit about it. But fuck 'em. I told her I'd help and I'll help."

"I told her to press charges," Jax said. "Christ! He raped her, that cokehead son of a bitch. I hope he gets life."

"Her so-called boyfriend didn't take the news very well. He's blaming *her*," Pat said. "What a dick!"

"You think it was about the rape? Or the fact that she got herself raped by a black guy?"

"Both." Pat changed the dribble from left to right, right to left. "This thing could destroy her."

Jax slipped the dribble away from Pat, then flipped the ball back to him. "You got any ideas what we can do for her?"

Pat held the ball against his hip. "I warned Sand and Watts about trying to cover it up. They're doing it to keep that asshole from the NBA, holding it over his head. The NBA can have him. I'll get your buddy Eddie Sanford." He hadn't answered the question, he realized as he bounced a pass to Jax.

"It's all gone nuts," Jax said. "Everybody's brain damaged from watching all the shoe commercials." He double-shuffled his feet and dribbled toward the basket. "Come on, old man. I'll school your ass one more time." He leaped into the air and slam-dunked the ball with two hands. The sound echoed around the empty field house.

They played one more game of Twenty-One, which Jax won easily.

As they were walking out several baseball players were opening the batting cages at the north end of the building.

The last sound Pat heard was the hum of the

pitching machine and the sharp clean crack of a bat on a baseball.

Clean. A nice word. A nice idea. Like his daughter Jennie . . .

Trying to recover from his workout with Jax Morrow, Pat was napping in his chair when his secretary Jan Dayton knocked on his front door. She was carrying videotapes of high-school players Pat was considering, mostly freshmen and sophomores.

"Come on in." He had fallen asleep thinking about his daughter.

The glow from the television was the only light in the living room. ESPN "SportsCenter" was on.

"Where've you been? I tried to call you for the last couple of days." Pat followed her into the dining room and watched her set the tapes with the others already stacked on the table.

"I was in Corpus, trying to remember if there was ever any magic in my marriage."

"Alone?"

"Alone." Jan turned on the lamp beside Pat's chair. "I made some decisions. And when I got back Don and I talked."

"I got a feeling I'm not going to like this."

"You knew it was coming before I did." She sat down on the couch and stared at the soundless television. Dick Vitale was gesticulating.

"I knew what was coming?"

The Conquering Heroes

"You rushing out of town to seduce some high-school basketball player," she said. "Then rushing back and fucking me to relax. It's like a pattern." Jan was twisting her wedding band.

"Do you really think what we've done has fouled up your marriage? I'd hate to think that . . ."

"No, no," Jan said. "You're a symptom, not a cause. Hey, I've loved my job, and I kind of love you. But it's time to change. This latest mess with Chuck Small has torn it for me."

"I think it's torn it for a lot of us," Pat said. "I don't know how much more of the bullshit I can take. No matter how much I tell myself that I owe it to the guys I recruit to try to help them hang in."

"So? How long are *you* going to hang in?"

Pat stood and walked to the front window. "I've at least got to see the Sullivan girl through it. I promised her I would. It'll mean going after Small."

"Is he gonna jump to the NBA?"

"When the shit finally comes down, he's going to jump straight up his own asshole. God, I feel old tonight."

"Too much time on the old recruiting trail. Pat, you have got to get out before it kills you."

"Hey, I thought you liked working for me."

"I changed my mind in Corpus. I can see what the job has done to you. I care about you, I don't want to see you die. It's sure no fun anymore."

Pat walked to the mantel and studied his Michigan High School State Championship medal that his mother had mounted and framed in a shadow box.

"When we won that I had fun and my biggest worry was the Bomb. Now I've got Brick Williams, Barry Sand, Sam Watts and all the good old boys in the Rebel Brigade."

"You left out yourself," Jan said. "You're sleeping with the enemy when you're in bed alone."

Pat laughed. "Don't quit on me, lady. I'm gonna really take the fight to them over the Sullivan girl."

"Well, I agree you *need* to fight this fight. I don't, but anyway I can support you better from outside the university."

They both turned to the television to relieve the tension that had built in the room. And staring back out at them was Medgar Evers High School coach O.K. Free.

Pat grabbed the remote and turned up the sound.

"Who's that?" Jan asked.

"O.K. Free, from Detroit."

"Jamail Jenks's coach?

"Bingo."

" . . . I've been handling all recruiting contacts to protect Jamail and make certain there are no NCAA violations," Free was saying.

"Amazing," Pat said. "I can't escape it . . .

basketball is floating through the air."

" . . . nobody was more honest and more concerned about Jamail's education and welfare than Pat Lee from Southwestern State . . ."

Free was cool, neatly dressed in a gray suit and button-down shirt and tie.

" . . . because of this we are happy to announce that out of the more than fifty schools pursuing Jamail he has reduced his choices to Southwestern State, UCLA and UNLV . . ."

Jan smiled and punched Pat on the shoulder.

"Well, I'll be dipped in shit and rolled in Cracker Jacks." Pat turned the sound down.

"Way to go, big man. Your stock just went up in the field house. What did you do in Detroit?"

Pat shook his head. "I don't remember. Maybe I blew the guy."

"Come on, really."

"I'm telling you the truth, I don't remember. I came to in Houston."

"Well, you did something right."

"Or, I did something very wrong."

"Don't be so picky," Jan said. "Congratulations."

"You're a little premature. UCLA and UNLV are still in it. And if I did blow 'em I ain't doing it again."

The phone rang. Pat jumped at the sound.

"Already, calls of congratulations, new job offers, big money." Jan laughed at him, picked up the phone and spoke into it.

"Pat Lee's residence."

Jan listened, then handed Pat the receiver.

"It's Doc Knight."

Pat took the phone and listened. His face was suddenly drained of color.

"I'll be right there."

"What's up?" Jan asked.

Pat's white face was her only answer.

Pat parked next to a campus police car in front of Owens Residence Hall, ran up the steps and through the lobby filled with crying students, officious-looking resident assistants, grim police.

He took the stairs to the second floor two at a time and into Cathy Sullivan's room.

Police and paramedics were milling around Dr. Knight, who was standing in the doorway to the bathroom. The doctor heard Pat come into the room and turned to face him.

Now Knight stepped out of the doorway, and Pat could see Cathy Sullivan, hanging by the neck in the shower stall, her face swollen and distorted.

Dr. Knight, Sgt. Jim Cash of the campus police, and a Dallas plainclothes detective were huddled in the middle of the room, speaking too low to be overheard.

Finally, Pat looked away from the dreadful sight in the bathroom. "What happened?"

"Suicide, obviously," Knight said, keeping his attention focused on Cash and the detective.

The Conquering Heroes

"Jesus Christ!" Pat stomped his foot and hit his leg with a clenched fist. "*Goddammit!* I knew this could happen, we should have—"

"Pat!" Knight stepped over to him and grabbed his arm. "Just calm down. This is not the place or the time to be placing blame."

Pat jerked his arm free. "Who found her?"

"Her roommate," Sgt. Jim Cash said, stepping away from the detective. "She'd been home for a few days and came back to find . . . I got the call in my car, I was the first one here." Cash seemed to avoid Pat's eyes as he told his story. "The paramedics came about two minutes later. They said she'd been dead awhile, there was nothing to do."

The plainclothes detective reread his notepad. He seemed blasé. Student suicides were not that unusual, apparently.

"For God's sake, why doesn't somebody cut her down?" Pat demanded.

"They were waiting for me, to declare her dead," Knight said. He seemed remarkably cool too, Pat thought.

"Well, *do* it, for Chrissakes!"

"Calm down," Knight said. "It's being done."

Pat watched while the paramedics cut down and bagged Cathy Sullivan's body, then wheeled it out of the bathroom onto a gurney. He kept watching until she was taken out of the room and down the hall.

While the detective and Sgt. Cash moved out into the hall Pat eased over to the bed and looked down at the nightstand. There on a notepad by the phone a message was scribbled.

"EIGHT P.M. DEFOR CLARK CALLED."

Pat quickly tore the note from the pad and put it in his shirt pocket.

"What are you doing?" Dr. Knight looked at Pat.

"Nothing. What time did she die?"

"According to the people Cash has talked to, sometime between eight and ten tonight." Knight studied Pat, careful not to challenge him but clearly annoyed by his question.

"Will there be an autopsy?"

"No, I shouldn't think so, Pat. It's finally time to put an end to this. What would be the point? It was a suicide. A sad and tragic thing, but there it is. Young people seem to be so vulnerable these days—"

"Vulnerable? Yeah, doc, Cathy Sullivan was *vulnerable* to rape, and you people won't be able to keep that quiet now."

Knight looked at Pat. "I respect your feelings, Pat. We all share them. But I'm afraid they just wheeled the alleged victim out of here."

"Jesus, *alleged* . . ."

Knight was searching his pocket for a pen. "It seems Mr. Small is going to get to the NBA, after all. Barry has lost his hold on Small."

The Conquering Heroes

Knight found the pen. "By the way, I suggest you get to Houston and secure the Sanford boy. Barry needs him even more now—"

"I can't *believe* you. Well, I guarantee you this isn't the end of it. You tell Barry and Watts I said so."

"I heard you've been threatening people, Pat. Not too healthy a thing to do for a fellow who lives in a glass house."

A paramedic returned just then with a clipboard on which Knight wrote with the pen he had gotten out of his pocket.

"You better have a shitload of stones, doc," Pat said.

"I sure as hell do, and I can't wait to start throwing."

Dr. Knight did not look up from the clipboard . . .

When Pat got home Jan was gone. No surprise. He opened a fifth of vodka and started drinking for black.

Soon the room started closing in on him.

After he finished the bottle he called a cab and rode to the airport, where he caught the last shuttle to Houston, falling asleep as soon as his head hit the back of the seat.

His dreams were filled with visions of the Mazurski brothers . . . Chuck Stanislawski . . . Dr. Knight . . . Chuck Small . . . Barry Sand . . . Cathy Sullivan . . .

*   *   *

Anne Sanford smiled pleasantly as Pat walked into the Derrick Lounge in Houston.

It was one-thirty in the morning.

"How about a triple Stoli on the rocks?"

"Getting a late start, are we, coach? Or just keeping a bad thing going good?"

"The latter."

"Where'd you start?"

"Dallas. I took the last shuttle out."

"And you can still remember everything that's happened to you since?"

"Unfortunately, yes . . . How's Eddie doing?"

"Fine. You in town to see him?"

She set the drink in front of Pat.

"Nope. I'm on the run from my sordid life in Dallas."

"When are we gonna see some new song-and-dance from you?"

"Soon, maybe not tomorrow. Anyway, Eddie knows all about SWS and unless you're interested in illegal inducements, which you're not, the whole scholarship procedure is pretty cut and dried."

"I took your advice and talked to Eddie. He likes you and Southwestern. He's pretty well decided."

"Whatever." Pat slugged down the rest of his drink and asked for another.

"You better slow up."

326

The Conquering Heroes

"I couldn't get drunk if I wanted to, and I want to."

Anne sat down. The bar was empty, as usual. "What's really bugging you?"

"Somebody I knew just killed herself."

"My God. Who?"

"A Southwestern student. A lovely girl, whole life in front of her, everything to live for."

"What happened to her?"

"Fucking lowlife happened to her and nobody was around to give her a hand. Including me."

"That's awful."

"Worse than that." Pat was tempted to tell her the whole story, but figured she didn't need all that laid on her.

"You can't take it personally. Nobody can be responsible for keeping another person alive—"

"They can be responsible if they help kill them."

"What do you mean?"

Pat finished his drink and again beat down the urge to tell the whole story of Chuck Small's rape of Cathy Sullivan and Barry Sand's attempts to use it to keep Small from the NBA.

"People mistreated her . . ."

"We all get mistreated, Pat. We don't all commit suicide."

"I know, right. But she got it all at once."

Anne touched his hand for a moment.

"Have a drink with me. I could use the company and some talk."

"One, then I'm closing up."

"Okay, good. Can I have another Stoli? I'll wait while you close up and walk you to your car."

"You don't have to do that."

"I'd like to. It's not like I've got any pressing engagements. Besides, making friends with Eddie Sanford's mother is the best thing that's happened to me in years."

Pat watched her while she closed up the bar and finished his drink as she walked over to his table with her blue cardigan sweater draped over her shoulder.

"Ready?" Anne Sanford was one attractive woman, no question. "I appreciate you walking me to my car. The north lot is poorly lit and this late at night it's kind of scary out there."

Anne Sanford was getting more attractive by the moment, and Pat wondered whether her attractiveness to him was genuine or somehow of a piece with the pressured panic of his emotional state. He was running, he realized, from the death of Cathy Sullivan. Was Anne just a port in the storm? Maybe . . . partly. Worse, was her attraction to him influenced by his need to land Eddie Sanford? Maybe . . . to hell with it . . . she *was* an attractive woman and she'd been damn nice to him. Don't look a gift horse, and so forth.

"Let's go." Anne stood over him.

As they rode down in the elevator, she said, "You know, actually I'm glad to see you. As aggravating as you can be, which is plenty, you at least seem like somebody who thinks and feels. Most people, especially the ones I meet, do neither. Believe me."

"Well, thanks . . . I guess. Mostly, though, I screw up in both departments."

"Well, as Joe E. Brown said, nobody's perfect." They both laughed at the line from the movie *Some Like it Hot.*

The elevator doors slid open and Pat followed her out into the muggy Houston night, then walked beside her into the darkened parking lot. She handed him the car keys when they were halfway across the empty tarmac.

"There it is," she said, and pointed to her gray Volkswagen Rabbit.

Pat was stopped beside the car, bending over to unlock the door, when out of the darkness two thickset men appeared. Anne saw them first and tried to warn Pat but they were on him immediately.

"Hey . . ." Pat felt a pair of heavy arms grab him and pin his arms behind his back. He tried to break free, but the man had a grip like a vise.

"This is a little warning not to go around threatening people." The taller of the two men stood in front of Pat.

Anne tried to force her way between Pat and the two men. The tall one set her aside. "Tell the lady to stay out."

"Anne . . ." Pat shook his head. "Just walk away."

"No—"

"*Please*, Anne. I'll be better off. The sooner they get started the sooner they'll finish."

"Better listen to him, lady," the tall one said. "I don't mind whacking a woman around if she gets in the way."

"He means it," Pat said. "These guys are serious people. Walk away . . ."

Anne backed away a few steps but didn't take her eyes off Pat—

The tall guy hit Pat with a quick flurry of blows to the stomach, chest, kidneys. The short man turned loose, and Pat fell face-first to the pavement. Both men then methodically worked their way up and down Pat's legs, kicking him in the thighs and shins.

"You're lucky. The boss told us not to break anything."

"Tell Mr. Watts I'm grateful."

They kicked Pat a couple more times.

"Don't act so smart. We don't know any Mr. Watts."

"Right," Pat growled. "And I never saw you two clowns standing around his limousine outside the field house."

The shorter, thicker man pulled Pat to his feet and slugged him twice more in the stomach. "You don't quit bein' the smart guy, I'll accidentally break you in half and start on the woman."

After he slammed Pat up against the Volkswagen, he and his partner walked off into the darkness as Pat slid down to the asphalt.

Shocked and terrified, Anne knelt next to him. "Are you all right?"

Pat winced. "Not really. Didn't you see those two guys just beat the piss outta me?"

"Oh, God, I'm sorry...*what* was that all about?"

"It's a long story." Pat groaned and tried to stand. "I shot off my mouth to the wrong people." He got to his knees, then fell back against the car. "I'm sorry you had to see this."

"You're apologizing?"

"It was stupid. I was upset over the girl's suicide."

"I don't understand."

"They think this'll keep me quiet about the Sullivan girl and Chuck Small."

"What are you talking about?"

"Nothing. I just made some people mad. It's a long story."

"I got time," Anne said. "We need to get you cleaned up. Can you make it back to your room? I'll clean you up and you can tell me the whole story."

Slowly Pat's swimming head came clear and he saw Anne and the parking lot and the towering hotel.

"Come on," Anne said, "let's get you back to your room. Do you think you're all right, should we go to a hospital?"

"No. I've had hangovers worse than this." He got to his feet. "You can tell Eddie how you saw me stand up for my principles."

"You didn't do a whole lot of standing."

"That's funny, I like that. Let's get out of here before your ex-husband shows up and pounds me for drill."

Anne took his arm and led him back to his hotel room and put an ice pack on the bruise where his face had hit the pavement.

Pat welcomed her tenderness, a nice side of her to go with the stand-up toughness he'd seen. He rested against the headboard and she sat beside him on the bed, took his shirt off and dabbed the welts on his ribs and back with the ice pack. They were silent for a long while as she tended to him. He leaned back and closed his eyes, enjoying the touch of her against his bare skin . . . He was aware of her free hand stroking the back of his neck, opened his eyes and turned toward her. As he did she pulled him to her and kissed him hard on the mouth.

Pat pulled her close and kissed her back.

"I've missed this," he said, after she pulled away.

"Kissing?"

"That too."

"What else?"

"Feeling close to somebody . . . sharing without holding back."

As soon as he said it he knew he wasn't being really straight with her.

"What's the matter?" She felt his body stiffen.

"I was lying."

"About what?"

"About sharing and not holding back. I've been holding back so long it's become part of my DNA code."

"Well . . ." She didn't move away but her voice took on an edge. "You better start decoding yourself or I'm outta here. And I can tell you that Eddie won't be far behind me. So?"

"Look, what I know right now is I don't want to lose you before I even know you. I'm scared and that's no lie. If I have any chance at something with you, I just don't want to blow it."

"You have a chance, we *both* have a chance," she said. "Take it easy, I'm not looking for Mr. Perfect. So what are you going to do?"

"Watch my ass, is the first step. As you noticed in the parking lot, there are people who will go to great lengths to make sure that their secrets are kept." He sat up suddenly. "Goddamn it, this girl killed herself last night. She was driven to it because some big shots in Dallas wanted to win some basketball games . . ."

"I said never mind being perfect. But it does

seem like it's up to you to set things right," Anne said. "If you don't expose whatever it is, you're part of it."

Pat sighed and shook his head. "I don't know . . ."

"You better, and pretty damn quick. You're fucking with my kid, Pat Lee."

He wanted to tell her everything, starting with the deal made over three decades ago to bring Barry Sand with him to SWS, through the betrayal of Terry Dixon and the creation of Plantation Basketball to the suicide of Cathy Sullivan.

"It's a long story," Pat finally said. "It started a long time ago. When I was young and JFK was president. It's got names in it like Vietnam, Greg Dunne, Brick Williams, Sam Watts, my brother Steve, Chuck Stanislawski, Ron Waters, the Frog . . ." He smiled briefly. "This may take a while."

"I've got all night," Anne said.

Anne stayed the night and listened to his story, much of it sounding like a confessional, a tale of the long and sometimes twisted road from Wood, Michigan, and the 1960 state championships to Southwestern State University, including the tragicomedy of recruiting and racial politics, finished off with the ghastly account of Chuck Small and Cathy Sullivan.

She saw how tangled he had become in the deceits and ambitions of other people, until he had trouble separating out his own thoughts and emotions. She saw how deeply he had loved his sport, how his passion had been turned against him to damage himself and others. And she saw how angered he was by the outrage that had resulted in the death of this Sullivan girl.

Afterward they made love slowly and carefully as the sun came up and he truly felt an intimacy, a closeness to her. The walls were falling away. He trusted her, and she seemed to trust and believe him. The feeling from that was exhilarating, liberating.

Enough so that he had to go back and make good on his promises. Not just to Anne, but to Cathy Sullivan, to Jax Morrow and Terry Dixon, all the way back to his brother Steve, Chuck Stanislawski and Ron Waters. Promises to the past and the future . . .

Anne left him sleeping at noon.

Steve lobbed the ball to him on the baseline. The center from West Lansing moved toward him. Pat kept the ball low, close to his left ankle, and rocked toward the big man's left side.

The West Lansing center crouched and spread his arms to stop the drive across the middle. Pat pulled back and lifted his head, eye-faking at the basket.

Rolling up on his toes, the center raised his left hand to block the shot.

It was all the room Pat needed.

Leading with a quick first step, Pat dropped his left shoulder, took a right-hand dribble under the upraised arm, slid past the center, drove the baseline and put in a reverse lay-up. The old armpit drive, and it worked like a charm.

Now they were all at the soda fountain of Sharpe's Drugstore in downtown Wood. All of them young, carefree. Pat and Steve, Ron Waters, Barry Sand, Larry "the Frog" Grant, Chuck Stanislawski . . . Something wasn't quite right. Chuck Stanislawski reached for his milkshake and his arm fell off. His chest exploded, there was a big bloody hole. Blood flowed from his nose, his eyes, his ears. The top of his head was peeled back.

Pat picked up Chuck's arm and tried to reattach it.

Mr. Sharpe had gotten out a box of Band-Aids.

Geena Keats and Rachael Golen walked in, screaming and crying.

Pat's ears began ringing from the sound of the screaming.

He dropped Chuck's arm and woke up in a cold sweat.

Pat took the shuttle back to Dallas the next afternoon feeling good about himself for the first time in a long time.

"Coach! Coach Lee!"

The Conquering Heroes

Pat stopped at the sound of his name being called inside the terminal and scanned the faces moving around him.

"Coach! Over here!"

It was that campus cop. Cash, Sgt. Jim Cash. He was waiting by the exit. He waved at Pat, glanced around, then walked up and stopped directly in Pat's path. He looked around again. "Coach? I've got to talk to you."

"Let me guess. Chuck Small pawned the basketball floor for an ounce of coke and a new nine millimeter."

Pat stepped around Cash and continued walking with a limp.

"Worse." Cash looked down at Pat's legs, then back at his face. "What happened to you?"

"I stepped on my dick. Why are you here?"

Cash turned a piece of paper over and over in his hand. He had read the words dozens of times. "I wish to God I'd never gotten involved in this mess. I've got to talk to somebody. You seemed to be the only one who cared anything about that girl. Coach Sand got me into this."

"And you think maybe I can get you out."

Cash handed the paper to Pat. "Read it."

Pat read, stepped back. "This is awful . . ." The hand holding the note fell to his side. He turned a cold-eyed gaze on Cash.

"Has anybody else seen this?"

Cash shook his head.

"Where the hell did it come from?"

"I was the first one there. It was pinned to her bathrobe. I just took it, I'm not sure why—"

"Yes, you are," Pat said. "After the rape, Barry sent you over to see her in the hospital and warn her to keep her mouth shut. Right?"

Cash slowly nodded. "I can't believe I did it, I should have helped her."

"We all should have helped her." Pat looked back at the note and read it again:

Dear Dad,

Please forgive me and try to understand. I can't stand the pressure of school anymore. Nobody here likes me. I am so terribly lonely. Please don't be sad. I am going to be with mother.

I love you.
CATHY

"This is typed," Pat said. "Even her name." He stared at Cash. "She never wrote this."

"I was afraid you'd think that, too. What are we going to do?"

"I want to know why this is typed and who typed it. Did you see a typewriter in her place?"

"No, but I didn't check out all the rooms. I did see fresh bruises on her arms and the back of her neck."

"Did Dr. Knight see them?"

The Conquering Heroes

"He told me to keep quiet."

"You are one chickenshit cop, you know that?"

"I know."

"She might have been *murdered*." Pat looked at the cop. "You know that, don't you?"

"Like I know she was raped."

"You were the original investigating officer on the rape charge, weren't you?"

Cash nodded.

"Is there any paperwork left?"

"No. They destroyed everything. Police and hospital records."

"How the hell do you live with yourself?"

"Maybe the same way you do, Mr. Lee. With great difficulty and large amounts of alcohol."

"I guess I deserved that. You got any suspects in mind?"

"You're the only one I was sure *wouldn't* kill her," Cash said. "I suspect everybody . . . from Sam Watts, Barry Sand and Chuck Small to the goddamn towel boy."

"What about the Dallas city detective who was there? Did he have any ideas?"

"Pettyman? He couldn't shove his thumb up his own ass. He just wrote what Dr. Knight told him."

"Did anybody see Small around the dorm?"

"The janitor said he saw a tall black guy coming out of the dorm around eight-thirty or nine. He didn't say it was Small. I should think he'd have recognized Small. Small being a big-shot sports celebrity."

"Maybe not." Pat thought a moment. "Do you know DeFor Clark? He's Sand's student assistant. He's black and about six-seven. He might have been in the area around eight."

"What makes you think that?"

"Later. I'm going back to the field house and look around. I'll get back to you."

Pat wheeled his car into the field house lot, parked and was getting out when a campus cop walked over.

"Sorry, coach, but you can't park there."

"What are you talking about? That's my space."

"I got my orders."

"From who?"

"Coach Sand. You don't work here anymore. It's on the front page of the morning paper. Mr. Williams fired you."

Pat walked into the coffee shop and found Cash waiting for him, reading the paper. Pat could read the headlines from across the room.

WATTS DEMANDS LEE'S HEAD, WILLIAMS CHOPS. SAND CITES POOR RECRUITING.

Pat sat down across from Cash and ordered coffee, acutely aware that every eye in the place was on him.

"Looks like they're already one jump ahead of us. A couple of guys warned me off last night in Houston."

"Knight probably went straight to Sam Watts after he left the girl's dorm room," Cash said. "You really got to him."

"Well, fucking excuse me. I didn't know we were talking about a murder. You could've said something earlier."

"You didn't give me much chance—"

"You were so forthcoming with everything else, like the rape and assault. Let's stop hassling each other and decide what to do now."

"Roust Chuck Small. See if we can rattle him."

"I'll do that, you go back over the girl's room." Pat dug down in his shirt pocket and pulled out the note he had picked off Cathy Sullivan's nightstand. "Look at this." He handed it to Cash. "I found it next to her phone."

" 'Eight P.M.' " Cash read aloud. " 'DeFor Clark called.' What do you think it means?"

"I think it means that DeFor Clark called her at eight that night, Sherlock. See what you can find out."

Pat knocked on the door to Chuck Small's apartment. Small jerked it open, looked at Pat and laughed long and loud.

"S'up coach. You looking for a handout?"

"Just wondered where you were last night?"

"Why? Your momma mad I didn't come fuck her?"

"Not too funny, considering the trouble your ass is in."

Small giggled and pounded the door. "The trouble *my* ass is in? I ain't the one just got fired. I just got me a real job."

A small dark-skinned man in an Armani suit stepped out from the apartment.

"Who's this guy, Chuckie babe?"

"*Chuckie?*" Pat echoed, and looked the man up and down. It was a short trip. "*Babe?*"

"Nickie"—Small pointed at Pat—"this needle dick motherfucker *use* to be a coach. Now he ain't shit."

"Well, don't waste any more time on him," Nickie said. "Piss off, pal."

Nickie babe started to shut the door. Pat kicked it back open.

"Who the fuck are you, you overdressed Billy Barty-looking jerk." Pat stepped into the doorway. "Chuckie here is a suspect in a rape and the victim has just been found dead," Pat said. "So I want some answers before I pull you out of that suit through the fly."

"Look, asshole, I'm Chuckie's agent and he was with me for the last two days *and* nights." The little man flushed red. "I just got him signed to a $12.5 million NBA contract. So take a fucking hike."

The Conquering Heroes

"Shuffle your has-been ass outta here." Small grinned. "That bitch hung herself and saved everybody a lot of trouble."

Suddenly Pat was taken over by a fury as he brought a punch from the floor, shoulder and legs pushing it, into Chuck Small's nose.

Small's head snapped back, blood flew, splattered the agent's thousand-dollar suit.

Slowly Small touched his nose and studied the blood on his fingers. He smiled, looked at Pat, and pasted him square on the jaw with his cement-block fist. Pat sailed backward and landed on his back on the sidewalk.

"Chill, coach." Small pointed at Pat, then slammed the door.

"Brilliant detective work," Pat groaned at himself. "Just fucking brilliant. You've definitely made a great new career move."

Sgt. Jim Cash cut through the CRIME SCENE— KEEP OUT tape and walked into Cathy Sullivan's dorm room. He searched the room, digging through her dresser drawers and clothes hamper. He walked into the bathroom and opened the medicine cabinet; a full bottle of sleeping capsules caught his attention. Back in the bedroom he noted the typewriter on Cathy's desk. Without the note, the police had had no reason to pay attention to the typewriter. He took the suicide note out of his pocket and laid it next to the typewriter.

He opened a drawer, took out a piece of stationery. It matched the suicide note paper. He rolled it into the typewriter and typed, then pulled the paper out of the typewriter and laid it alongside the suicide note. The typefaces matched.

When he reached down to close the desk drawer he saw part of an envelope, uncovered when he had reached in for the stationery. He dug down under the rest of the stationery, and pulled out a thick SOUTHWESTERN BASKETBALL DEPARTMENT envelope. Inside, wrapped in a piece of notepaper with FROM THE DESK OF SAM WATTS hand-printed across the top, was a bundle of hundred dollar bills.

"What do you mean, you can't find the recruiting files?" Barry erupted into the intercom phone. He listened, then threw a playbook against the wall. "Well, goddammit, DeFor, find 'em or I'll fire you too." He slammed down the receiver.

Suzie stuck her head through the door. "Did you call me?"

"No, I didn't call you. What the fuck is the matter around here? Can't anybody do their job?"

"You might check on the dipshit who's got his fat ass planted in your chair," Suzie said, then slammed the door.

Barry grabbed another playbook and threw it at the door as his phone rang.

"What?"

The Conquering Heroes

All he got back was silence.

"Who the hell is this?"

"*This* is O.K. Free, head basketball coach at Medgar Evers High School. Who the hell is this?"

Barry froze in his chair.

"I asked a question." O.K. Free's voice came through loud and clear. "Who in hell thinks they can talk to O.K. Free in that tone of voice?"

"Oh . . . hey, I'm sorry, Coach Free. Things have been kind of crazy around here and—"

"I asked who this was?" Free's voice was cold.

"Well . . . coach . . . this is Barry Sand. Sorry about the way I answered the phone but I've been getting crank calls all day—"

"Look, Sand, I don't give a shit about your calls. I want to talk to Pat Lee. Get him for me."

"Well, coach, Pat's not here just this minute. Is there something I can do for you?"

"No, you can't do nothin'. But if you want Jamail Jenks at Southwestern you better hook me up with Pat, and fast."

"Well, he's out for a while. I'm sure I can help you with anything Pat could do. After all, he works for me."

"I'd say that's his problem. I want to talk to Pat Lee. Are you deaf or something?"

"No, coach, it's just that Coach Lee's indisposed right now. I'm sure I can—"

"I'm sure you can't. Lee has an understanding with me, something you don't have. So unindispose his ass. Otherwise, Jamail Jenks is gonna be heading to UCLA this fall. You get my drift?"

"It's just that Pat's outta pocket today—"

"Well, you get him back in pocket by six o'clock tomorrow Detroit time if you want Jamail to be taking you to the Final Four. Understand?"

"You bet, coach. He'll be here."

"I'll call back then."

Christ! He'd needed Pat Lee all his life. Whatever made him think he could do without him now?

He had spent all day just looking for the damn recruiting files, and even if he found them he wouldn't know what to do with them.

Pat had been his best friend . . .

Goddamn Sara! She'd split them up. She'd cheated on Pat. Okay, he shouldn't have let her seduce him, but if it hadn't been him it would have been someone else. The bitch, she'd cheated on his buddy while he was off recruiting and building the SWS program. She *tried* to ruin their friendship. Well, from now on it would be a cold day in hell before he'd let a blow job get between him and his oldest best friend Pat Lee . . .

He stood and paced his office, nodding to himself, convincing himself, overlooking in his burst of renewed friendship for Pat that he'd stolen Geena Keats from Pat during their senior year in Wood, had used and betrayed him ever since.

The Conquering Heroes

He picked up the intercom phone. "Suzie! Find Pat Lee immediately and get him over here."

In the outer office Suzie held the phone away from her ear, wincing at the sound of his voice. She put the phone down and inspected her nails.

"Fat fucking chance."

Sgt. Jim Cash drove his patrol car around the industrial park six miles from the campus with Pat Lee in the passenger seat studying the SOUTHWESTERN BASKETBALL DEPARTMENT envelope, FROM THE DESK OF SAM WATTS, and the bundle of hundred dollar bills.

"I found a full bottle of sleeping pills in the bathroom," Cash was saying. "You'd think if she was gonna do herself in she'd have taken the pills."

"This looks exactly like one of the envelopes Sam Watts gave DeFor Clark," Pat said. "I saw him with at least two of them filled with money and wrapped in this kind of paper."

"Then DeFor Clark may have been in her room . . ."

Pat nodded.

"But," Cash said as he turned a corner, "if Watts sent him to buy her off and she took the money, why would Clark kill her?"

"I give up. And why type a phony suicide note?"

"Campus two-one, this is dispatch."

Cash snatched up the microphone. "Dispatch? This is two-one."

347

"The captain wants you to find Pat Lee. They want him over at the basketball office and he isn't answering his home phone."

"I thought he was fired," Cash said, looking at Pat. "Any idea where he is?"

"Drive by his house. If he isn't there check all the bars on the Drag. Or somewhere around the campus. Just *find* him."

"What's the big hurry?"

"Scuttlebutt is that the blue chips aren't gonna fall for Barry Sand unless Lee's back in the fold . . ."

Pat and Cash exchanged looks.

" . . . Apparently Lee went to Houston and wrapped up that seven-foot kid from Country Day. Now the kid's mother has heard about the firing and is threatening to send the kid to SMU. Ditto some kid's coach from Michigan. Just find Lee and get him to the basketball offices."

Cash signed off and looked at Pat. "You sign that Sanford kid?"

"It's news to me," Pat said, and it was. He'd just been hoping. "Let's play this out." Pat held up the money. "Meantime, why don't you hunt down DeFor Clark. Ask him about this and watch the shit run down his leg."

"Pat." Sam Watts was sitting at the head of the conference table in the AD's office. "It looks like we owe you an apology."

The Conquering Heroes

"You owe me more than that," Pat said, looking at Williams, who was cleaning his glasses, and at Barry Sand, who just looked red-faced.

"Don't worry, you'll get it," Watts said quickly. "You landed the two top blue chips in the nation. We're on the road back to the big dance—"

"Spare me the commercial."

Barry Sand chewed on his thumb.

"Pat, we're all agreed. A $25,000-a-year raise, the title of assistant head coach, a new car every year, a one-time bonus of $55,000 if you come back to work today . . ."

Watts's smile was a mile wide. Pat wanted to tell him to stuff it, that he intended to see them all in hell for what they had done. But he restrained himself, figuring it would be better to let them think they'd bought him, including his cooperation in their murderous conspiracy.

"I guess that'll do for now," he said, "and now, you'll excuse me, I got to catch a plane to Detroit."

He stood and walked to the door, stopped and turned back.

"Oh, Barry, by the way, fuck you very much."

Pat Lee and O.K. Free were sitting in a small bar near Medgar Evers High School cutting the final deal for Jamail Jenks.

"Have you discussed it with him?"

"Pat, my boys go and play where I tell them. I'm

the one with a college education." He signaled the waiter for another round. "If I let them in on the deal before it was closed they'd end up settling for a new pair of Reeboks and a used Datsun."

"Okay," Pat said, "but run the offer back by me so we know we're on the same page. It was a kind of long night and I'm a little hazy on the details."

"Hazy?" Free laughed. "That's a new name for it."

"So let's have it."

"Well, you refused to name a campus building after me but I got most everything else I wanted for Jamail."

"As long as it just costs money I don't give a shit. It's Sam Watts's money, and he owes all the Jamail Jenkses for a long time."

"A $250,000 signing bonus and $250,000 back-end money for staying four years," Free said, smiling.

"Okay."

"The $5,000 a month is fine," Free went on, "but I don't want you to get him a new car his first year. I know that boy. He needs a year of seasoning and growing up before he gets too mobile. Get him the car his second year. Put it in his mother's name and buy it from this dealer."

Free passed Pat a business card.

"Now, my end is $50,000 for services rendered."

The Conquering Heroes

Actually Pat didn't remember offering Free anything but the $15,000 to set up the first meeting with Jamail. "Okay," he said. "I just want your word that Jamail doesn't have a coke or heroin habit."

"He's a great kid." Free held up his left hand and covered his heart with his right. "I guarantee it."

"I'm making this deal with Sam Watts's money, and if you fuck him Watts will send two flat-nosed guys up here. Personally, I don't really care."

"Look, he's a ghetto kid," Free said, hedging. "He's got problems, sure, but he's a great talent. You got to work with him."

"I know." Pat nodded. "That's my specialty."

"Then you got yourself a deal, and thanks," Free said, and they shook on it.

"I know everybody in the business thinks I'm a greedy asshole," Free said. "But I look out for my kids. I got to get my kids off the streets and this is the only way."

"Who knows," Pat said, "maybe you're doing some good. Maybe we both are. I sure need to believe that right now."

"These kids couldn't survive without money. Do you think it's wrong?"

"It isn't wrong, it's against the rules."

"The rich man, the white man's rules, not mine."

"I hear you," Pat said. "The NCAA protects

the system and buries the player. Without the Recruiter's Code of Silence you and I would be picking shit with the chickens."

"Ain't that the truth. Hey, I'm glad you understand."

"I'm trying," Pat said. "I'm trying."

"Christ!" Sam Watts howled. "This guy don't want much!"

"I had Jamail for $100,000 at both ends and Free had settled for the $15 K we'd already paid." Pat looked at the other three men assembled in the AD's office. "But Free smelled blood when he talked to Barry on the phone. He was upset that I was leaving and our program was coming apart."

"So it's my fault?"

"That's what it sounds like, Barry," Brick Williams said.

"Thanks for the support, Brick. Don't hurt your back bending over to kiss his ass—"

"Barry," Sam Watts cut in, "you're missing the point. This isn't about personalities, it's about protecting and preserving the *program*. Since you lost Chuck Small we had to have Jamail Jenks *and* Eddie Sanford."

"You're blaming me for Small?"

"Well, Small did rape her," Watts said, "and he's your star that we're now going to lose."

"Jesus, it's my fault the girl killed herself?"

The Conquering Heroes

Nobody touched that one. It was clear, though, Pat thought, that right now Watts and Williams were piling on Barry and implying without saying it that his job could be on the line and Pat Lee could be his successor. Good . . . let them all think he'd go along with the program. *His* program was to bring them all down.

"How much is Sanford going to cost?" Barry finally asked.

"Fortunately, you didn't get a chance to fuck that up," Pat said.

"Well, what does he want?"

"The kid just wants a scholarship and the promise of my coaching. Recruiting isn't always deals and money."

"Well, now, that's better." Watts clapped his hands and rubbed them together. "If we amortize two players, it's a pretty fair deal—"

"You ain't amortizing dick," Pat broke in. "Don't even suggest that Sanford's getting money. He even gets a sniff that something like that goes on and he'll be gone. And so will I."

"They think I want the head coaching job under Watts and Williams," Pat was saying to Jim Cash under the bell tower, where they had met to update each other.

"Well," Cash said, "I guess that's good if they think you're one of them."

"That's the idea. Where to now?"

"I'm on my way back to Owens Hall to talk to the janitor," Cash said. "Remember, he saw a tall black guy coming out of the Sullivan girl's dorm around 9:00 P.M."

"Can he ID him now?"

"He says he thinks it was one of the boys he saw in the team picture in yesterday's paper. It was seeing the paper that reminded him. I'll try to get him to be more specific."

"Have you asked DeFor Clark about the envelope?"

"Not yet. I'll see what the janitor has to say first. I'm supposed to meet Clark back here tonight."

"Anything new about Small?"

"Yeah. His agent lied. I found people, hangers-on, who said they didn't meet until after midnight the night the Sullivan girl died. His alibi looks real shaky."

"Okay, I'll go after Small again . . ." As he said it, Pat touched the welt on his jaw where Small had landed his punch. "I'll meet you tonight at the tower after you talk to Clark."

"I should be there by ten. Be careful, coach."

Pat tracked down Chuck Small walking along the creek . . . a real nature lover . . . and pulled up alongside in his car and got out.

"What the hell do you want now?"

"Same thing, Chuck. The campus police have witnesses that say you didn't meet your agent

354

until after the Sullivan girl died."

Small glared at Pat. He was truly a frightening man.

"Prove it, motherfucker. I ain't some field nigger anymore. I got serious money and important people behind me."

"So you stick with the lie and hope your midget agent will risk a fall himself on a conspiracy charge? They won't let him wear his Armani suit in Huntsville." Pat stared at Small. "Of course, you may want to take him along as your bitch. I'm sure he'll dig that."

Small counterattacked. "If they had any real proof the cops would be here, not a wash-out like you."

"The cops are showing your picture to a witness right now. They'll be along."

"Fuck you. Fuck them." He turned and headed down the bank to the creek.

"You better practice walking on water, you sorry bastard," Pat called after him, " 'cause you're gonna have to miracle your ass out of this one."

Pat was back in his office when Jax Morrow stopped by. It was 6:00 P.M.

"Where you at, coach?" Jax stood in the doorway. His huge frame filled the opening.

"Trying to clean up the mess these assholes made of Cathy Sullivan."

"Right . . . I couldn't believe it when I heard.

She was a real nice kid." Jax shoved his hands into the pockets of his baggy pants. "Killed herself, huh?"

"No," Pat said, "somebody killed her, and I'm pretty sure I know who."

Jax's face went slack. "I thought it was suicide."

Pat leaned back in his chair and locked his hands behind his head. "It was murder, Jax. This is between us."

Jax moved into the room and closed the door. "You sure? I can't believe it."

"Believe it. I just finished rousting Small. He lied about where he was on the night she was killed."

"Small killed her?"

"We'll know soon enough. Jim Cash is over showing the team picture to the janitor at Owens Hall. The guy saw somebody leaving the dorm that night. He told Cash he thought he recognized him from the team picture."

"And you figure it's Small?"

"Him or that errand boy DeFor Clark."

"DeFor Clark?"

"Yeah, he's in the team picture and he looks like a player. I think Watts and Sand had Clark taking money to Cathy. They were trying to buy her silence. Cash found a basketball-department envelope full of cash buried in her desk. I saw Clark with cash-filled envelopes on two separate occasions . . ."

Jax just looked at him, seemingly stunned.

"And this wasn't your standard plain white envelope," Pat said. "Or the standard amount of cash."

"But if she took the money—"

"I know nothing makes much sense, but I'm working. I don't really think it's Clark, my pick is Small."

"When do you figure you'll know?"

"I'm meeting Cash at the bell tower around ten tonight. By then he'll have talked to the janitor and to Clark. After we nail one of them, Small or Clark, I'm gonna use him to fry Watts and Barry. This whole thing starts with them."

Jax shrugged, hesitated, then said, "Well, you know how it works, they'll walk away clean, nobody's gonna blame them—"

"I will."

"Sorry, but I don't think who you blame is gonna carry that much weight. Maybe you overestimate the value of recruiting Jamail or Eddie. You're not that powerful. Everybody'll walk, except Small. Not that I bleed for him . . ."

"Small's just signed for $12.5 million."

"That'll buy a lot of lawyers."

"Maybe not enough," Pat said.

Jax stared at the floor for a moment, then stood up. "Well, I better go."

"Did you want something?"

357

"Well, I wanted to talk about my scholarship," Jax said. "But I can see you got more important things to do."

"I told you, don't worry about your scholarship. When this thing blows I'll be the one passing out scholarships and cleaning house."

Jax smiled tightly, turned and left. He really seemed wired, Pat thought.

It was after 10:00 P.M. by the time Pat pulled up behind Jim Cash's squad car and got out. He could see Cash sitting in the driver's seat as he walked up beside the car, rapped on the window and looked in.

It was not a pretty sight.

The top of Cash's head was blown away. The inside of the car was splattered red, white and gray.

Pat opened the door and caught Cash's limp body. His holster was empty and his Smith and Wesson, model 19 .357 Magnum revolver, was gone. The Southwestern Basketball Department envelope slid off Cash's lap and onto the road. Pat pushed the body back in the car and picked up the envelope—

He caught a flash of movement out of the corner of his eye. Somebody up by the bell tower.

"Hey!" Pat yelled, realizing as he did so that it wasn't the smartest thing to do. A man took off, running.

The Conquering Heroes

* * *

DeFor Clark . . . trapped by the creek. Pat cut straight through the underbrush for the footbridge and was waiting by the time Clark got there. He stepped from the shadows and jammed Clark at the shoulder, knocking him down hard on his right arm and ribs.

"You sick sorry son of a bitch." Pat stood over him. "Where is it?"

Pat kicked him in the left shoulder.

"What? Where's what?" Clark tried to sit up and Pat kicked him down.

"The gun. I will kick the living shit out of you—"

"Stop. Jesus Christ, stop."

"Last call . . . sicko. Where's Cash's gun?"

"Don't you have it?"

"Cut the shit. What did you do, throw it away after you shot him?"

"*I didn't shoot him.* I just got there, for Christ sakes. I was late for our meeting and I saw you holding his body and all that blood. Hey, I thought you killed him—"

"Why would *I* kill him?"

"Why would *I*?"

Pat slapped Clark across the face with the Southwestern Basketball Department envelope filled with hundred dollar bills. "*This* is why." Pat held the envelope in front of Clark's face. "You knew Cash found it in the Sullivan girl's room."

"I don't know what that is, I never saw it before."

"Bullshit. I saw Sam Watts give you this envelope and money the other day at the office. You had another one in Barry's office. Both of them filled with money, just like this."

Clark looked at the envelope and back up at Pat. "That's not the same envelope."

"Try again. I *saw* the money. The Watts letterhead. Watts wanted you to pay off Cathy Sullivan with it. I found a note in her room with her name on it saying you called at eight the night she died. She was murdered between eight and ten."

"Murdered? I thought she killed herself." Clark's surprise actually seemed genuine.

"She was killed between eight and ten that night." Pat studied Clark's face. "You called her at eight."

"I called but I did not go to her room—"

"Bullshit! What happened? Did something go wrong after you gave her the money?"

"No! I called to see if she wanted to go for a ride that night. She wasn't there. Her roommate took the message."

"For a ride? Where the hell were you gonna go?"

Clark stalled, looked around.

"I can't tell you."

Pat slapped him across the mouth with the envelope.

360

"Then you'll tell the cops."

"Okay, okay . . . I met Cathy through Jax Morrow. I liked her. I heard what Small had done. I called to offer her a ride home to San Antonio. I thought she might want to get away from the campus and see her father. I knew she was being harassed something awful—"

"Why would you go to San Antonio?"

"I wasn't. I was going to Nuevo Laredo. I was going to drop her off at her father's house on the way. I was just trying to do her a favor—"

"Like giving her this money."

"That's not the money I had. I took that money to Nuevo Laredo for Mr. Watts."

"For Watts? Why?"

"He owns a *farmacia* down there. I go down there and . . . and buy steroids and growth hormone for the athletic department. You can check it out. It took me all night to go down there and back."

Pat looked hard at him. "Watts has you trafficking in steroids and HGH?"

"Yeah, for two years. I pick up Dexedrine and codeine too. They pay me extra for the risk."

"Jesus Christ! I don't fucking believe this."

"You're surprised? Watts and Sand told me it was you who handed the stuff out to the players."

"You believed *that?*" He shook his head. "Yeah, you probably did . . . you're so used to doing their

361

shit you'd swallow anything. How long has this been going on?"

"I've been making runs for two years. How do you think Chuck Small put on all that weight? He was only 220 when he came here . . . Jesus, you kicked the shit out me."

"Sorry. Fuck it, I quit. The bad guys win, the good guys lose. Leo Durocher was right."

Clark looked at Pat. "I don't believe you. Hey, I know what you think of me. And you're at least half-right. If it walks like a duck and quacks like a duck it's a duck. But that's not the whole story. Just because I work for guys like Watts and Barry doesn't mean I want to be like them. Things can change and I want to be part of the change. Hey, you're my fucking White Hope." He rubbed his left shoulder and winced. "I've watched blacks get fucked over around here for years. We've never gotten along but I knew you were the only guy who cared a rat's ass about black players. Any players."

"Then why did you give me so much shit?"

"I'm no hero, I admit. But how long do you think I'd have lasted if I had taken your side against Barry and Watts? You're always about to get your ass fired. These guys hate you. At least I could maybe be in a position to do you some good by being your enemy. As long as I acted like one of them you really had one enemy less."

Pat shook his head. "That's pretty complicated

for my weary brain right now." Pat got to his feet. "But I'll go along with it until something proves you're full of shit."

"So, what do we do now?"

"You wait with Cash's body. I'll call the campus police. Then I'm gonna drive over to the field house, pick up another team picture and go see a janitor about a murderer."

"You still think Small did it."

"I know he did it and I'm gonna burn him," Pat said.

"Then I'm gonna burn Sam Watts, Brick Williams and Barry Sand. They'll make a swell fire."

"Way to go, coach," Clark said, and seemed to mean it.

Pat turned on the light in his office, searched through his key ring and unlocked the large cabinet behind his desk, in which he found an eight by ten picture he had in the hidden recruiting files.

He turned out the lights, locked up and was walking through the dimly lit lobby of the field house when he heard the sound of breaking glass at the front entrance.

He moved across the tile floor to the top of the wide staircase and stood by the door to the office of the ticket-sales director.

A tall shadow moved at the foot of the stairs.

"Who's there?"

The boom of the gunshot and the splintering of the door-frame was simultaneous.

Pat stumbled back, tripped and fell.

The shot was wide of the mark.

A second shot made a hole in the ticket manager's door.

Pat lay silent on the floor. He heard footsteps climbing toward him. He scuttled across the lobby on all fours. He could hear the scuffing sound of shoes on stairs, climbing higher. The only light in the lobby came from the trophy and picture cases that covered all three walls, but Pat figured it was enough light to see and shoot by.

Before the shooter reached the lobby Pat knew he had to get into the hallway that emptied onto the staircase leading down onto the field-house arena.

The footsteps grew louder.

Pat clambered across the tiles, skinning hands and knees. Suddenly the trophy case above his head exploded in shattered glass. He kept scrambling, the broken glass shredding his skin, his hands and knees cut and bleeding.

The next shot blew air across the back of his neck and smashed into the National Championship Trophy case.

Pat dove into the hallway. Once in the darkness he was up and running toward the light that marked the exit down to the arena floor. He kept waiting for the next bullet. The hall seemed to stretch forever. The door wasn't getting any closer; it seemed to be moving farther away.

He kept waiting for the gunshot. He kept running and running, waiting and waiting. Was this how Cathy Sullivan felt as she tried to get away from Chuck Small the night he attacked her?

When he hit the bar lever to open the door he drove glass shards deeper into his hands and his fingers went numb. He stumbled down the blackness of the stairwell, making it about halfway to the first landing before misstepping and skidding forward. He caught his arm on the railing, half-falling and half-sliding the rest of the way. His shoulder slammed into the rail post, stopping his descent. He got his feet back under him and turned the corner on the landing, started down the last flight of stairs.

Above, the door slammed open.

At least now the shooter was hindered by the darkness as much as he was. He dismissed the idea of waiting on the stairs and ambushing the guy in the dark. Even unarmed Chuck Small was more than a match for Pat Lee. He had proof of that.

Holding tight to the banister, Pat made his way down the last flight of stairs, bursting through the door and falling face first onto the dirt floor of the arena.

A single light illuminated the basketball floor.

The lights in the press box glowed down on the west-side bleachers. The rest of the arena was in semidarkness. Pat took off running on the indoor track, hoping that no one had been practicing the hurdles.

He had reached the north end of the building, somewhere near the batting cages, when he heard the door bang open behind him. Crouching down with one hand waving in front of him, Pat worked his way off the track and felt his way toward the batting cages hidden somewhere in the blackness below the balcony.

His outstretched hand hit the heavy netting that lined the cage sides. Working his way along the net, hand over hand, he found the cage door.

If he could get to the far side of the cages and slide between them and the wall, the shooter would never find him. He pulled himself around the door and stepped into a rack of bats, spilling them onto the ground with an awful noise.

The footsteps started up the track toward him.

He grabbed a bat and slid into the first cage.

As he looked back he could see the tall shadow outlined against the faint light illuminating the floor and the press-box light flooding down on the west-side bleachers.

Backing into the cage, keeping his eyes on the slow-moving shadow of the shooter, Pat moved back further into the cage until he bumped into the pitching machine. His eyes were adjusting to the minimal light. He crouched behind the machine and watched as the shooter moved up the track, following the Tartan surface. The only sound was the scuffing of the man's shoes on the track.

With only the track to follow, the man might just walk right past the batting cages hidden in the darkness, Pat hoped. But just as he was about to follow the curve of the track away from Pat, the cage door slowly swung open.

Pat could see the tall shadow stop and turn toward him, toward the noise.

The shooter was still dimly backlit, and as he moved forward Pat kept shifting around the pitching machine to keep the man between him and the available light.

The man walked smack into the open cage door.

He knew Pat was inside and stepped carefully through the opening.

Pat gripped the bat tightly and kept moving around the machine to keep the man backlit.

There was nowhere to go.

The shooter stopped, apparently waiting for his eyes to adjust to the dark. And once that happened, Pat knew, he could start cutting off the cage like a boxer stalking the canvas, making sure his opponent had no avenue of escape.

Now the shooter was standing directly in front of the plate—Pat quickly turned on the pitching machine. The man fired at the click of the switch; sparks flew off the top of the machine.

Pat rolled away, the sound of his movement covered by the humming of the machine.

The man stood and fired at the humming sound until the hammer slammed down on an empty cartridge with a flat snap. Pat could see him fumbling with the gun, heard the cylinder release and the spent shells fall to the dirt. He had a speedloader he must have taken from Jim Cash and was refilling the chambers, too quickly for Pat to try and rush him with the bat. Anyway, Pat wasn't even sure he was capable of rushing anymore. Soon the man's eyes would adjust to the dark and he would see Pat crouched in the corner of the cage, trapped.

It was only a matter of time.

The man straightened up and squinted back into the darkness.

The hum of the machine increased in pitch. Suddenly it pulsated and Pat heard the metal arm whine and snap. There was a dull thud as the baseball hit the man in the chest and he staggered backward. The second ball hit him in the stomach and he slipped to his knees. The third ball hit him in the forehead and he flopped backward, arms flying up and the pistol sailing off into the dark.

Pat used the bat to push himself to his feet, moved over to the machine and switched it off.

The Conquering Heroes

By now his eyes were accustomed to the dark and he walked slowly up onto the prone form sprawled out just behind home plate. A splinter of light from the press box splattered across the man's head.

"Small, you son of a bitch . . ." Pat moved up to him. "You won't get out of this."

The man moaned and began to roll over.

"Come on, asshole, give me a reason to finish you." He lifted the bat above his head.

Pat looked closer—couldn't believe what he saw.

He was looking down not at Chuck Small. He was looking down at *Jax Morrow* . . .

"*Jax?* What the hell . . . ?"

Jax stared up at Pat, eyes empty, seeing but not seeing. He spoke in a barely audible whisper. "It was me . . ."

"What are you talking about? It wasn't you. Small raped her—"

"I didn't rape her . . ."

"I know you didn't—"

"I killed her."

"*What?*"

"I didn't mean to, it was an accident—"

"An *accident?* Jax, why, what the hell were you doing with her . . . ?"

Jax tried to prop himself up and fell back, still dizzy from the blow to the head. "Barry . . . he gave me money for Cathy, told me to go see her, knew I was a friend . . . oh, shit, you knew he was going to take my scholarship away, you knew what it meant to me, I figured I had to go along . . . he said if I got Cathy to keep quiet about Chuck he'd let me keep my scholarship."

Pat shook his head, not believing, not wanting to believe what he was hearing. He waited for more.

"She didn't want the money, I should have known she wouldn't . . . but I had to try, or I thought I did. I pushed it on her, put it in her desk drawer. She went crazy, accused me of going along with the rest of them. She said Small wasn't going to get away with it. And then she was all over me, hitting and scratching and I tried to stop her, calm her down, and . . . all of a sudden she was falling backwards. She hit her head on the edge of the desk . . ."

Pat was just staring at the man he had cared most about of all of them . . . "Jax, I told you I threatened to quit if they took your scholarship—"

"Big fucking deal. You quit, I'm still fucked if I don't do what they want. And do you know what they were going to do to her if she didn't keep quiet . . . ? Smear her all over the press, call her a whore who was hot for black guys and then yelled rape . . . Wasn't it better that she take some money and avoid that? . . . You never really understood why that scholarship means so much to me. It's not just me, it's my family, they've killed themselves for me all my life, sacrificed, I owe it, I owe. . . ." His voice trailed off; he was looking away from Pat as he talked.

"What about Cash?" Pat said. "Was that an accident too?"

"What? I didn't kill Cash. I found him dead when I got to the car. I don't know who did that, but I can guess and so can you. You said he was getting close to exposing those guys . . . I took his gun 'cause I was scared."

Pat could believe that. Watts and his people would do anything to keep what they had, to avoid being exposed . . .

"What about how they found her, Jax? She was found hanging by the neck, for God's sake."

Now Jax did look directly at him. "You think I'd do that? I'm out of my mind, I admit, but I'm no animal. She was lying on the floor when I ran out of there."

Barry? Sam Watts? Pat couldn't quite believe that even they would be able to stomach that. More likely somebody like Nickie Babe, Chuck Small's agent, who once he heard about Cathy's death would realize his million-dollar client was sure to be blamed, since alive Cathy was the biggest threat to Small and his future and all the money Nickie would make from it. Nickie had the friends with bent noses who could manage it . . .

"But what about his crazy shooting at me, Jax?

371

It's pure luck you didn't hit me."

Jax looked at him, almost smiled. "Figure I really didn't want to. But I've been out of my goddamn mind. I knew you were going to get an identification on me from that witness. I lost it, Pat. I just totally lost it . . ."

Pat looked down at him. "You did that, Jax. You sure as hell did lose it. You lost it all."

Texas attorney general Laude VanMeer was in bed when Pat called him at his home in West Lake Hills outside of Austin at midnight.

After his postings south of the border VanMeer had moved to D.C. and took a job working with Benjamin Pankin at the Justice Department. He returned to Texas when Nixon was elected and served as an assistant prosecutor under Henry Wade in Dallas. Winning the attorney general's job his first time out in statewide politics had been just what he needed, and he was already laying plans and building a network for a run for Congress.

Pat figured VanMeer was especially going to like this call, involving as it did his old nemesis Sam Watts, who had come out strongly against Laude when he announced for attorney general. Watts had spent half a million dollars of his own money supporting "any candidate whose dedication to the rule of law will not be twisted by his deviant sexual practices and gender orientation."

The Conquering Heroes

He was exploiting VanMeer's having come out of the closet.

"I know it's late, Laude," Pat said. "I wouldn't call if it wasn't important . . . How bad do you want to get Sam Watts?"

"I'd like to ram a gatepost up his ass. Why? What have you got?"

"Sam Watts," Pat said. "By the balls."

"Hold that thought."

Bread and Circuses

They were preparing to broadcast live from the Greg Dunne Memorial Field House. The satellite uplinks were in place. Part of the extravaganza was the signing of Jamail Jenks, but there would be more, much more.

When it became known that Pat Lee had prevailed on a major singing star to open the ceremonies with Southwestern's fight song and another celebrity to sing the national anthem, The Nashville Network decided to piggyback coverage on CNN.

When approving the plans for the construction of the Greg Dunne Memorial Field House, Athletic Director Dr. Brick Williams had insisted on a private luxury box. It was furnished with a bar, closed-circuit television, plush carpet, two large convertible sofa beds and twelve leather captain's chairs mounted on swivels. The box was built on two levels with the captain's chairs down in front for people who actually wanted to watch the basketball. Above and back were the bar, sofas and television. The suite was a place for gossip, political hacking, a place where deals were cut, where people were made and broken.

Pat leaned back now in one of the captain's chairs, sipped his Russian vodka and studied the Picasso that Dr. Williams had "borrowed" from the Samuel Watts Collection at the SWS Art Museum. Studying the abstract painting, Pat began to see Greg Dunne's liver. It was appropriate.

Sam Watts, Brick Williams and Barry Sand had agreed to pay half a million dollars to an eighteen-year-old kid who couldn't read at a junior high school level in return for his promise to exercise his basketball skills for Southwestern State University.

Sam Watts was not stupid. He was an astute international businessman who had partnered with people like the Emir of Kuwait, the Saudi oil sheiks, Ferdinand Marcos, the PRI of Mexico, PEMEX, BCCI. If Sam Watts thought it was a good investment to give $500,000 to a kid with a cocaine habit and a Browning nine-millimeter stuffed in his belt under his expensive bloused yellow leather jacket, so be it.

The crowd was filling the seats.

Chuck Small, NBA-bound, was going to be on the dais to greet Jamail and to give a thankful farewell to SWS.

It was still an hour until show time. Pat downed the vodka and made his way out of the AD's suite to the AD's private elevator.

It was going off like clockwork. The crowd was ecstatic. The stars had been terrific. Dr. Brick Williams gave a brief speech about the SWS basketball tradition.

Sam Watts had been introduced.

Brick Williams had been introduced.

Barry Sand had been introduced.

Chuck Small had been introduced.

Then Jamail Jenks was introduced.

Pat Lee walked from the tunnel straight to the dais and stepped up to the microphone.

"Folks, let's move right to the special film high-light." He pointed toward the two huge Diamond-vision replay screens as the lights went down and the recorded music came up.

"Tonight, as one era ends . . ." the dulcet tones of the video narrator boomed out into the arena, " . . . another begins. Tonight as we say goodbye to Chuck Small and wish him continued success let us one more time thrill to the many feats of this multitalented man . . ."

The Conquering Heroes

The screens were filled with exploding colors, then a long lens slow-motion shot showed Chuck Small swooping down the floor on a fast break, leaping for a high feed and slam dunking the ball.

The crowd roared.

The music blared.

Suddenly the screens went black. The music stopped. The crowd became restless.

Then the screens lit up again in black and white, except that now Pat Lee began to speak, describing the black and white still shots.

Crime-scene photographs that Pat had gotten from Jim Cash's widow and had transferred onto videotape. Sergeant Cash took the photos after he had removed the phony suicide note pinned to Cathy Sullivan's bathrobe.

The crowd gasped.

"But"—Pat's voice was almost shrill—"Chuck Small's accomplishments were not limited to the basketball floor. Neither were Barry Sand's, or Brick Williams's, or Sam Watts's . . ."

The huge screens displayed the body of Cathy Sullivan hanging by the neck.

"This, for instance, is what Chuck Small, Barry Sand and Sam Watts were able to do for a young Southwestern student who had the misfortune to get caught in the rain on her way to her humanities class . . . And because her desperate search for help and justice interfered with the plans of the basketball department, she died. It was *not* suicide . . ." Pat's voice echoed throughout Greg Dunne Memorial Field House.

There was total silence, as if everyone in the arena was holding their breath.

Barry Sand looked around, started to stand, to go after Lee, but Sam Watts put his hand on his arm.

"You stay right here," Watts said as he slipped off the dais.

People could be heard crying as Barry Sand watched the shadowy figures around him move off the dais. Brick Williams. Jamail Jenks. Chuck Small.

Pat walked from the microphone to the tunnel entrance, where Attorney General VanMeer waited with a brace of Texas Rangers, on hand to arrest Sam Watts, Chuck Small and Barry Sand.

It was VanMeer's idea to stage this elaborate bust, and Pat was willing to go along, realizing as he did that Laude's overwhelming interest was in generating support for his run for Congress. He would be "tough on crime" live and in color.

The lights came up now and Barry Sand found himself alone on the dais, facing a very hostile group of spectators, Attorney General VanMeer and several Texas Rangers.

Chuck Small had tried to sneak his seven-foot 270-pound frame out a side door, which had been anticipated. He was cuffed and wadded into a squad car.

The Conquering Heroes

Sam Watts had disappeared, and his lawyer had already materialized, talking about cutting a deal.

It had been quite a show.

It was a cold clear late-November day when Pat Lee walked from his parents' house to the blinking light and what remained of the two blocks of downtown Wood.

He was on his way to meet Ron Waters at Sharpe's Drugstore just as they had met so many times after high-school basketball games in the fifties and sixties.

Two years earlier Angelo had installed new pumps at the service station. Last year he had a stroke and medical bills had taken his savings. Now he was back at work, though with a crippled right side.

When Pat had worked for Angelo in the fifties he had seemed indestructible. Today, old and feeble, he tried with his one good hand to wash the windshield of an old '87 Buick. The oil company Angelo had partnered with for forty-five years was cutting his gas allotment and upping his rent. The company wanted the land for their new self-serve gas stations and convenience stores. The oil shortage they had been planning on for years was here to stay and the pieces were all in place. No more full-service operations. Ten skilled mechanics' jobs reduced to two minimum-wage cashiers.

A young Pat Lee was no longer needed to wash cars, change oil or pump gas.

Pat walked past the abandoned Wood Dairy, bought out by the larger Harbor City Dairy, which had closed it down. Twelve people lost their jobs. There was no more free home delivery. For a moment Pat thought he could hear the rattle of milk bottles as they ran down the line. But only for a moment.

The IGA grocery store, William's Hardware and the Smoke Shop had all been bought out and razed by the A-1 Supermarket chain, which had built a new combination supermarket, dry goods and liquor store. A-l sold at discount rates and drove Water's grocery store out of business. Now they could bump their prices back up to what they were charging at their fifteen other stores.

Gone was the Smoke Shop, along with the old men, the smell of tobacco and the ongoing card game. Gone was the blue-white haze of cigarette, cigar and pipe smoke. People weren't smoking anymore. Everybody was going to live forever.

Gold's Five and Ten, where Pat had whiled away much of his youth staring in wonder at all the stuff "Made in Japan" for less than a dollar, was still holding on, if barely.

In the vacant window of the Wood Men's Shop, mannequins lay in dusty disarray and disassembly. Heads, arms, legs, torsos were scattered about the floor. Across Main Street Don's Barber Shop and Dee's Beauty Shop were still open, but the liquor store had fallen victim to A-1's marketing strategy.

Red's Hobby Shop was closed. Hobbies had been replaced by interactive video, personal computers, high-definition television and liquid crystal display. The Wood Elevator and Fruit Exchange, next to the railroad tracks, was still open and in need of repair.

The train did not stop in Wood anymore.

The small farms had failed and the land was bought up by Chicago real-estate speculators. The big farms survived by dealing directly with Fred Thomas's Benton Harbor Juice and Canning. After forty years in the House, U.S. Representative Fred Thomas mostly set the price for produce in this part of Michigan. Yet the people continued to return him to Washington, where he continued to steal from them by chairing or controlling House committees and subcommittees on agricultural policy, price supports and farm export-import.

Jon of Jon's Ford dealership, the same Jon who had so pissed off Jim Lee and ruined Pat and Steve's teenage driving years, had done three years in jail for selling floor-planned cars and not repaying the bank. Now he was up north working in a Native American gambling casino; Jon turned out to be one-quarter Potawatamie.

Standing in front of the empty Water's Grocery

Store, Pat remembered the 1960 white Ford convertible with the blue interior that had been in the showroom window those last months of high school. It had listed for $2,199.

Keats Metal and Coil was closed. David Keats had finally moved all his manufacturing to Mexico rather than pay UAW wages and deal with the lawsuits for contaminating the Birch River and the town's water supply. The plant had dumped heavy metals and dioxin into the river and the ground for years. Keats took the money to Texas and left the garbage in Michigan. When he closed down the plant David Keats made a good profit, claiming the Wood plant as a loss and getting a capital write-down. Keats had dissolved his old corporation and reincorporated as Keats Defense Industries, Inc., a Delaware corporation with all its physical plants in Texas and Mexico.

The town of Pat Lee's youth was almost gone. What had not gone seemed to be going. It was an old story that Pat had tried to tell Rachael way back in the summer of 1960.

All the old Jewish resorts had been razed and replaced by condos during the building boom of the eighties. Waterfront property commanded a premium price, even if the water was said to be radioactive. In nearby Colins, the nuclear plant was in its twenty-fifth year of operation, although rated one of the ten most dangerous nuclear plants in the United States. The plant had been fined in the early eighties for having vented radioactive steam directly into the atmosphere every day for twelve years. Yet recently the Nuclear Regulatory Agency gave Midwest Utilities permission to store high-level nuclear waste on-site and above ground in containers less than one hundred yards from Lake Michigan. The containers began leaking.

When he returned from Vietnam Pat's buddy Ron Waters had gotten a construction job at the plant. He was not impressed by the quality of work. But Colins still had a great basketball team with a brand-new gym paid for by taxes on Midwest Utilities nuclear plant.

The short-term profits were good. The long-term costs were in terms of respiratory diseases, cancers, stillbirth and genetic damage.

"I was talking to my union steward, the other day," Ron said to Pat after they met at Sharpe's. "The original construction was so screwed up we'll have permanent jobs repairing the original work on the plant."

"I thought the plant was to be decommissioned after thirty years," Pat said.

"And do what? They ain't got a clue what to do with it. They have no plan, so they'll just keep on running it."

Ron had married Barb Coles after Pat's brother Steve had gone off to college. "We're like strangers," he said. "She never left Wood. I don't think I ever got back."

"You'll make it," Pat said. "You're a winner and a survivor. Nobody adjusted better than you. You made it back alive and in one piece. Chuck didn't do either."

"Sometimes I wonder," Ron said.

"We all do," Pat said. "Hey, I barely made it back and all I did was coach basketball and recruit and . . ." He didn't finish the sentence.

"Everything's changed."

Pat nodded. "This doesn't look much like the town we left," he said. "But it's here somewhere."

The interior of Sharpe's Drugstore had been remodeled. The soda fountain had been reduced from twelve to six stools, the booths were gone. Mr. Sharpe had died of cancer in 1970, one of the early victims of the epidemic that was finally traced to the heavy metals Keats Metal and Coil had dumped into the ground water.

The jukebox was still there.

Pat sat at the soda fountain while Ron walked back to the jukebox.

Pat looked back at Ron, leaning against the jukebox, smiling.

"Can you believe it?" Ron said, "the songs are still the same."

The Conquering Heroes

*   *   *

Later that day they rolled into Harbor City in Ron's red Pontiac convertible.

The North Beach and the Birch River were lined with condominiums. The water looked deceptively clean, the days of the big fish kills were past. The Michigan Department of Conservation began planting trout and salmon in Lake Michigan rivers in the sixties, and the game fish had survived in enough numbers to start a growing sport-fishing industry. It would thrive even if people eventually figured out that fish grown in toxic water became toxic fish. It just took them twenty years. Then all the Department of Natural Resources did was print a warning on all fishing licenses that the fish would kill you if you ate them.

Ron Waters drove down the alley where Melvin Purvis and his FBI agents hunting John Dillinger accidentally killed his grandfather. The same place where Pat and Steve beat the shit out of the five Mazurski brothers with a VW door and a Sears catalogue.

Tommy Mazurski had finally bullied the wrong guy and took four slugs from a .22 automatic in the head. The guy was doing life in Jackson. Tommy was doing eternity in the Harbor City Cemetery.

There were lots of new Yuppie restaurants and boutiques.

No more Chicago comedians, polka bands or Jewish girls on vacation.

An era had ended and a new one had begun.

Tourism was the second largest industry in Michigan. People paid good money to live by, swim in and fish from radioactive water diluted with heavy metals and dioxins.

Go figure. Nothing was perfect.

The Last
State Champions

The Wood Cemetery was on the west side of Wilson's Hill overlooking the Mill Pond and the old iron bridge.

Pat Lee stood at the foot of Chuck Stanislawski's grave. The headstone was white marble. Mrs. Stanislawski had Chuck's name, dates of birth and death carved in English on the stone.

Chuck had been dead a long time now. Along with JFK, RFK, MLK, Medgar Evers and over 60,000 others who had been killed as a direct result of trying to find meaning in the sixties.

It had been a strange decade. Pat's decade. Pat Lee became a man in the sixties. He took his beatings, passed his rites. The sixties had taken a special toll on the American Dream. There was a huge black wall of names of the dead in D.C.

Nobody was bulletproof. The last thirty years had proved that.

The last generation.

Pat stopped at Ron Waters's fresh grave. The tumors in his brain that had started as headaches began to grow and migrated to his spine. He was gone within a week after the University of Michigan specialists finally decided what to call his disease.

Pat walked on to his car and stopped to look at the beauty of the Mill Pond and the iron bridge.

A developer from Chicago was trying to promote a housing development. He had commissioned an environmental study from Michigan State University and was paying to reinforce the old dam at the Grist Mill to create an artificial lake. He planned to build houses along the shoreline. In return, the Michigan Department of Resources was going to plant salmon in Birch River.

They were going to have a fish ladder and everything.

Pat looked at the river and shook his head. He didn't have to wait on a study from Michigan State to know that with all the mutagens in the water the fish would have legs by the time the ladder and the development were finished.

But people from Chicago didn't know or seem to care. The Greater Fool was still around.

The Conquering Heroes

America was going to get moving again. The Cold War was over but there was fighting in the Balkans. The Serbs and Croats and Muslims were at one another, again.

It was all on the wheel.

Well, the next generation was going to have to look out for itself, just like the last one.

The day was clear, the sun bright. The sky was a high blue with a few scattered cirrus clouds for texture. The Mill Pond glittered a deep silver blue. The first snow of the season had fallen. It looked like a White Christmas was in the offing.

Pat started his old Lincoln and drove down the hill through Wood. Most of the cars he passed were made in Japan or Germany. Pat would drive Detroit Iron. It gave him the feeling—the illusion?—he was ahead of the socio-economic curve.

The NCAA administered the death penalty to Southwestern State University with a relish seldom seen since Henry VIII was saving on the cost of divorces.

Brick Williams moved to Washington, D.C., to lobby for the NCAA.

After cutting a deal for secret testimony and campaign financing with Laude VanMeer, Sam Watts moved the majority of his business operations to the Far East. It had been in his long-range plans for years. The Cathy Sullivan–Chuck

389

Small incident had just pushed up his timetable by a few years.

Laude VanMeer won election to Congress from Texas.

People from Grand Rapids were hanging around the White House, again.

Jamail Jenks enrolled at a major West Coast college where he ended up shooting and wounding an assistant coach in an argument over his shot selection.

His final shot selection on that occasion was a nine-millimeter parabellum.

A shooting dispute over a shooting dispute.

O.K. Free still ran the program at Medgar Evers High School in Detroit and shopped his players to the highest bidder. It was rumored that he put together a $1 million deal for a seven-foot-five kid with no guarantee the kid wouldn't turn pro. Or would learn to speak English.

The players and the money got bigger every day. Soon a top blue chip from the inner city could afford to equip an armored division.

The U.S. Olympic basketball team was made up almost entirely of professional players. Before their fall Brick Williams and Barry Sand were instrumental in changing the eligibility rules to make that possible.

Eddie Sanford ended up going to an Ivy League school on a government grant-in-aid. He dominated the league, with no plans to go professional.

The Conquering Heroes

Pat and Eddie's mother Anne talked on the phone and wrote letters. Anne said she was thinking about visiting him again in the spring.

Geena and Barry stayed married. Given a five-year suspended sentence for conspiracy, Barry was banned from coaching for life. He and Geena moved to Phoenix, where Barry drank, scouted for the NBA and sold used cars. Geena got money from her father.

Jax Morrow turned state's evidence for a reduced charge of manslaughter. He named names, including his suspicions about who faked Cathy Sullivan's suicide, but only Chuck Small went to Huntsville. He would be eligible for parole in the year 2005. A wiseacre sportscaster said that "the layoff will definitely cost him his chance to go in the First Round."

Nickie Babe, Small's agent, claimed the whole affair "was a plot to bring down my demands for a fair wage for this gifted athlete . . ."

Nickie had also filed an appeal against the IOC's lifelong ban against "any player convicted of a violent felony involving the use of a firearm." In that particular case his client was Jamail Jenks. The lawyer was convinced he'd win.

Pat was advised by his lawyer not to make accusations about Sgt. Cash's death. He had no evidence, and would undermine his own credibility. A lose-lose situation, the lawyer said. The case stayed unsolved. The same went for who faked Cathy's suicide.

The Lincoln rolled to a stop outside the old high-school gym.

Once inside, Pat watched the fifth and sixth graders chase the basketball up and down the court. It was as if the ball controlled the kids.

The game was spontaneous, joyous and, best of all for Pat, fun to watch.

The game was still the same. Everything else was different, except his daughter Jennie, who was enrolled at Yale and seemed happy. Pat was looking forward to her first visit at Christmas. And his oldest son James was working at Universal Pictures as a producer. He got the job when he married the Japanese woman running the studio. His first production was a docudrama for television based on Chuck Small's upcoming book, *Technical Foul.* Nickie Babe, still at it, negotiated a six-figure deal for the rights.

Ray was still in school at Southwestern and living at home with his mother Sara. Sara remarried. Her husband became the new SWS head basketball coach. Perfect.

Pat studied the old gym carefully. More than three decades earlier it had been his whole world. Now it was used for physical education classes and elementary school basketball games.

Finally Pat thought he understood what *decade*

meant. It was never going to be 1949 again. Or 1959 or . . .

The new high school west of town had a brand new gym. It was a state-of-the-art building but it produced mediocre basketball. The coaches learned their techniques from watching television.

So did the players.

And they played not to lose.

Pat looked around the gym, grabbed his whistle, blew the game to an end and had all the kids line up.

"Now," Pat said, "we're going to work on fundamentals and mental attitude."

He held up a new leather basketball and ordered the kids to look at it.

"Remember, this game is about playing. You work on anticipation and execution. You never worry about winning or losing. Play the game right and the winning takes care of itself.

"It's how you play the game that matters. That's the truth. I don't care who tells you it's corny."

He tossed the basketball to the kid farthest away.

"And remember, never take your eyes off the ball."

He hadn't really gone that far away after all.

SPECIAL
30TH ANNIVERSARY EDITION

JACKIE O.
Hedda Lyons Watney
Thirty years after the tragedy in Dallas, she's still the world's most fascinating woman!

Thirty seconds in Dallas changed her life—and the world—forever. Now, thirty years later, the glamorous, fabulously wealthy, yet tragic Jacqueline Bouvier Kennedy Onassis has made an indelible impression on our time.

Despite the glare of publicity that surrounds her, she remains a mystery. Discover the surprising secrets of the most sought after, most admired woman ever.

16 PAGES OF INTIMATE PHOTOS!

_3555-3 $4.99 US/$5.99 CAN

RED TIDE
R. KARL LARGENT

"A writer to watch!" —*Publishers Weekly*

COUNTDOWN: 72 HOURS

Aboard a yacht on the peaceful Caribbean, a secret meeting between the leaders of the U.S. and the former Soviet Union is set to take place. Protected by the most sophisticated technology known to man, they will have nothing to fear— if one of their own isn't a traitor.

OBJECTIVE: DESTROY THE NEW WORLD ORDER

In a tangled battle of nerves and wits, Commander T.C. Bogner has to use his high-tech equipment to defeat a ruthless and cunning foe. If he fails, the ultimate machines of war will plunge the world into nuclear holocaust.

_3366-6 $4.99 US/$5.99 CAN

CHARMED LIFE

By Bernard Taylor

Bestselling Author of *Mother's Boys*
"Move over, Stephen King!" —*New York Daily News*

Time and again, Guy Holman eludes death. No disease or disaster seems capable of killing him; no injury can do him mortal harm. But for all his good fortune, he loses everyone he has ever loved. Then a young woman who bears an eerie resemblance to his dead wife appears, and he thinks his luck has changed. But unknown to Holman, he is the innocent pawn in an age-old battle between the forces of good and evil. Blessed by some miracle or damned by some horror, Holman has the power to change the destiny of the world— the power to decimate or spare the souls of untold millions— the power that can only be realized by saving or destroying his charmed life.

__3561-8 $4.50

BORDERLAND

S. K. EPPERSON

"A First-rate Thriller!" —*Booklist*

Not much has changed in remote Denke, Kansas, since the pioneer days: descendants of the same families still walk the streets; the same customs still hold the residents together; the same fears still force the people to hide their dark secrets from unwanted visitors. For over one hundred years, the citizens of Denke have worked far outside the laws of man and nature, hunting down strangers, stealing their money and their lives. But the time has come at last for every one of them to pay for their unspeakable crimes....

_3435-2 $4.50 US/$5.50 CAN